"Is this the way to Livesey Village?" Ash asked, and Rosalind felt the earth shift under her feet as his deep voice echoed around in her reeling head and she looked up at him like a simpleton.

Had her silly dreams conjured him up, then?

Idiot! she accused herself as she stood staring at him as if turned to stone. *You could have said no and hidden your face.*

"Ah, I see it is. Well met, wife," said the sixth Duke of Cherwell, with a harsh parody of his old smile that made her heart ache.

She had to peer up at him through the black spots dancing in front of her eyes and she could hardly hear his mocking words past the thunder of her frantically pounding heart.

Author Note

When a woman married during the British Regency period, she took a huge risk. In the eyes of the law she became her husband's chattel and divorce was nearly impossible. She could be setting out on a loving and lifelong partnership or end up locked inside a marriage neither of them wanted to live with anymore. So what would happen to a couple who began their marriage convinced they loved one another for life, then bitter misunderstanding left them still married but oceans apart?

Thinking about that question led me to Rosalind and Ash and their tale of young love, elopement, marriage, headlong desire, then a furious parting. *The Duchess's Secret* pushes them back together in a marriage of convenience as they both agree to try again. I hope you enjoy reading about Rosalind and Ash's struggle to untangle the mess they made of their great romance, and at least they have a second chance at living together, now they are older and maybe a little bit wiser. I would also like to thank you for being my wonderful, tolerant and loyal readers.

ELIZABETH BEACON

The Duchess's Secret

ISBN-13: 978-1-335-63538-9

The Duchess's Secret

This edition published by arrangement with Harlequin Books S.A.

For questions and comments about the quality of this book, please contact us at CustomerService@Harlequin.com.

Printed in U.S.A.

Elizabeth Beacon has a passion for history and storytelling and, with the English West Country on her doorstep, never lacks a glorious setting for her books. Elizabeth tried horticulture, higher education as a mature student, briefly taught English and worked in an office before finally turning her daydreams about dashing piratical heroes and their stubborn and independent heroines into her dream job: writing Regency romances for Harlequin Historical.

Books by Elizabeth Beacon

Harlequin Historical

A Rake to the Rescue
The Duchess's Secret

The Alstone Family

A Less Than Perfect Lady
Rebellious Rake, Innocent Governess
One Final Season
A Most Unladylike Adventure
A Wedding for the Scandalous Heiress

A Year of Scandal

The Viscount's Frozen Heart
The Marquis's Awakening
Lord Laughraine's Summer Promise
Redemption of the Rake
The Winterley Scandal
The Governess Heiress

Visit the Author Profile page
at Harlequin.com for more titles.

Prologue

1811

'I love you so much, Ash,' Rosalind told her new husband, with such joy in her heart she wanted to say it over and over again. *'My husband,'* she whispered to herself. *'My one and only love.'*

'And I love you, Mrs Hartfield,' Asher Hartfield said, with such love looking back from smoky grey eyes it was better than any love poem.

'Enough to come all the way to Gretna to marry me when my stepfather said no,' she agreed happily as the hired carriage headed back to England.

Travelling by mail coach had been an adventure, but Rosalind was looking forward to a leisurely trip home now they were man and wife and nobody could ever part them again.

'I would go to the ends of the earth to marry you,' Ash told her and when their eyes met the fire under all that smoke was plain to see.

Rosalind felt warmed and cherished and eager for the first intimate inn along the way Ash had promised her as they travelled relentlessly, snatching sleep when the roads were smooth enough, never daring to nap in warm taprooms for fear they would be left behind. It had been an odd combination of restless haste, anxiety her stepfather, the Earl of Lackbourne, would catch up and stop them and the boredom and discomfort of travelling at such a pace, but she would do it again a hundred times over in order to marry Ash.

'Husband,' she whispered and slipped off a soft tan glove to stare down at the gold band he had placed on her finger less than an hour ago.

'Wife,' he said, as if she was a fantasy he had been promising himself since they first laid eyes on one another as well. It had only taken his long, hot stare to send her spinning out of a Mayfair ballroom into this new world made only for them. Rosalind had tumbled fathoms deep in love and Ash had blinded her to other men. The wonder was he felt the same when their two worlds met and they became *us two, Ros and Ash, lovers until the end of time.*

Rosalind imagined she would be wary of wild young men after her experience of the man who lied to her when she was younger and a lot more naïve, but apparently she could not resist a rogue. But this one was different and Ash Hartfield really was the true love of her life.

'How far must we travel today?' she asked breathlessly, thinking even waiting until early nightfall at this wintry time of year would feel like riding a knife-edge when she wanted him so urgently she had no idea how they had managed to keep their hands off each other all the way to Gretna Green.

Ash would be a caring and passionate lover—the fire in his eyes when he met hers said how difficult it was for him to wait—but he had done so all the way from London. Her heart ached with the hugeness of love and she would not even think of the rogue who had lied about how impossible it was for a man to control his base passions in the presence of true beauty right now. Or remember how she had cursed her looks until she met Ash's eyes across that ballroom. Nothing about *Ash's* need for her at the heart of his life felt base or wrong. He was warmth and care and strength. Other men only wanted to possess her body and never mind the contents of her head, or her hopes and dreams—but this man was so different she wanted to pinch herself until she could believe this was really happening and he really loved her.

'Carlisle,' he murmured as if even the word was temptation enough for a man so close to the end of his tether.

'Good,' she said just as sparsely because she felt as if this lovely fire was eating her from the inside out as well.

By the time they got to the border between Scotland and England, crossed into that fortified and often fought-over city and found a cosy inn off the main coaching routes, it was getting dark and the fire and frustration inside her were almost out of control. Rosalind went into her husband's arms with a hunger and sweetness only Ash could arouse in her and knew she was home. This was where she belonged, she decided foggily, as he planted a delicate mesh of kisses down her exposed throat. He filled her senses and thoughts until she had no idea when he undid her laces. As well they had got this far, though, a sane part of her cautioned, because the rest of her did not really care if they were in this private and fire-lit chamber or out in the marketplace and the freezing cold January air. Ash was all that mattered to her, all she wanted to know about in the whole wide world, and wanting this and him felt like everything to her.

'Rosalind,' he gasped softly and, on a long sigh, 'My Ros...a...lind...' He stretched out her name between gentle nips at her earlobe as he worked his way around to a place she never knew was so responsive until now. He had been saving that revelation until they were like this together, she decided, as heat shot through her and she moaned out his name in an echo of his huskier tones.

Would there was more of it, she decided as breathily she whispered, 'Asher...' It felt brief and insufficient 'Asher Hart...'

'Enough,' he murmured as if it would be a command if he had the strictness left to make it so.

'Yes, it is. Asher, my Heart. That's enough for me,' she whispered as that busy mouth of his went back to trailing urgent kisses down her throat and settled on the racing pulse at the base of her neck. So close to her that he must have felt the lurch and race of her heartbeat when he moved from one pulse to the other as if he had to reassure himself both marched to the same beat.

'Love me, Ash,' she boldly encouraged him as she wound her arms about his neck and tugged him further down to whisper kisses over the bared slopes of her breasts. It only took a little wriggle to slide the unlaced gown and lacy shift off her shoulders, then he did the rest. She might have found it a little too much intimacy, a little too hasty but for the tremble in his caressing hands. He had felt it, too then, the novelty and bravery of total intimacy. Knowing that, she could let go of her doubts and leap headlong into Mr and Mrs Hartfield. She left him to take the lead and know how to make this fine and good. She trusted him; she knew him. This was right.

The next morning she still thought so. Ash knew her inside and out now and they had made love so many times last night she could not recall whether it was three or four trips up that lovely road to ecstasy they had travelled before sleep finally overcame them. Now she wasn't afraid of any thought in his head or touch of his hands, because this was love and he was her first, last and forever. Rosalind loved being his wife so much she could hardly believe it was possible to be so happy, so completely content when she woke up to see Ash watching her with such warmth and tenderness in his intent gaze her heart raced with longing for him all over again.

'We still have to face our families,' she reminded

them both, feeling some of her blissful joy tumble back to earth. 'Your grandfather the Duke and my stepfather the Earl will not be very pleased about our elopement. They are sure to look down their long noses and threaten to cut us out of their lives,' she added and shivered against Ash's bare shoulder at the thought of those two arrogant old men making their displeasure plain to them and then the rest of the world.

'My grandfather threatens to do so at regular intervals, but he never does it. They will pretend it was their idea all along and inform the world what a fine match it is when they see I am a reformed man. I don't know why your stepfather was so against our marriage when I did promise him I would settle down and help Grandfather manage the estates during Charlie's minority. Now we are wed they will admit we are a well-matched pair and not to be put asunder by a couple of jealous old fools,' Ash drawled lazily, as if he could not see any need to worry now the deed was well and truly done.

Rosalind felt a superstitious shiver run through her like ice. A wicked old god might be listening and blight this glorious love of theirs if they were too bold and rash with it. 'It seems like tempting fate to take anything for granted,' she told him carefully, turning to look up at him and very ready to be distracted if he was not quite done with being her new husband yet.

'Nothing can part us now, my love,' he told her and ran a soothing hand down her bare back as if he had felt that shiver of apprehension run down it and was fascinated by where that shiver could take them.

'Truly? Nothing I could tell you would stop you loving me?'

'What could? I love you; you love me. There's nothing a couple of bitter old men and a pack of gawping fools can do about it now.'

Rosalind thought about the nasty little secret her stepfather had held over her for the last two years to keep her obedient and half-heartedly attracting the best offer her looks could draw in while a shadow loomed over her happiness. What would the Earl do now his hopes of arranging a profitable marriage for his penniless stepdaughter were ruined? She ought to tell Ash in order to draw the sting out of the story Lord Lackbourne would tell him with relish when he found out what they had done. His lordship's price for housing her since her mother had died could not be paid by the second son of a second son, even if Ash was the grandson of a duke. Ash had warned her from the start that his father had gambled and caroused most of his fortune away before breaking his neck on the hunting field. Ash had gone on to admit his own misdeeds and his wild ways, but he did not gamble and that seemed a very good thing to his future wife. But the fact remained Lord Lackbourne would not squeeze much in the way of settlements out of Rosalind's husband. The thought of his frustrated fury when he had been expecting the golden good looks she had inherited from her famously beautiful late mother to attract fortune and influence instead of a rackety young man made her shiver again.

'What is it? Why are you so worried about admitting we are married?' Ash said, pushing himself further up in the bed so he could look down at her face in a shaft of midwinter sunshine peeking nosily in through a gap in the innkeeper's best bed hangings.

It wasn't a tale Rosalind wanted to tell, but did she dare keep it to herself? What if the Earl and Ash's military brother caught up with them today? Any chance she might have to explain her folly two years ago would fly out of the window under their critical eyes and her stepfather had never loved her, so what was to stop him telling Ash about her youthful stupidity? Even the thought of Ash looking at her with horror instead of love made her flinch from saying anything, though. Maybe the Earl would be struck by lightning and so changed he became her kind and gentle protector instead of the impatient and penny-pinching autocrat she knew him to be.

'Are you really sure nothing could part us?' she asked, sitting up in bed as well and turning her face up to meet his gaze again with every ounce of sincerity she had in her while she tried to gauge his inner thoughts.

'Do you mean to be faithful to me?' he demanded with a hard note under his usually flexible deep voice and in his smoke-grey eyes.

'Of course I do, to my dying day,' she swore as ardently as if they were in front of an archbishop, because anything less than total fidelity to this fine and brilliant young man felt unthinkable.

'Then we have nothing to worry about,' he told her with an only-for-her smile on his slightly stubbly face and a gleam in his eyes she simply had to resist until she had confided her silly story and got the last obstacle to their happiness out of the way.

'What did you say?'

'I should have told you before, but—'

'No,' Ash roared and leapt out of bed, 'there is no "but" in the world important enough to stop you telling me until you had my ring on your finger. You lied; you *used* me,' he added and the revulsion in his voice was straight out of her worst nightmares, but at the same time too real to hope she would wake up and find she had dreamt it.

Rosalind watched her husband throw on his clothes as if it felt wrong to be naked with her now and shock held her frozen, like an abandoned houri after a night of unimaginable sin. Her mother had been right then; she should never have told her husband what a fool she was at sixteen. She should have kept it to herself that young and silly Rosalind Feldon had let a handsome young rogue convince her she was the love of his life before she found the touchstone of true love the moment she saw Ash. She had been so blinded by the grown-up glow and glamour of her first love affair she had let that rogue convince her the punch at her first grown-up party was made with spices and lemon juice and honey and wouldn't harm a baby. Later he told her a man like him couldn't help himself in the company of such a beautiful girl. Rosalind had been so intoxicated with rum and dreams he had managed to seduce her while she was so dazed and loose-limbed she had hardly known her own name and thought it a strange and oddly uncomfortable dream. Waking to an appalling headache and the terrible realisation it had truly happened, Rosalind had discovered the furtive rogue had left at daybreak for his new posting at the Russian court without even a note to say sorry.

'No, I never actually lied and I *do* love you. I was a fool to believe a word that man said, but I refuse to let a careless rake ruin my life, then or now. It cost a great deal of heartache to put my life back together, but I know the difference between real love and pretend—I know you love me as he never could. He was too selfish to ever love like you do, with every bit of your heart and soul. My mother was dying when he did what he did,' Rosalind added and paused for a moment to find enough strength to carry on talking with the memory of that terrible, precious time clogging her throat with tears. Mama had urged her to be strong and not tell anyone else, ever, and she was so right. 'She made me promise not to let him ruin my life,' she whispered sadly now.

'Yet he has managed it anyway,' her Ash said bleakly and he hadn't been listening after she told him her dark secret, had he? He had made up his own story about her fall from grace, but that would not stop her fighting for her marriage and this new, true lovers' life they were so eager to begin.

'No, that makes him the winner. I refuse to be used and ruined because of one foolish action when I was little more than a child, Ash. He was a cold-hearted rogue who took advantage of me, then left.' She got out of bed at last to face his stony gaze bravely as she reached for her hastily discarded clothes and began to scramble into them.

'So you say. That's your version of what happened and how can I ever trust that again? You have had a lover and you didn't tell me. This so-called rogue of yours didn't sit by my side all the way to Scotland so we could marry in haste and repent at leisure. You were ready, willing and eager to elope with a lovesick fool. Who else was going to marry a soiled dove, Rosalind? I really thought you were an angel in human form and you look like one, on the outside.' He must have seen her flinch at that tired description of her golden looks and his stare turned cynical. 'You gave an exquisitely polished performance. Your unspoilt grace and sweetly hesitant manner were masterly. I suppose you already have a lover waiting to keep you in style.'

'No. I am still the person you married. The same woman you swore you loved to the edge of madness last night.'

'You are not a woman, but a silly little girl dressed up in fine clothes. You are a liar, though. I cannot live with one of those for the rest of my life.'

'That means you cannot endure yourself, since you swore you loved me only a few minutes ago and it must have been a bare-faced lie.' Even to her own ears Rosalind sounded childish. It seemed to confirm everything Ash said about her, but it was either that or sob and plead for forgiveness—miserable defiance it was then.

'I loved someone who does not exist,' he said stiffly,

as if his pride was offended. 'How can I love a woman who is a liar? Three whole months have passed since we met and you have never managed to find a single moment to tell me you are not what you seem? Oh, no, you made sure we were well and truly married before you told me the truth, when it was too late to escape your clutches.'

'If that was my plan, I did not need to tell you at all. You *can* trust me, Ash, I swear you can. It wasn't my fault.' She heard her own defensive and, yes, childish response to his fury and despaired, but it was defend herself against his bitter fury or weep and she refused to when he was glaring at her as if she was his enemy.

'It wasn't my fault,' he parodied cruelly. 'That's what *she* said,' he burst out as if it hurt him to talk about the reason he felt so betrayed by her failure to tell him of her sad misadventure until now.

Wild jealousy rocked Rosalind as well as an echo of his pain. Despite sobs tearing at her throat she was too proud to let out, and a sense of injustice burning inside her, she still loved him. His hurt felt like hers. Maybe he had never cared about her as he swore he did from the moment he first laid eyes on her. Maybe he was the true liar out of the two of them, but this accusation belonged to a guiltier woman. 'Who said it?' she said bleakly. 'Who was she?'

'My mother.'

'Your *mother*? I thought you must have been betrayed by a lover. I almost felt sorry for you, but, no, you turned on me because of your mother. I never expected to trail in her footsteps,' she said, fury so strong it buoyed her up even as her world fell apart. 'What did she do, drop you on your head as a baby?'

'She told us she was going to be at a house party in the next county, although she was really flitting off to join *her* latest lover.'

'And that's all?'

'Of course not, but she made it impossible to find her when our little sister was taken ill. Our mother came back a week after the funeral in her mourning weeds, telling anyone *it wasn't her fault*.'

Ash's voice sounded as if he was reliving his agony and even after all the terrible things he had said to her Rosalind pitied him. 'Maybe it wasn't,' she said. 'She might not have been able to save your sister even if she had sat at her bedside the whole time.'

'Maybe not, but my brother Jas took it so hard you would think he had killed her himself. I hated my mother for lying over and over again and believing it. I did not go to her funeral; I did not owe her enough love.'

And there were the bleak, unsaid words between them: *I would not bother to turn up for yours either.*

'I am truly sorry you lost your sister so tragically, Ash, but I promise I am not lying when I say I love you,' Rosalind said, but felt the faith she had been clinging to until now began to fail as the dogged reason he was so angry ate it up and spat out the bones.

'Not enough to tell me the truth,' he said bleakly and left the room as if she was a stranger he did not care for.

Chapter One

1818

Ash stopped pacing his austerely opulent office in the sticky heat to glare between the gaps in the window screens at the lush landscape outside. It was monsoon season and most of his neighbours had departed for the hills with their families, but he had no family. He stayed to watch the relentless miracle of the rains enrich this exotic, fascinating land and to seize the odd business opportunity they were too far away to grasp.

He swung away from the view and cursed the steamy heat for sapping his energy and dulling his mind, then strode to his desk and picked up the letter to reread impossible news. Stupid to hope his eyes had deceived him and he must have imagined those dire words in neat script on hot pressed paper.

The outside of the letter was almost unmarked by its long journey, as if to prove he was now a very important man. Even his letters must be taken great care of aboard a busy merchantman. Not for this cursed thing a sack in the hold with the cargo.

He blamed the form of address the prestigious firm of London lawyers used to direct it: *To A. Hartfield of Calcutta*; with the words, *Sixth Duke of Cherwell, Marquess of Asham and Earl Morfield* added in smaller letters, as if to warn of terrible news.

> *It is with great regret we must carry out our sad duty as the Fifth Duke of Cherwell's legal representatives and executors and inform you of His Grace's untimely death.*
>
> *The day before yesterday your cousin, Charles Edward Frederick Louis Hartfield, died in a terrible carriage accident on his way to spend the summer months at Brighton...*

Ash could not make himself read any more, now or when the first shock of those words bit like steel. The shining young hope of the Hartfield family, his scapegrace cousin Charlie was gone. The lad could only have been four and twenty. Ash pictured the gangling seventeen-year-old youth he had last seen seven years ago and sadness beyond tears caught him by the throat. He wanted to yell defiance at the gods. Was his whole race cursed to die before their allotted span on earth? *No*, reason stepped in and argued—his grandfather, the Fourth Duke, had lived to be an upright, if irascible, eighty-eight and even Ash's father, Lord John Hartfield, managed to survive into his forties before he met his end drunk on the hunting field. Yet three years after Waterloo, Ash's mind flinched at the dreadful truth that his brother Jasper was dead, left among the piles of dead on that bloodiest of battlefields until his batman found him. All over Europe there were fathers and brothers, sons, husbands and lovers dead so many decades before their time because of the war. He was not the only one to feel this aching loss day after weary day, but he never thought Charlie would join in and make Ash feel blighted and guilty that he was alive when two better men were cold in the ground.

There was no point blaming himself for not being there to protect his little cousin from every ill wind that blew, but he still did. Charlie would have hated it after growing up under Grandfather's stern gaze until the old man gave up his fierce grip on life five years ago. Better be glad Charlie had had a few years as a handsome young duke with the world at his feet than curse the gods for taking him so long before his time. No, why the devil not? He was right to be furious. Except stamping about the room blaspheming and trying to pretend his eyes must be deceiving him did not make him feel better and heavy tears were still aching in his throat.

Ash glanced at the date below the formal listing of the lawyers' partnership and chambers. He hated the scribe who had set it out so neatly he clearly did not care about the tragedy he outlined. Ash had been Sixth Duke of Cherwell for six months of blissful ignorance. The letter had made its slow way through Biscay, past Spain and Portugal, down the coast of Africa to the Cape of Good Hope until it got to the

Indian Ocean and at last to here. If he went home he would have to wear the heaviest coronet below the weight of a crown on state occasions. He shuddered; Charlie or Jasper should be there to lead what was left of the Hartfield clan.

Ash cursed again and paced and cursed a bit more. The vexing problem of what to do about the slightly smaller and lighter coronet of a duchess crept into his head like a bad fairy. He had a vision of Ros in it before he bit out a choice epithet to add to the collection echoing around this lofty room like malicious flies. He did *not* want to be haunted by visions of the loveliest girl he'd ever seen gloriously grown into her looks after eight years apart from her hoodwinked husband. Eight years without him to catalogue her by the changing seasons and count the lovers she was sure to have cuckolded him with by now. Only a handful of people even knew of his misbegotten marriage; two were dead and the rest had kept quiet so divorce might not be the nightmare it was for other noble cuckolds. They had been apart for so long there would be discarded lovers aplenty in Rosalind Feldon's wake. He could take his pick of deluded fools to sue for criminal conversation with his wife, then seek a bill of divorce in the House.

No, it was foolish to delude himself it would be so easy and there could be no hiding his youthful idiocy now. The public dissolution of his marriage would be chewed over and chuckled at in every newssheet in the land. At least when they realised the sad depths of his youthful folly his peers would send his Bill of Divorce through unopposed and there was sure to be plenty of evidence; no woman as fiery, passionate and silly as his wife could have fooled her own kind she was virtuous for so long and she could hardly marry one of her lovers with a husband still alive.

The thought of Rosalind in the arms of whoever was keeping her now sent a roar of fury through him that hurt like a whip. As well he had so many weary weeks aboard ship to look forward to, then. By the time he got home and tracked down his Duchess he would be cold as ice. Neither Jas nor Charlie had lived long enough to wed and have children, so it was up to Ash to sire legitimate heirs to the family honours and next time he would make sure he picked a plain and dutiful wife. His new Duchess would not blind him to her true character with breathtaking looks and fine acting and they would enjoy a marriage of convenience. He could not be like his father, careless and wild himself and managing to ignore his wife's parade of lovers once she had provided him with an heir and a spare. That sort of marriage was not for him and he needed a dutiful wife without a head full of silly dreams. Love and lies made a tangled trap he had no intention of ever falling into again.

Six Months Later

Ever since she had seen the notice of Charles Hartfield, Fifth Duke of Cherwell's tragic death in a week-old copy of the *Morning Post* almost a year ago Mrs Rose Meadows had been waiting for trouble to strike. Charlie Hartfield's early demise would force Ash into divorcing her now and what a harsh and humiliating business it promised to be. She had sent a letter to his family solicitor by a very roundabout route to tell their noble client she had no wish to remain a duchess by accident. If she had to go to London and set herself up as a brazen hussy to deflect attention from Livesey Village and her real life, she would do that as well. She would do anything to keep Ash away from Livesey and her dearest secret.

'More tea?' Joan asked when she bustled into the little parlour to clear the breakfast dishes and frowned at Rosalind's untouched plate.

'No, thank you.' Rosalind had already let two cups go cold and it was a luxury they could not afford to waste.

'Are you feeling badly?' Joan asked her bluntly.

'I am perfectly well, thank you.'

'You ain't been right for months, my girl,' she thought she heard Joan murmur as she went back to the kitchen bearing cold tea and limp toast.

They lived a spartan life in the cottage Rosalind had bought with a small legacy from her paternal grandmother. Considering Grandmother Feldon was a clergyman's widow whose schoolmaster son had to attend a famous charity school after her husband died, it was a wonder she had managed to leave anything at all to her only grandchild. Mama once whispered Grandmama Feldon ran a lodging house in a not-very-respectable part of town to pay for her son to go to Cambridge, but least said soonest mended. There were a lot of small secrets in the late Lady Lackbourne's life and Rosalind wondered now if growing up keeping the mesh of little white lies that held up her mother's splendid second marriage had caused her to take a cavalier attitude to the truth as well. Perhaps Ash was right to call her a liar.

And perhaps not, Rosalind, her inner critic argued sternly. *No point forgiving him for what he did when he is about to divorce you.*

She sighed and recalled Mama telling her about how she was going to have a new stepfather to distract herself from the horrid prospect before her. Apparently his lordship fell in love when he called on a canon of his local cathedral and met the canon's beautiful widowed daughter. Mama thought his lordship had a good heart under the cool reserve he showed the world, but that sounded like another comfortable lie to Rosalind now. The women of her family did not have much luck with love and marriage, did they? At least, thanks to Grandmother Feldon, there was enough money to buy Furze Cottage with a little left over for emergencies. Ash's return as Duke of Cherwell was one of those in anyone's book and she had no intention of letting him ruin her new life. Even the thought of Ash in the same country again, walking the same earth and breathing the same air, felt disturbing, but at least when their marriage was officially ended she would finally be able to forget him.

'Mama, Mama, please can I go to the vicarage to play with Hal and Ally?' Miss Imogen Meadows, known as Jenny, burst into the parlour to ask her mother. 'Mrs Belstone sent you a note.'

'Oh, and Mrs Belstone addressed it to *me*, did she?' Rosalind asked her daughter, raising her eyebrows since Jenny seemed to know the contents of it already.

'Yes, and she would have sealed it if she didn't want me to know.'

'Maybe she thought you such a good little girl you would not dream of reading your mother's letters,' Rosalind said, but the irony went over her daughter's head and this did not feel like a good time to drill some manners into her.

Rosalind read her good friend Judith's account of Christmas at the vicarage with three lively children, another baby on the way and a hard-working husband to support at one of his busiest time of year, then smiled at her friend's invitation to please allow Jenny to come and divert her darlings from trying to kill one another for a few hours.

'Promise you will do as Miss Galvestone, the Vicar and Mrs Belstone say and try to be a good girl?' Rosalind said warily, having learnt to add conditions before rather than after agreeing to anything, since Jenny's ears seemed to go deaf as soon as she got what she wanted.

'Of course, Mama.'

'Ah, but what sort of a promise is that?'

'I promise to be good and do as I am bid,' Jenny parroted with the usual martyred sigh.

'Then I will try to believe you, but please don't break anything.'

'As if I would,' Jenny said with a cheeky grin and a glint of mischief in grey eyes that looked too much like her father's. Jenny had dark hair and was built like a sprite instead of a lanky Hartfield, but her smoky gaze was pure Ash.

'You should respect your aged mother, Imogen Meadows,' Rosalind told her headstrong daughter, who grinned happily, held up her face for a kiss, then ran off to meet her next adventure.

Now the silence in the spotless little house felt oppressive and Rosalind decided a good walk was what she needed. Her pupils were absorbed in family life or absent from home at this time of year so she had nothing much to do, for once. Joan kept the house clean and neat as a new pin and digging over the neat vegetable plot behind the house ready for spring crops would not distract her from the treadmill of her thoughts long enough. A ramble up on to the high heath above Furze Cottage was what she needed to help her forget Ash until he was actually home and even more eager for his freedom than her.

The ancient stuff gown she kept for rough chores was good enough for rough exercise. Rosalind plaited her corn-gold hair tightly and wound it around her head, then sighed and let it down again. This time she twisted it in a loose knot and pinned it more gently to take the pressure off the headache that had become all too familiar since she read about Charlie Hartfield's tragic demise. She eyed the reflection of her pure oval face, finely moulded features and deep blue eyes in the mirror with a frown, then turned away before she could change her mind about the cap she usually hid behind. The stark white linen would stand out against the heath and she preferred not to be seen.

'You look like a tramping woman,' Joan said when she saw Rosalind standing at the back door scanning the lane for onlookers.

'I'm going out,' she replied absently.

'Where to and why?'

'Just out,' Rosalind said stubbornly. 'You have no respect.'

'You don't deserve any dressed like that, *Your Grace*.'

'I am Mrs Meadows, plain and simple.'

'Nothing plain or simple about you, my girl. Easier if there was.'

'And you could not keep up, even if I was willing to wait while you put on your boots and fuss for half an hour about fires and pots.'

'At least I know my duty and you are a lady born, like it or not.'

'I don't—a lady is not supposed to have opinions or lift anything heavier than a teapot or embroidery frame. I would rather be a quiz than endure such idleness ever again.'

'You are still young and beautiful, despite all those dull clothes and that daft cap you think makes you look invisible. A girl like you should not be flitting about the countryside alone just because you need to think about them as don't deserve it,' Joan said with a significant glance at Rosalind's left hand.

Rosalind had kept Ash's ring to give her story weight when she came here with his baby growing in her belly. 'I cannot help but think about him now,' she snapped disgustedly, then strode up the grassy lane so fast that her russet countrywoman's cloak swung out behind her like a banner.

She had to stop and draw breath as soon as she was out of sight of the cottage and now she had a stitch and must stand still until it went.

Look where intemperate feelings get you and learn your lesson, Rose Meadows, her inner schoolmistress nagged.

It *was* only fury that made Ash seem close enough to feel her rage today. Only a man could make a divorce and even then he had to be an aristocrat. Ash had always been one of those to his very fingertips and she dreaded to think how arrogant he must be now. Eight years ago he had turned his back on her as if she were dross and then left the country to avoid her. She would not let him fill her life now as she had for so long after he left her. There, that was him recalled, dismissed and done with. Now she could turn her thoughts to gallant winter sunshine and a clear blue sky.

The wind had dropped after weeks of storm and tempest and she was tired of feeling hollow inside when Ash must have forgotten he even had a wife until the dukedom landed in his lap. There now, drat the man, but she was thinking about him again. It would not do; she had time to walk to the old stone circle at the highest point on the heath and be home again before dark and she must watch her step. If her thoughts wandered to him on that rough path she might blunder into a foul-smelling bog or tangle herself in a sneaky thicket of brambles. So this was exactly the sort of vigorous exercise she needed until she reached the brow of the hill and could stand in awe of the wide view across the heath and out to the distant sea before she strolled on and reached the stone circle.

When Ros reached her objective without letting her mind wander or think of the unthinkable more than once or twice, she rested against one of the lichen-covered stones in the January sun to get her breath back. The heath had a strange, secretive beauty at this time of year and she wished she could paint it and take a reminder home for times when the walls of her cottage seemed to close in. Even the pale ribbon of sea on the horizon looked serene as a millpond after weeks of storm and turmoil and only the faintest of breezes stirred the wisps of her hair escaping from its knot to tickle her flushed cheeks.

'Would I was so calm,' she murmured and searched the pocket no lady of fashion would dream of allowing to spoil the smooth lines of her gown. Luckily fashion was a stranger to her nowadays so she did not have to worry about such things. Here was the gold half-hunter watch she had bought for Ash as an engagement present and he later thrust back at her as if he wanted no reminders of what they had been to one another before they wed. She calculated how long it would take to walk downhill by the bridleway down to Livesey Village as her fingers ran absently over finely chased metal warm from her body. So many times she had decided to sell it, then put it back in her pocket or hung it by her bed again. Now the familiar details pulled her traitor memory back and she was eighteen again, rounding the corner of a secluded walk in Green Park with her heart hammering with eager anticipation.

Yes, there he was; impatiently waiting for her as he had promised last night when he daringly climbed up to her bedroom window at Lackbourne House to kiss her goodnight and beg her to meet him here in the morning. Here was her love, her Asher Hartfield, handsome, carelessly elegant and infinitely dear. And, wonder of wonders, he must love her back or he would never risk her stepfather's wrath and a crashing fall just to wish her goodnight. She had been quite right to ignore all the warnings that he was too young to settle down with one woman and as wild and untameable as a feral moorland pony. One look into his warm grey eyes and she knew here was her one and only and what else was there to know?

'You are precisely ten and a half minutes late, my darling,' he had told her that morning, closing the watch she had given him as a secret betrothal gift and putting it away so she could run into his arms. Then he was close enough for her to feel his warm chuckle against her skin.

'I missed you so much I—' she said, but he stopped her mouth with hot sweet kisses until they both forgot about words for a while.

The sharp cawing of rooks nearby brought Rosalind back to now with a thump. Oh, for goodness sake! Here she was, lolling against the ancient stone with a foolish smile on her face. Cross with herself for reliving that silly, broken dream, she stood upright hastily and hoped nobody had seen her. No, the heath was as empty as usual at this time of year. Even the almost-wild heath ponies kept to lower ground and sheep were safe in winter pastures. She heaved a sigh of relief. Rosalind Feldon, one-time society beauty, was still safely hidden under Mrs Meadows's stern disguise. Cold nipped at her fingers now so she pulled on knitted gloves, wrapped her shabby cloak closer to her chilled body and waited to feel warmer, but the cold seemed to have crept into her bones.

Hunger, she told herself practically and ate the small pie she had put in that useful pocket as she left the house. It was time she set off for home if all she could do up here was brood on the past. She soon found the bridle path that would take her back by an easier route and settled to a steady pace. She wondered why those rooks were still complaining like harsh-voiced old women discussing a scandal, but a clump of stunted pines hid the track from Dorchester so she could not see what the fuss was about. At last she heard a horse on the old pack road and wished she had worn the stark white cap after all. And why the devil had she been crying over the bittersweet memory of how much she and Ash once thought they were going to love each other for the rest of their lives?

She pulled her hood up to hide her face and hoped the rider would pass by with a brief *Good day.* The horse's hooves were so close now she could actually feel the vibration of its coming through the lightly grassed-over chalk under her feet. The animal snorted as it came alongside and tried to jib at something about her it decided not to like. It was swiftly controlled and she risked a hurried sideways glance. A fine grey gelding—good, his wealthy owner would have no time for shabby countrywomen. She got ready to bob a curtsy and walk stoically on, as if she was only intent on getting home before the early dark of a winter afternoon cut her off up here with only ghosts and creatures of the night for company.

'Is this the way to Livesey Village?' Ash asked and Rosalind felt the earth shift under her feet as his deep voice echoed around in her reeling head and she looked up at him like a simpleton.

Had her silly dreams conjured him up then?

Idiot! she accused herself as she stood staring at him as if turned to stone. *You could have said no and hidden your face.*

Then she would be free to run home on paths a stranger could not know about and escape before he got there.

Aye, and pigs will grow wings and fly, a mocking inner voice argued.

She numbly added up the time it would take her to whisk Jenny into hiding and let Joan know she had been forced to run away without even a toothbrush.

'Ah, I see it is. Well met, Wife,' said the Sixth Duke of Cherwell, with a harsh parody of his old smile that made her heart ache.

She had to peer up at him through the black spots dancing in front of her eyes and she could hardly hear his mocking words past the thunder of her frantically pounding heart. Maybe she was still leaning on the ancient stone inside its eerie circle, dreaming impossible things. Yes, that was it; she had fallen under a malevolent spell. Local legend promised terror to anyone silly enough to dally there and her Ash had been lean and self-conscious about his height, whereas this man sat his horse like a Roman emperor posing for a triumphal statue. She had taken great pains to hide her tracks when they came here as well and had never contacted anyone from her former life, except the Hartfield family solicitor by the most devious route she could think of, so nobody could have betrayed her to him, therefore he could not really be here.

'Go back to hell,' she ordered the spectre and crossed her fingers under her cloak to ward off evil.

'Only if you come with me,' it said coolly. 'Cat got your tongue?' he added in a darker version of the voice she remembered so well her hopes he was an illusion were beginning to waver.

'I have nothing to say to you.'

'Not even "Where have you been all these years?"'

'No.'

'Yet I am very curious about you, Mrs Meadows. My lawyer tells me you live alone except for a maid and teach music and dancing to aspiring young ladies. Is your latest lover a wanderer, too, then? Does he have a different lovebird in every parish as a reason for not keeping you in style?'

'You never knew me at all,' she said distantly, silently blessing her close-mouthed neighbours for not being at all helpful to any official-looking strangers asking questions along a coast where smuggling was rife.

'I know everything there is to know.'

Ha! her inner rebel argued. 'You know nothing,' she said out loud.

'I know enough,' he said icily. 'And as I need a duchess rather badly now you are damnably in the way.'

'Have you come to kill me and bury my body up here where nobody will ever find it?' her inner idiot challenged, but somehow she still trusted him not to physically hurt her. Disconcerting, she decided, as she met his eyes without a single shudder for her safety. He was shaking her world to its core yet again and she could not bring herself to hate him wholeheartedly even now. Still, if she irritated him enough, maybe he would ride away and never get any closer to Livesey and find out she had borne him a child.

'And wait another seven years before I can have you declared dead?' he said with a cynical smile. 'Even I am not that stupid.'

'Do you have your next Duchess picked out and waiting, then?' she asked just as cynically back, in order to mask the fact it had hurt her that he seemed to think disposing of her merely stupid, instead of unthinkable after what they had been to one another, once upon a time.

'No, but I should be able to find a gentle and biddable young lady with no illusions about love and a practical mind easily enough once I am free to wed her, what with me being a duke and under the age of thirty.'

Arrogant of him to think it would be that easy even if he was right. He was also formidably handsome and obviously rich and should have no trouble finding a suitable candidate among the debutantes, even if they were secretly terrified of such an awe-inspiring aristocrat. He meant his next wife to be her very opposite. Good again—a romantic fool like Rosalind Feldon would have her heart broken and no man should be able to do that to two wives in a lifetime.

'I wish you joy of one another,' she said coolly, thinking it sounded as empty and joyless a union as he deserved. When she considered how deeply they had meant to love one another the day they married over the anvil, his new version of marriage sounded as frozen as an Arctic waste. She shivered at the thought of all the dash and promise he had at one and twenty turning into this cold man with a cold heart, aiming for an even colder marriage. What a relief he meant to divorce her if that was what he wanted from a wife. He might look like Ash, but this man was very different under the skin. There were still glimpses of young Ash in his smoky gaze and tawny hair and she eyed him sideways and longed for things she didn't understand. She recognised the Ash of eight years ago under the hard shell and she wanted him, not this hard cold man he had become. That was the only reason for this thrill of attraction still so annoyingly alive under *her* armour against *him*.

Chapter Two

Ash would have been relieved to know Rosalind thought he was hard and emotionless. All it took was one look at her white, closed face and she had divided him in two again. One half was doing and saying cool and rational things while the other slid about on thin ice like the boy he was when they first met. And she was so lovely now she took his breath away. He felt his inner boy grieve for the light-hearted girl she had once been, but a beautiful face could never make up for a fickle heart and shallow nature. Yet there was something about her now that even made cynical, grown-up Ash wonder how best to describe her. She was pared down—that was as close as he could get.

Her old sidelong looks of girlish uncertainty and a puppy-like need for approval were gone. She was the woman she had not yet found room to be when he fell in love with her and he wanted her so urgently it hurt. He refused to brood over the lovers she had no doubt enjoyed, told himself he didn't care who had enjoyed her richer curves and the privilege of exploring the sweeter, tighter hollows of her silky skin with the slavish attention of a lover. Except he did; he envied them like the devil. Temper at the thought of another man exploring her secrets would hand her victory in this battle of wills and that would never do. He had come here to do business with his wife, it was just a shame he could not remember what it was right now.

Remember, Ash, he cautioned himself and tried to see the little changes that would make him feel repelled by her shop-soiled charm.

There was a faint trail of freckles across her high cheekbones and she had the slightly gilded skin of a woman careless about wearing a hat on unladylike tramps around the countryside, but that was all.

You would have thought time would write 'liar' across her purely beautiful face, wouldn't you?

No sign of it that he could see. Well, his mother could act the innocent so beautifully a saint might be taken in and he was no saint. He still eyed the high neck of Rosalind's disreputable stuff gown and simple cotton collar and caught himself longing to trace the line of sun-exposed skin where it met whiter, even softer, Rosalind with passionate kisses. Devil take the woman; he had come here to make sure he could finally be rid of her, not to fall under her witchy spell again. His body wanted to lead him about by an organ far more wilful and troublesome than his nose and if he wasn't careful his sex would betray him. He had come for his freedom and didn't want his heart mangled by his confounded wife again.

'Why are you dressed like a dowd?' he heard himself ask even so.

'Because I am one?' she said cautiously, as if she didn't understand why he was asking either.

And he had never been able to accuse her of vanity, had he? 'Not if you wrapped yourself up in chainmail and put on a suit of armour to try and snuff out your sex altogether,' he scoffed.

There, young Ash was even speaking for him now. He wanted to kick the immature fool where it hurt and ride away, but since that was impossible he watched her muffle her thoughts with a bland, blue stare and wondered what was going on in her head. Maybe he had put that curb on her passions when he left, but he could not afford a conscience about it now. He needed his new Duchess and his heirs and her sceptical gaze said she would rather have the poor life she lived now than bend the knee to any man and what a humbling thought that was. He eyed her rough clothing and recalled the little life his lawyer reported when he had finally found her after months of false leads and well-hidden tracks.

It really had been high time he rid himself of the man, despite that clever feat of detection. The lawyer had made little or no effort to find Mrs Asher Hartfield after Ash left for India, so the income from the tiny fortune Ash inherited at one and twenty had not gone to his wife as he had intended but into the fat lawyer's pockets. At least news his client was the next Duke of Cherwell stirred the man into tracking Rosalind down, despite all those false leads and dead ends she scattered in his path. Ash had never meant his wife to earn her own bread and eke out a spartan existence in a cottage. When he was an angry boy he had not wanted to use the law firm his family had always employed though, because he hadn't wanted his grandfather to find out he had eloped with Ros, then run away. That would have been the final nail in the coffin of any love they had had as grandson and grandfather and he could not have endured the old man thinking so badly of him when he was on the other side of the world. Coward, he accused that boy now. He should have known better than to have trusted an obscure lawyer he had found more or less at random with all the money he had had at the time. Given the wild races he used to ride over any terrain Ash knew he was a challenge for his grandfather to love. Little wonder Grandfather had sent him abroad with a flea in his ear and said he might as well risk death doing something useful instead of wasting his life on aimless adventures. Just one day of marriage before he had given up on Mr and Mrs Hartfield would have added contempt to Grandfather's despair at his least important grandson's wildness. Ash was far too cowardly to admit to the old man that he had married and deserted the Earl of Lackbourne's stepdaughter because she had told him a lie and he thought she might grow like his mother. The thought of his grandfather's contempt made him feel uneasy even now the man had been dead five years, but he had been right to go, hadn't he? Once a liar, always a liar. Rosalind could never have loved him if she thought it was all right to marry him without telling the truth about her lover first.

Right; that was the past back in its rightful place then, now where was he? Ah, yes, the lawyer. Ash had dismissed the man as soon as he had told him Rosalind's new name and humble address. Then he made himself come here himself to make sure the Mrs Meadows the man had come across living so obscurely really was the former Rosalind Feldon. A dishonest lawyer could always lay his hands on a dishonest woman, so Ash had to see for himself before he believed the man. If not for that, Ash would have been happy to do as the impudent letter she sent to his family lawyers after Charlie died suggested and divorce her *in absentia.*

Rosalind shifted under Ash's coldly critical scrutiny. When he jumped down from his horse to confront her on level ground it still seemed impossible this was really was him. Standing on the same earth as he was an assault on her senses and she didn't trust a single one as he calmly held the mighty grey's reins and studied her like a portrait. By summoning all the strength and self-reliance the last eight years taught her, she just about managed not to flinch under his stony scrutiny.

'You look like a duchess in disguise,' he mocked, but there was something in his eyes that reminded her how it felt to truly be his wife, for one passionate and largely sleepless night.

'Nonsense, I am a simple countrywoman,' she argued. She tugged the watch from her pocket to avoid his puzzling stare. 'One who must hurry home or be very late for an engagement,' she lied, closing the case with a snap. There was a flicker of feeling in his eyes at the sight of the watch she had once spent all her pin money on, so he could count the hours until they were together again. He had left it behind so it could not really mean anything to him.

'You kept it, then?' he asked huskily.

'I needed a timepiece and it cost nothing.'

'A laudably practical attitude,' he said with a frown that disagreed.

'I am a prosaic creature.'

'I very much doubt it,' he argued, looked about to smile, then changed his mind.

'Country widows need to be,' she insisted.

'Not when they are not widows at all they don't.'

'Since you must have come about a divorce I suppose the whole world will soon know I am still wed,' she said gloomily and now he had tracked her down that was probably true, one way or another.

'They don't have to.'

'The only way I shall not be notorious now is if you hire an actress to pretend to be me and I stay quiet and pretend not to be me under yet another name.'

'A tempting idea, but lies have a habit of catching up with a person, don't they?'

'That's cruel and even a little bit mean of you, my lord Duke. I don't think we need to descend to name calling when our divorce will be humiliating enough as far as I am concerned to satisfy even you.'

'I am not that vindictive, but you are right. I apologise,' he said and Rosalind did not quite know what to make of him now.

'It will be appalling,' she said with a shudder.

'I suppose we could always employ someone desperate to pretend to be you,' he almost offered and it was tempting, for a moment.

'We would be a laughing stock when she sold her story to whoever offered the most money and you might not get your divorce.'

'True,' he said with a disgusted shake of the head for the very idea of being tied to her for the rest of his life and that was good. As long as he was being the opposite of her dashing, charming and funny lover of long ago she could face him with indifference. It was when he reminded her of the young Ash who had loved her that he was dangerous.

'I don't know why you are here. I have already offered to come to London and face the mob so you can pillory me for my imagined sins—and you will have to imagine them because I never ignored *my* marriage vows.' Drat, why had she let that slip? He would know she was jealous of the idea of him lying in another woman's arms if she wasn't careful. But if she didn't care, how could she be jealous? *Good question, Rosalind*, her inner schoolmistress observed.

'I had to make sure it was you and not some actress my former lawyer set up here to take the money I intend to settle on you after the divorce. He took what little I had when I left the country and thought I was leaving it behind to support you.'

'Did you do that? I had no idea.'

'I was right then, he made no effort to find you before you disappeared and I cannot help but wonder why you did that, Rosalind?'

Don't wonder too hard, she silently urged and faced him with raised eyebrows, as if to say she thought it was too obvious to need explaining.

'Why didn't you tell the world about us?' he ignored her sceptical stare to ask as if that puzzle had been plaguing him for years.

'Hadn't you made enough of a fool out of me without the rest of the world knowing?' she parried. She wasn't going to tell him she hadn't cared about anything much at all after he left. When she had finally woken up to the new life they had made between them on their wedding night she had had good reason to slip away from the *ton* as if she had never existed and she definitely didn't want him to know about that. Every time she needed or wanted to tell him about Jenny over the years she would remember him turning on her the day after their wedding and know it was impossible. Except now he was so close to their daughter panic goaded her heartbeat to a gallop again.

'I thought the shoe was on the other foot,' he said cynically and he would, wouldn't he? The young man he once was had been dashing and handsome and entirely wonderful as far as young Rosalind knew, before they wed, but he was also hot-tempered and arrogantly convinced he was always right.

'I cannot imagine how you intend to stay anonymous now I am home and you can hardly go unremarked even here looking as you do,' he said.

'Looks give no hint of a person's inner life. You are handsome in a gruff sort of way on the surface, but you are not the man I fell in love with.'

'Pah—*love*,' he said with a revolted expression, as if she had said blasphemed.

'Yes, love. It is vital to me, which is why I want a divorce every bit as fervently as you do. You have been away from me for eight years and I doubt very much you stuck to the marriage vows you thought you were deceived into making with me,' she challenged him with a very straight look that defied him to lie. He avoided it for a moment, then met it defiantly and she knew she was right. *As expected, Rosalind, as expected*, she reminded herself and hoped she was managing to look scornful about it when confirmation he had been enjoying himself as if he had never married her made her want to scream and lash out at him, but that would never do, it would look as if she cared. 'One of us has been unfaithful to our marriage promises, so that will have to do for both our consciences while you lie it was me who took lovers, since only a wife's adultery can dissolve a marriage. Imagine that; me having to live a lie to cover up yours, after all you had to say about me being a liar when you left.'

He looked offended and defensive and ducal so she must have caught him on the raw with that barb and she really must stop sniping at him. She wrapped her arms across her shivering body at the thought of what a disaster it would be if he ever found out about Jenny. However much he had wronged her, she could not sue *him* for divorce since the law did not recognise her as a sentient human being, merely as her husband's chattel. And if he was furious with her for lying by omission when he left her, how would he feel if he found out she had borne his child? Somehow she must get him to leave.

'I am ready to do what you want because it is what I want as well. So you can go away with my promise to turn up to be insulted and defamed, now you have satisfied yourself I am really me,' she said lightly.

She would leave Livesey first and make sure there was no trail for his bloodhound to follow this time. Then she could set out for London by an indirect route to act the adulteress for him, since that was the only way out of this prison they had made for each other all those years ago when they wed over the anvil.

'You will bolt as soon as I turn my back,' he said abruptly and that was annoyingly perceptive of him.

'I agree to let you fabricate grounds for a divorce and I do not go back on my word.'

'Hmm, we shall see about that.'

Inside she was raging at him for pretending her failure to confide in him before marriage was a deliberate lie, but that paled to nothing besides her worry his former lawyer would tell Ash the truth even if she did manage to get away without him finding out he had a daughter. The lawyer must know about Jenny, so why had he kept her secret? Blackmail, she decided. If what Ash said was true he had made provision for her before he left and someone stole it. The lawyer must be venal and lazy and if he could make money out of her to pay back what Ash would demand he returned to him he would still win, wouldn't he? Most of that settlement, the conscience money Ash had intended to settle on her, would have to go on paying the man to keep quiet but it would be worth it, she assured herself as she shot this hard-faced stranger a sideways look. The headache she had come up here to cure thundered in her temples now as a new hazard was added to her list and how she wished Ash would leave her in peace to try to work out a way around them.

'They expect me at the inn in Livesey, by the way, before you try to tell me the place is full to the rafters with benighted travellers.'

'Why? What more can you want from me than a promise to go quietly?' she asked rather desperately.

'Nothing, but I knew I would be cold and weary after riding from London as fast as my horse can carry me. My former lawyer told me the inn at Livesey is comfortable and clean and Peg needs a rest even more than I do.'

'Peg?' she echoed hollowly and shock could make the strangest things seem important. It sounded a very odd name for such a noble steed.

'Short for Pegasus—his last owner had high-flying ideas to go with his huge debts.'

'Oh, I see,' she replied vaguely and she wasn't really interested in him or his horse, was she? 'You could get stuck there and you would not want that, would you?' she said as she fought those silly tears back and focused on the yellowish band of cloud now creeping across the sea and realised what it meant.

'Why?'

'Have you been away from England so long you have forgotten what yonder sky means?'

He followed her pointing finger as if he didn't trust her to know snow clouds from a hole in her shoe. 'Aye, you're right,' he finally had to admit. 'There is a goodly fall of snow on its way.'

'Best hurry back to Dorchester and be comfortable there for however long it lasts, then. I promise to be on my way as soon as the roads allow travel again,' she urged, hoping she could escape while his back was turned and she wasn't exactly lying, was she? She did plan to scoop Jenny up and run as fast as she could go in the opposite direction. She had not said where she would be on the road to—how could she when she had no idea herself?

'I am not the soft aristocrat you seem to think me. A village inn will do me very well,' he argued with a suspicious look that asked why she was so determined to get him away from her humble home.

She managed to shrug as if she didn't care what he did. 'Well, I am going home anyway. I have a great deal to do before it snows,' she said with a warning glare as if to say *Don't even think about hauling me on to that great horse and making us ride double.*

'Chickens and things, I suppose,' he said, Duke to peasant.

The old, impulsive Rosalind would have smacked his smug face for that taunt, but this one gave him a look of icy contempt and marched away from the bridle path he would have to follow as a stranger to the heath.

'Don't get bogged down, Your Grace,' he shouted after her and she strode on even faster to stop herself turning around and sticking her tongue out like a street urchin.

What a fool—what a *lunatic* he was. Why not do as she said and avoid her until he had to see her again for whatever reason the lawyers dictated? He had this stupid, boyish impulse to break through her determined serenity because his body wanted her, so his tongue had said things he cursed it for even when he was saying them. Ash urged his horse along the track to Livesey someone told him was shorter than the toll road and with a fine view—nowhere near as fine as the one he found at the top of it. If only he had been prepared for the sight of Rosalind there he might not have sniped at her and given himself away as far less calm and cold about this divorce business than he thought he was until he saw her again. It was that silly boy talking; the one who wanted to jump off the grey and chase his wife down the snaky track he had not even seen until she bolted down it as if the devil was on her tail. A little bit of logic survived and wondered why was she so intent on getting back to the village so fast she was prepared to risk a sprained ankle as well as very muddy legs and torn skirts. He stared after her as she neatly twisted and turned to avoid hazards until she was lost to his sight. Then he shook his head to try to settle some sense back into it and sighed.

The boy he once was still wanted her mercilessly, but it was the man who said stupid things then stuck to them as if taking it back would be a sign of weakness. He didn't really want to go to Livesey Village in the middle of nowhere and risk seeing her every time he walked down a road or looked out of the taproom windows. One look at the fine gold curls that had escaped the severe knot she had skewered it into and shining like a halo in the winter sun, those deep blue eyes and that glorious feminine mouth and he wanted her nearly as badly as he had on their wedding night. He should never have come here alone; better still he should have found another lawyer and sent *him* to bargain with the Duke of Cherwell's unwanted wife. Instead he recalled her extraordinary beauty and decided not to trust even the most staid lawyer with the task, but he didn't appear to be that trustworthy in the face of it either.

Despite his impatience with himself Ash managed to ride down to the village as if he was not in a hurry. Even running recklessly over rough ground and jumping streams and walls Rosalind could not beat him there by many minutes. He had been lucky to find this fine beast for sale at a livery stable to pay the bill his last owner could not afford and he had no intention of ruining the gelding's legs by galloping on unfamiliar ground. Time for the Duke of Cherwell to pretend he was just a modestly well off gentleman with business in the area, except why on earth had he booked that room in the name of Meadows? Rosalind seemed to be pretending to be a widow and a snowstorm ought to stop her grabbing whatever treasures she had and bolting off into the blue to hide under another name in another obscure place for reasons best known to herself.

Chapter Three

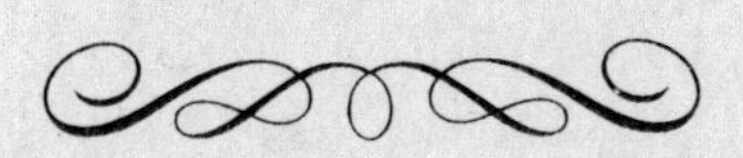

'Joan, Joan—where on earth are you?'

'Here, Miss Rosalind.' Joan emerged from the little bakehouse-cum-scullery with the delicious smell wafting out behind her. 'Heavens above, just look at the state of you,' the maid gasped and took in Rosalind's torn and muddied petticoats and wild-looking hair half-up and half-down after she had lost most of her hairpins on her reckless dash home.

'He's here; we have to leave before it snows and we are stranded in this village with him for goodness knows how long until it melts again.'

'We can't risk being snowbound out in the open.'

'Yes, we can; we have to. We must leave this place now he has come here. He cannot be allowed to find out about Jenny; he will take her away from me.'

'If he's putting up at the Duck and Feathers it won't take five minutes for someone to tell him about her. Since he's sixpence short of a shilling it could take ten for him to work out the lamb is his, but that's not long enough for us to get out of here before the snow starts.'

'But once he knows he will take her away from me,' Rosalind said numbly, wondering if every penny she had could buy Seth Paxton's neat cob and a light cart. There was the gold watch; it was worth a fair bit and she had often told herself that was why she kept it—to barter when she was desperate and heaven knew she was desperate now.

'It's too late if he is already in the village, but are you sure it's him?'

'Yes, I met him up on the heath. We spoke.'

'Then you are well and truly caught and I should have told you about the fat ferret who stayed at the Duck and Feathers and asked a lot of questions a couple of months ago.'

'You knew an investigator was looking for me?'

'No, I would have told you if I was sure he was after you, but the ferret asked about half the village. Luckily Seth Paxton and his dad don't like outcomers who ask too many questions and they didn't say much.'

'Yes, and I can imagine why,' Rosalind said absently, wondering again what the lawyer's motives were for concealing Jenny's existence.

Never mind the lawyer now; she had more urgent problems. Jenny was quite small for her age so she might convince Ash she was not his. Why had she told him she had stayed faithful to her marriage vows when they were up on the heath? Idiot, she condemned herself, even as jealousy shot through her again at the thought of the mistresses he must have had since the night he made love to her as if she was the only woman on earth who would ever matter to him.

'Rogues, the lot of them,' Joan condemned most of the south coast. 'But never mind them now. Somebody is sure to tell the Duke about your daughter and there's no use pretending they won't.'

'A fine Job's comforter you are,' Rosalind said grumpily. 'I am going to run across to the Vicarage to fetch Jenny and you can pack a couple of bags and put out the fires so we can leave the moment we get back.'

'Very well, Miss Ros,' Joan said with a shrug that said she thought Rosalind was wasting her time, but that she had promised her late mistress she would look after her child as best she could and a promise was a promise.

Ash approved his neat and spotless bedchamber at the inn. After the neat and spotless landlady went away he had a very necessary wash after his ride through the Dorsetshire hills in midwinter. He shivered in this confoundedly cold climate as he rubbed himself dry and hurried into clean clothes, then went to make sure his horse was being looked after.

'A fine beast, sir,' the groom told him and jarred him out of yet another daydream of Rosalind looking breathtakingly beautiful against a blue sky.

'Aye, I only bought him last week, but he's already proved a trooper.'

'Cavalry man, sir?'

'No, but my brother was.'

'Ah, a sad business the Great War,' the groom said with a shake of his head at Ash's use of the past tense.

'God send we never suffer the like again,' he agreed soberly.

Grief made his heart twist every time he thought of Jas dead at the end of that terrible conflict and he wanted to remember his brother with a smile and a *See you again one day, big brother* salute, instead of this aching gap in his life now he was back in England to feel it even more.

'I'll not argue with— Whatever are you three little devils doing up there?' the middle-aged groom broke off to admonish a pair of unlikely looking cherubs peering down at them from the hayloft and taking in every word.

Ash narrowed his eyes to see exactly who was giggling and shuffling about up there in order to spy on the latest stranger at the inn. As his eyes adjusted to the gloom he picked out what looked like a brother and sister, as both had brownish hair and dark eyes, currently wide with curiosity and apprehension. He was about to grin and reassure them he was not going to give them away, if they could persuade the groom not to either, when the third little demon pushed her way to the front as if she had to know what was going on even if it cost her a scold as well.

He thought seeing Rosalind again was shock enough, but Ash felt his head spin with the sheer impossibility of what his eyes were telling him now. He was looking up into his dead sister's face. Amanda had looked just so when caught out in mischief—a little bit wary of the consequences underneath, but as bold and uncaring as a baby lioness on the surface. He was mad, then. Or sick. Yes, sick—he didn't want to be mad. He blinked hard to try to clear his wandering senses. She was still there, looking back at him with puzzled grey eyes so like his own he wondered briefly if his father had strayed around these parts and she was his grandchild, or maybe Jas had left his mark on the world after all?

'He's gone ever so pale,' the older girl whispered as if she was almost as worried about his health as he was.

'Hard to tell when the sun has turned him so brown,' her brother said critically.

'Are you a sailor?' the girl with his little sister's face demanded and leaned over her friend's shoulder to peer down at him more closely.

The truth clicked into place like a perfectly timed mechanism. Not the ghost of his little sister Amanda, or Lord John, or Captain Jasper Hartfield's by-blow then—she was *his* child! His daughter. God forgive him, but he wanted to kill Rosalind as soon as that frozen moment of recognition relaxed its grip enough for him to think at all. His wife had kept him in ignorance of this perfect little miracle for seven years. He revised the perfect bit when his imp wrinkled her brow at his silence and gave him a very haughty look, but he still wasn't letting his wife off the hook for making him a stranger to his own child. Rosalind would have to pay for this somehow. As if anyone could repay him seven and a quarter years of his daughter's life in this world. He was a rich man now, but the whole of his fortune could not cover that loss, no amount of money ever could.

'You are very rude not to answer a direct question,' his imp informed him as if she had been born a queen instead of a pretend Meadows.

'It ain't rude to spy on your elders and betters and ask this gentleman a mort of nosy questions, then, Miss Jenny?' the groom demanded since Ash showed no signs of doing it.

'He is very brown for a gentleman. Mr Wentmore from the Towers is pale as a ghost and his sister told me only seamen and labourers ruin their complexions out in the sun and wind in all weathers.'

The groom muttered something uncomplimentary about the pale and interesting Mr Wentmore while Ash tried to gather his senses.

'I only got back to England last week,' he defended himself, as if his unfashionable suntan mattered a jot. So her name was Jenny, was it? Lady Jenny Hartfield did not have a very stately ring to it, but he liked the name anyway. He badly wanted to tell her what he was to her and she to him. He imagined Rosalind's version of where her child's father had got off to and bit back an oath his daughter should never have to hear, especially from him. He could rage at Rosalind later, after he had made it clear she and his child were not going far without him ever again, unless she wanted to relinquish all rights to her child as well as a duchess's responsibilities. There was no question of a divorce now; he would make sure his child stayed under one of his roofs from now on and whatever plans his wife was making to whisk Jenny away again would be stopped by the coming snow, so he had time to convince her she was not parting him from his child ever again. Jenny changed everything. In an instant he had learned the lesson most parents had months to get used to—this little life was far more important than his own and whatever plans he had about the future without any trace of Rosalind in it must now be forgotten.

'Where have you come from?' his imp demanded.

'India,' he said and waited in vain for her to say, *Oh, yes, my papa lives there*, so there was not even that much cover for his absence from his daughter's life. Ash wondered how Rosalind would get around the fact he was staying here as Mr Meadows, since being a duke would have caused an even bigger sensation and some strange impulse had made him sign himself so when he was still furious with Rosalind for hiding in the middle of nowhere to pretend he didn't exist. He still wondered why he had done it, but at least it would make removing his daughter from this backwater a lot easier. Not even Rosalind could deny they were man and wife with this child between them to prove it. He felt sure she would go wherever her child went, even if she loathed the girl's father and she must do so to have done this to him for the last eight years.

'Are your saddlebags stuffed with rubies and pearls?' the boy asked as if he thought such jewels must be scattered on the ground in exotic countries for anyone to pick up and bring home.

'No, I keep them in a bank vault,' he joked to stop himself promising his child the run of his treasury if she would only love him as her father. Adorning her with diamonds and pearls and all the riches he had gained in eight driven years of hard work could not buy a child's loyalty. He only wished he did not have to make her Lady Jenny before he had much of a chance to get to know his own child. *I have a child*, he whispered it in his head—as if someone might leap in and take her away again if he dared to say it out loud.

'Did you catch a fever while you were out there?' she asked as if that might explain his dazzled silence and make him a bit more interesting.

'Not that I know of,' he said feebly, still not quite sure this was really happening even now.

'My father says India is too dangerous for English women and children because fevers are rife. He was going to live there until he met Mama, but he agreed to come here instead so Grandpapa Waters would let them marry one another and have us. Grandpapa says he would rather put a knife in Mama than send her out there to die in all that heat and—' The girl must have given her talkative little brother a sharp elbow in the ribs since he grunted a startled breath then glared at her.

'He might like it, Hal, since he didn't take a fever there and you should not have been listening when Grandpapa thought we weren't there,' she lectured from the advantage of what looked like a couple of years' seniority.

'You were there as well, so neither should you.'

Obviously thinking the siblings were about to forget all about Ash and his fine horse and everything else except their latest quarrel, Jenny ignored them and continued to stare down at Ash as if she knew he was important to her somehow. 'When I grow up I am going to be a sultana,' she told him solemnly.

Even Ash could not quite hide a grin and the boy forgot to fight with his sister to laugh so hard he began to cough and splutter, until his sister thumped him on the back so hard he begged for mercy. 'You'll kill me,' he accused her breathlessly, then recalled the reason why he had been laughing in the first place. 'Raisins are nicer than sultanas, Jenny, so why not be one of those instead?' he taunted Jenny.

Ash had to bite back a stern rebuke to stop the lad teasing his child, even if she didn't know she was instantly precious to this tongue-tied stranger.

'She's been reading that book about Aladdin and whoever else is in there again,' the older girl told her brother with a shrug. 'Anyway, you're the fool for not knowing a sultan's wife is called a sultana. Not that you can marry one, Jenny, because your mother wouldn't want you to live so far away.'

'I could if he loved me and I loved him,' Jenny said stubbornly.

Ash silently cursed Rosalind for putting such nonsense in her head when she ought to know better by now. Love was not real; had she learnt nothing from their fiasco of a marriage?

Yes, how to lie even better than she did before it, an inner voice whispered sternly in his ear.

'Yuk, what soppy stuff and I thought *you* knew better,' the boy said, pulling a revolted face. Ash almost nodded his agreement before he met his daughter's reproachful gaze. She could not even be eight years old for months, so he had years and years to fight that battle before she was old enough to marry anyone, let alone a sultan.

'Be quiet, you two, someone's coming,' the older girl hushed the fight about to break out between her brother and their friend as Jenny took exception to the boy's scornful superiority.

'Hide,' the boy ordered and there was a great deal of wriggling and whispering as the trio drew back into the loft and Ash wanted to shout a protest and call them back. This was not the right time. He must make himself wait to claim his child until he had confronted her mother with her latest sins and got her to admit the truth. Then they could find a way to tell Jenny who she really was and get ready to leave for Edenhope as soon as the weather was right for such a long journey.

'Seth said he thought those two eldest demons of the Vicar's had been sneaking around the yard again and I won't have it, Enoch. If they was to tumble into a stall and get themselves trampled half to death after scaring the horses, that Mrs Belstone would be on our tails sharpish and we'd never hear the last of it. Vicar might have his head in the clouds when it ain't in a book, but his missus's tongue's sharp enough to cut a duke down to size if she was to turn her mind to it.'

The only Duke available managed to look too modest to need a trimming while he listened to those three furtive children creeping down from their perch by whatever means they got up there in the first place. A few moments later there were delighted squeals outside and he looked through the door the innkeeper's elderly father had left open when he came in here and saw a fat flake of snow drifting to earth like down. He didn't want to be snowbound in a village that thought his wife's husband must have died before his daughter was born, but it looked as if he would be staying here until the snow was gone whether he liked it or not.

By the time he stepped outside with directions to Furze Cottage and a frown from Enoch to wonder what this stranger wanted with a respectable widow, Jenny and her not very saintly friends were long gone. Ash jammed his expensive beaver hat on his head, pulled his collar up around his ears and hoped those three scamps were safely back at the vicarage having nursery tea by the time he got to Rosalind's house, because he didn't think he could wait to talk about their past, present and future until his daughter was supposed to be asleep tonight.

Now the snow had actually arrived Rosalind had to accept it was ridiculous to even try to travel, so she almost welcomed the cool slide of a fat snowflake against her flushed cheek. She scurried away from the vicarage with a promise from the Belstones and a delighted Jenny happy to stay the night while Rosalind attended to unexpected business. Judith Belstone shot Rosalind a sharp look, as if she could see how agitated she was under the pretend calm, but she agreed the children would be happy to play together in the heavy fall of snow it looked as if they would have by morning.

Now her daughter was safe with the Belstones she could hope against hope Ash would make a hasty retreat to Dorchester after all, so she and Jenny could sneak off in the opposite direction as soon as the coast was clear. If this desultory snow was all they were going to get he might even be able to leave first thing in the morning. So there was still a slim chance he might never find out about Jenny, if she kept her fingers crossed and a myriad of small chances all went her way. She rushed across the churchyard and out on to the lane leading to Furze Cottage, eager to grasp a last straw of hope.

'Ah, there you are.' Ash's deep voice rumbled on the still air. What a giveaway to put a hand to her racing heart to stop it leaping clean out of her ribcage. She blinked at him and thought he looked stonier than ever.

'Yes,' she agreed warily, 'here I am.'

'On the way home?'

'Yes,' she said, deciding it would be silly to deny it when anyone in the village could have directed him there. He loomed over her in this murky half-light as snowflakes began a slow dance around them. Earlier there was still a hint of the old humour in his voice, but now it sounded so hard and stern she wanted to shiver. A moment ago she felt almost too warm from hurrying down the hill, then dashing about the village to find Jenny, but now cold was nipping at her fingers and toes and she was shivering.

'Good, I was on my way to see you,' he said grimly.

'Why? It will only stir up gossip.'

'Your neighbours will be even more interested if

I throw you over my shoulder and carry you there, if that's the only way we can talk out of the cold.'

'I didn't make you turn up here like a bad penny. I will struggle and cry out if you even try it and they will all come to my aid.'

'If you prefer us to have an open and honest discussion of the past and the state of our marriage right here and now, where anyone can listen who cares to risk frostbite, then let's get on with it. I don't care what a pack of strangers think of me, but I suspect you do.'

'I don't want my friends to think ill of me.'

'They don't really know you, though, do they?'

She shivered at his implied threat to say who she really was and gave in. Jenny wasn't there, so did it matter if Ash was inside her home? Except it had been her sanctuary for so long and he would look down his aristocratic nose at its humble proportions and low-beamed ceilings. Telling herself his contempt for her humble home was the least of her worries, Rosalind led the way. The snow was still only an odd flake of feathery whiteness, but heavy clouds were cutting out more and more daylight. They walked in silence, but she was conscious of every muscle and sinew of this newly powerful man loping alongside her. He even *felt* furious, as if suppressed rage might keep winter at bay. A familiar ache deep inside shocked her with stupid fantasies of his newly powerful body intimately entwined with her own and how could it betray her at a time like this? Maybe she had longed for him so much it hurt at times during the last eight years, but she was only six and twenty and she still had the usual womanly needs. She dreamt of him as well—warm and loving again as he was for one glorious night all those years ago. Then she would wake up with tears on her cheeks and feel so terribly lonely it hurt. Now here he was, about to rip her whole world apart again and those eight years of longing felt like a traitor force inside her defences. She frowned up at him before she tapped on her own back door to warn Joan she was back. She opened it just wide enough for him to follow her in before even more warmth escaped.

'It's only me, Joan,' she called out as they stood in the narrow hallway shaking snowflakes off their outer wrappings. Through the half-open door to the kitchen she could see a fire still burning and there was no sign of hasty preparations for a reckless journey. Rosalind sighed at her own idiocy—fancy her believing there was any chance of getting away in such weather.

'There's going to be far too much snow for us to go anywhere until—' Joan stopped on the stairs as soon as she was far enough down them to see Ash's towering figure in the tiny hall where the shadows cast by the rush light burning in its holder made him look even more alien. Joan glared at him before descending the rest of the way in tight-lipped silence.

'Do continue,' he invited so smoothly Rosalind glared at him as well.

'I have nothing good to say to you, young man,' Joan said sharply.

'You used to like me,' he said, a half-smile smoothing away the thunderclouds for a moment as if he was pleased to see her.

'I used to be a fool then.'

'No, I think Rosalind and I were those,' he said with a hint of regret in his voice to make Rosalind think so as well, until she remembered why he was here and hardened her heart.

Joan glanced warily at Rosalind, who shrugged and could not say where Jenny was in front of Ash, since there was still the faintest chance he would not find out about her.

'I know I have a child,' he announced as if he could read their hastily exchanged looks far too easily. 'I presume you left her at the local vicarage to keep her out of my way?'

'Yes, and my daughter is very happy at the thought of snowball fights and sledging before breakfast in the morning before you accuse me of neglecting her or being a bad mother,' Rosalind said defensively. Not only had she almost agreed Jenny was his, but they were back on the treadmill of accusation and defence she remembered so clearly from the time they travelled back to London together, yet so very far apart.

'Did I do anything of the sort?' he asked Joan.

'Don't drag me into your arguments. You two must talk through your differences for the sake of the child now you have finally arrived home. I am going out now, but if you ever hurt Miss Rosalind again you will have me to deal with. And the child will never take to anyone who makes her mother miserable, so think on that as you pick over your grievances.'

'Yes, ma'am,' Ash said to Joan's back as she seized Ros's russet cloak from where it was drying in front of the fire in the kitchen and marched past them and out of the back door. Her grand exit fell flat when she came back for her boots, but she pushed her feet into them without doing up the laces and stamped out without another word. 'Where will she go?' he asked Rosalind and she tried not to like him for sounding anxious about her oldest friend.

'The Duck and Feathers; Mrs Seth Paxton is her bosom bow.'

'Then we had best do as we were bid before she comes back.'

'I do not want to talk to you. You left, I survived and so did my daughter. That is the beginning and end of the story.'

'And at no time in the last eight years did you think it was wrong for a child to grow up without a father?'

'No, and she is not yours.'

'I don't believe you, but you can hardly claim to have given her such a wonderful life even if I did,' he said with a cool look around the narrow hallway with its glimpses of the warm kitchen and shadowy little parlour where Joan had not had time to relight the fire. 'And our child should not be growing up in a cottage at the back of beyond.'

'It's not that remote here and at least people accept us as we are. This is the real world most of us have to live in, Your Grace, and you are welcome to be bowed and scraped to in your own finicky circle, but there was always too much gossip and backbiting in it for me to miss the gilded pleasures and day-to-day luxuries the *haut ton* take for granted.'

'As my wife you will have to endure them all the same,' he said as if finding out about Jenny changed everything. The thought of being truly married to this cold and self-contained aristocrat made her want to run again and never mind the weather.

'I am not your wife though, am I? You walked away from our marriage.'

'And you decided to punish me by withholding my child.'

Rosalind had thought she had covered her tracks so well he would never find her and somehow she had to protect herself and her child from a man who distrusted every word she said. No, wait, she did not have to tell him the real reason she came here to save her sanity and cut herself off from polite society. She had not admitted Jenny was his yet and he had only spent one night in their marriage bed, so why not lie? He expected her to, after all, so she might as well oblige him and he might even believe her.

'Ah, that folly again. You may have met my daughter but she is not yours, my lord Duke.'

'Liar,' he accused her flatly.

'No,' she insisted as if half-amused by his persistence.

'Yes. Don't waste your breath arguing black is white. The child I just saw peering down at me from the hayloft at the inn is mine as surely as you are still my lawfully wedded Duchess, Rosalind. That little girl is a Hartfield through and through and you will never persuade me otherwise.'

Rosalind's heart sank into her plain countrywoman's boots, but she tried again. 'Nonsense; you are seeing what you want to see, not what is. My child is dark where we are both fair for one thing and she is small for her age, whereas you Hartfields are unusually tall. My Jenny is not like you for the very good reason she is not your child,' she insisted as he watched with cynical eyes.

She was damning herself and Jenny in the eyes of the law and the church, but the thought of losing her daughter to him was far worse than lying. Being present at Jenny's conception did not make him a father. Being with them when she was born, caring for her when Jenny was sick or unhappy, even sitting with her when Rosalind was so weary she sometimes tumbled out of the chair at her daughter's bedside during that terrible week when Jenny had scarlet fever so badly they almost despaired of her life—now *that* could have made him Jenny's father in more than a biological fact, but he hadn't been there, had he? No, he had been far too busy being hurt and angry with her mother for a lie that had had never felt like a lie to bother with them at all. Then the dukedom fell in his lap and goaded him to come and find his discarded wife so he could be rid of her for good. Ash did not deserve such a unique and wonderful child. Rosalind did shift under his brooding gaze when she recalled the letter she had written begging him to come and share the heart-stopping anxiety of watching their child struggle with a raging fever, then shake with teeth-rattling chills when bathing her in cold water must have brought her temperature down too far. Of course she had ripped the letter to shreds the day Jenny's fever broke, so relieved she had not sent it when she imagined him storming home to take her child away from her. She slept on a pallet at Jenny's bedside for a week in case she had a relapse and they slowly began to live again, without this man who thought he had a right to call Jenny his when he had never been there when they truly needed him.

Chapter Four

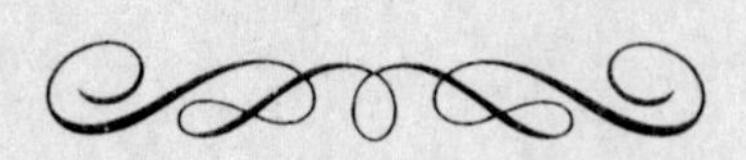

'The child I saw earlier today is mine,' Ash insisted, prepared to stand in this infernally draughty corridor all night if that was what it took to get her to admit the truth. 'And she must have come as a shock to you after we spent only that one night together,' he conceded clumsily.

Why had he never even thought about the chance of a child when he left Rosalind on her stepfather's doorstep? He had departed for India so he could not weaken and beg her to give their marriage another try. He wasn't ready to be sorry he had gone yet, though. Not when the shock and fury of finding out he had been a father all this time felt too huge to brush aside and blame himself for. He thought of all the birthdays he could not share with his daughter, all the first times he would never see. He had not been here to watch his child walk or talk for the first time. He had no idea how it felt to rock his baby to sleep. He had missed so many small details of his little girl's life he felt a deep sense of loss for days that could never come again. Yes, he had left, but Rosalind had deliberately kept the fact she had borne him a child secret.

'I will not let you put my daughter at risk because you are so desperate to get her away from me you seem to have lost any sense you ever had,' he told her sternly.

'There's no need to be rude and I told you, she is not your get. You left me, so why would I stay faithful? I lied up on the heath to make you feel guilty, but Jenny is not your child,' she insisted as if her hopes of keeping the lie going much longer felt hollow even to her, but she could not stop trying.

'Ours, then,' he said wearily.

'*No*, you are mistaken.'

'It might save a lot of time if I tell you I have a miniature of my little sister Amanda in my luggage that will prove your daughter is my child beyond doubt. It will be all the confirmation any court could need to say she is my legitimate child if you persist in this farce and I have to prove it.'

'You are turning a chance resemblance into full-blown fact.'

'Amanda lives again in the little girl I saw in that hayloft. You might have been able to fool me with dark hair and small stature if I had not lived with my sister for the whole of her short life, but since the likeness is uncanny you might as well give up now.'

'What use would a mere girl be to a duke anyway?' she said rather sulkily, as if she was beginning to give up on the idea of deceiving him.

'I don't care if the dukedom dies with me,' he finally said and it was true, now he had a daughter it didn't seem to matter a jot if the title died with him if she turned out to be his only child. 'But what the devil do you think I've been doing all these years, Ros? I have a fortune to pass on to my children and, as her father, I have a legal right to decide where my child lives. Now I have an heiress I could decide to do without the Duchess who goes with her.' Maybe it was cruel to hint at parting Ros from her child, but she had parted him from his all this time. She deserved to pay for that, even if this did change everything.

'No!' Rosalind heard agony in her own voice, but what was the point in trying to conceal her feelings now he knew everything? 'Imogen changed me the instant the midwife laid her in my arms and you do not know me now. I am a different person.' Memory of her child so innocent and perfect and totally herself in every way still made tears stand in her eyes. The memory would not allow her to lie any longer and it did not come naturally to her, whatever he thought of her past sins and omissions. 'Oh, very well, I admit it; she is yours,' she said with a mighty sigh. 'But if you truly wanted to be a father you should have been with me while I laboured to bring her into the world and through all the anxiety and sleepless nights afterwards. If you want a say in our lives now, you should not have been on the other side of the world nursing your grievances when we needed you so much. I know you had no idea she was on her way, but even if I had somehow managed to get news to you I was with child you would not have been back in time to be with us when she was born and I hurt so much I was afraid we were both going to die.'

He went pale at her words, but that must be because he might never have met his child, not because she might have died giving birth to her. 'I am still her father, though, you should have told me,' he said as if that cancelled out all the things he had done and it really did not.

'But I am her mother,' she said quietly. 'And you still left me.'

'Faults on both sides, Rosalind,' he replied as if her inability to tell him the whole truth about her past when they eloped still cancelled out his desertion of her and it felt like a huge gulf between them.

She grasped her hands together to stop them shaking. 'You haven't changed at all.'

'I am sorry, that was a low blow, but really, Ros—could you not even write a single letter informing me I have a child in all this time ? Do you think you have nothing to reproach yourself for when Jenny had to get this far without me knowing she exists?'

'We shall never agree, but you still have to free us from this ghost of a marriage to find your docile Duchess. All I want is to raise our child without your ridiculous dukedom destroying her peace of mind. She will never know who her real friends are if you drag her to Edenhope and make her live such an unnatural life.'

'She is my daughter, Ros. And at the risk of repeating myself, a father always has custody of his children after divorce. You admitted when we met on the heath that the only legal grounds for one is adultery on the part of the wife. Such a woman is deemed to have given up all claims to being a fit mother and that sounds a stark choice to me. Lie and live alone or tell the truth and stay with Jenny and be bound to me for the rest of your life.'

'Do you want her to hate you as well?' Even the thought of being parted from her child hurt. Without her Jenny might endure a jealous stepmother, always favouring her own children over his discarded first wife's daughter.

He sighed. 'Face it, Ros; I am a very rich man. You told me the truth when you said you had been faithful to our marriage didn't you?'

'Yes,' she said with a huge sigh, because lying wasn't going to work.

'So we are trapped,' he said with an equally gusty sigh. 'Our daughter will be hunted like a doe the moment she is of marriageable age if we two sit on our hands and leave her as my sole heiress. Her life will be made a misery by fortune hunters and worse if you refuse to be my Duchess.'

'If you divorce me and disclaim her, there would be no fortune hunters.'

'Just careless rakehells eager to corrupt your bastard daughter,' he pointed out starkly and he was right. Jenny would lose her chance of a decent life and respectable marriage if her mother became notorious as a divorced woman. 'If we agree to put a brave face on things for our daughter's sake, it will save her from an uncertain future,' he added as if he wasn't any more thrilled by the idea than she was, but he was ready to be a realist.

He had had years of practice at being cynical about love and marriage, though, hadn't he? Given his docile and undemanding ideal Duchess, he had a very different version of marriage in mind to any Rosalind considered tolerable. She would do almost anything for Jenny, though—even stay wed to this cynical version of her wild young love. 'I will not let you part me from my child.'

'And I will not leave here without one or both of you,' he told her as if nothing would change his mind either, so this was stalemate.

She had to consider enduring a marriage of convenience with him. 'You don't want me; I don't think you ever could have done deep down after the way you left me as if I don't matter.'

'Nonsense—one look from your beautiful blue eyes turned me into your lapdog the day we met,' he said in the rough velvet voice that used to make her go weak at the knees.

It sent a tingle of recognition shivering down her spine even now. Heat followed it to remind her of the passionate lovers they once were. 'Did it? I had forgotten,' she still managed to lie.

'Now I think you remember every hour we spent together and I know your body has not forgotten mine,' he murmured as his grey eyes challenged her to deny it.

'Why would I recall what happened so long ago?'

'Because my ring is on your finger and we are

bound by God and man? You are my Duchess, Rosalind, like it or not,' he insisted as if at the end of his patience.

'I am Rose Meadows,' she insisted. Rose was a better, stronger woman than Miss Rosalind Feldon or Mrs Asher Hartfield and she needed to remember how much she had changed.

'That's another form of your real name, but can we argue the rest somewhere warm?' He shivered and huddled into his multi-caped greatcoat. 'Damnable climate,' he muttered so gruffly she almost laughed.

'Do you think the sky will fall in if a duke sits in a kitchen?'

'Confound being a duke; if I don't get warm soon you won't even have to pretend to be a widow.'

'Don't say that,' she protested with a shudder that shook her to the bone. 'I might not want to be married to you, but I have never wished you dead.'

'Always an asset in a wife,' he joked as they passed from hallway to kitchen and shut the door behind them to keep the warmth in.

He held his hands out to the fire she stirred into more vigorous life with the poker and she heard his sigh of relief as he flexed his cold hands in front of its glowing warmth. 'You will get chilblains,' she warned and was about to shut all the other doors to keep the warmth in when she remembered Joan was baking this afternoon when she came back, so she searched the larder for something to eat.

'Thank you, suddenly I see advantages to living in

he could wall out his hurts and fears by hating a person she had never been.

'I had Jenny to make me a mother. Without her I hate to think what I might have become,' she admitted and it was true. If not for her child, what would she have done with herself over the last eight years? She hated to think and almost pitied him for not having a Jenny in his life to make it purposeful.

'Maybe she can make me a father and change me too.' He sighed and finally seemed to realise he still had his outer garments on. He shucked off his heavy greatcoat and she was impressed with the breadth of shoulder underneath and the power in them to get such a weight of damp wool off so easily without having to ask for help. Yes, he was dressed like a rich man trying to fit into a modest man's life. She recognised the cut of a master tailor and wondered how much it must have cost him to assemble a comprehensive wardrobe in the brief time he must have been back in London after his long voyage. His riding breeches and boots were the best quality and his linen snowy and immaculate, but the old Ash would have scorned such a plain and workmanlike waistcoat. As for the muffler this Ash could not yet bring himself to part with, he would have given that one glance of contempt and written his future self off as a middle-aged quiz with no sense of fashion.

Whereas Rosalind rather liked him; or she would, if she was the sort of idle society beauty who had time to spare for casting long, thoughtful sideways glances at a gentleman's powerful shoulders and those

a cottage,' he said and bit hungrily into the pasty she handed him.

'They are a lot easier and cheaper to keep warm than a mansion. My room at Lackbourne Hall was so cold in winter I used to beg Cook to let me stay in her chair by the kitchen fire all night instead of going upstairs to bed.'

'And did she?'

'No, she was too frightened of my stepfather. He said there was no point bringing me up soft since my father left me penniless and who knew whom I might have to marry when it came down to it. I think he only tolerated me because my mother had refused to marry him if he had me packed off to school until I was old enough to be married off to someone of my father's standing in life, like a curate or another schoolmaster.'

'He spent lavishly enough on your debut.'

'Because the *ton* would have raised their eyebrows if he did not by then. I was very much like my mother and she was a famous beauty so he could hardly pretend he didn't have a stepdaughter when I was growing up under his roof. He did grudgingly admit I had grown into my looks even if he despaired of my common sense, but our elopement must have been the final straw for him. I feel sorry for him now I look back. I was confused and angry after my mother died and it cannot have been easy for him to be saddled with another man's child when he and Mama had not managed to have a family of their own.'

'At least he did not throw you out because you

married me. My lawyer told me you left Lackbourne House a couple of months after we were wed.'

'I could not endure being a duty to him for the rest of my life. If he had discovered I was pregnant after my ill-advised defiance, as he called our elopement, he would have insisted the world knew we had married and you left me within days of our wedding. I could not endure the public scandal and derision and he did not deserve it. So I chose to make a new start. My life here feels better than any other on offer after you were gone.'

'She is my child as well. I would have done everything I could to support you both in comfort.'

'I never wanted my child to be a duty the way I was to Lord Lackbourne when I was growing up. Jenny has always known she is loved and she has never had to go without any of the true essentials of life. Imagine how it would have been for us if we had had to live on my stepfather's charity, always knowing we were a burden on him and a constant source of shame while you were living on the far side of the world from us.'

'I never thought about consequences,' he admitted, looking a little shamefaced about his younger self.

'You were too busy making me into a monster in your head to look at anything from my side. Your grandfather was right to say you were headlong and heedless and to prod you into making something of your life.'

'I wish I had been man enough to tell him about you before I took his not very attractive offer of a useful life in another country while I grew up, in return for

him paying off my debts and suppressing the worst of my misdeeds while I was at Oxford. He was quite right about me being an expensive young fool, but even he never knew what a heedless idiot I can be.'

'Neither did you,' she said as she contrasted his manner with her up on the heath to his slightly chastened one now he had found out about Jenny.

He refused to meet her eyes and reminded her of a boy with a cricket bat in his hand, a nearby broken window and a saintly expression on his face. Great vigorous man as he was, he looked a bit like Jenny's friend Hal caught in the wrong, but steadfastly refusing to admit it. 'Maybe I didn't grow up in India after all,' he finally admitted. He did have the air of a rich and successful man about him as he brooded over his sins and almost admitted he had been wrong, so maybe he really had made his fortune on the other side of the world and that was another factor to weigh up as they eyed each other warily across Joan's spotlessly clean kitchen.

What could she say to his grudging admission? I had been such a boy to carry all that fury across many miles of ocean, then unloaded it at the other like heavy baggage for storage until he was read unlock it one day and see what it really contain that day ever came. He must have been skirting a it ever since, telling himself she was everyth painted her after he found her out in a lie and she was just like his mother on the slenderes dence. If he had not done so much damage, s even feel sorry for the rootless young Ash wh

narrow flanks so temptingly displayed in the more modest fashion he aped today. As she was only his wife she did her best not to think those thoughts and turned away to put another lump of coal on the already glowing fire. He was obviously still cold and that was about as wifely as she was prepared to be under the circumstances.

'If you are trying to make me feel small, it's certainly working,' he told her after that long and thoughtful silence. 'I did arrange for the interest on the very small fortune I had left back then to be paid to you every quarter when I left for India,' he said, looking grim again as he eyed the mismatched plates on the dresser and the rag rug in front of the fire as if they were all the confirmation he needed she never received a penny of his money.

'So I could go from one charity to another? I had quite enough of being an unwanted dependent under Lord Lackbourne's roof, thank you very much. Even if I had known about it, I would not have been very grateful for your conscience money.'

'Not charity—I had a duty to provide for my wife although we were estranged and you could have starved for all my lawyer cared. My grandfather paid for my passage and arranged a post as a clerk to the Company when I reached Calcutta, then he told me I would have to live off my pay and expect no more help from him. But at least I thought you were provided for as best I could—you could have lived better than this on it anyway.'

'We live well enough, we are warm and well fed

and decently clothed, but it was harsh of your grandfather to cut you off without a shilling.'

'Not really, I was a wild and expensive young idiot so I suppose I deserved it. I promised Jasper not to gamble wildly or drink to excess like our father when I went off to Oxford and he went to war, but I never could resist a dare to relieve the boredom of being the extra spare grandson of a duke. Grandfather thought I was becoming as big a wastrel as my father and needed a shock to make something of myself before it was too late. He thought he had failed with his second son so he was determined to make me do something useful. His last throw of the dice with me was timed just right; I had an excuse to run away from my responsibility for you and any child we might have. I never even thought of such a consequence when I left you, which only goes to prove what a careless young idiot I was.'

'It was only one night and I expect he planned to get you away from me as well as forcing you to take some responsibility,' she pointed out as if she was defending him.

Everyone must have known Ash was besotted with Lord Lackbourne's penniless stepdaughter back then. They had thought it such a delicious secret to meet even after her stepfather had turned down Ash's suit, but with hindsight it was probably obvious to the gossips. Someone must have told Ash's grandfather the affair was not as nipped in the bud by that refusal as he and her stepfather had thought. Sending his grandson to India was the perfect solution for a duke faced with supporting the feckless pair she and Ash would have been if they had been allowed to marry openly and carry on with their lives as if the ravens would feed them like Elijah. Rosalind was glad she had been left free to bring Jenny up as an ordinary human being, until Ash came back, but his family were not to know when he was sent away for his own good that they had eloped together before he went.

'He never knew I had married you,' Ash said.

'Maybe not, but he never made an effort to meet me and judge for himself if I was a good enough wife for you. My father must have been a good man since my mother loved him, but the real truth is I can never have looked like a suitable match for a true aristocrat like you.'

Ash shifted in the Windsor chair he had sunk into as the fire warmed him, as if he didn't want to admit even now that he no longer loved her. 'The dukedom was so unlikely to fall on me I was no more than a gentleman when we married. If I had told him what we meant to do, he and your stepfather would have felt obliged to stop the wedding simply because we were so young and foolish we could not be trusted to know our minds,' he pointed out with the wisdom of hindsight.

'True, but once the deed was done and neither of them could do anything about it, why did you not tell him then?' she asked, thinking he must have been ashamed of his poor catch and scorned bride. He still looked as if he would rather not discuss the past now they had so much of Jenny's future to consider, but it felt vital for her to at least try to understand why he did and said what he had back then. Even a convenient wife needed some sense of the ground under her feet and she had always vowed she would do anything to keep her daughter safe and happy, hadn't she?

'We parted so quickly it seemed best not to advertise what an idiot I had been. And he would have raged at me for spoiling your life as well as my own. I thought providing for you as best I could was enough and went to India fully expecting his furious letter disowning me to follow as soon as he found out what a coward I had been.' Again his chair creaked as he fidgeted in it as if the thought of his boyish irresponsibility made him feel uncomfortable now it was too late to remedy.

'Do you expect me to cheer you for admitting it?'

'No, I was a cur. Grandfather and my brother Jasper and even my little cousin Charlie would have been so disappointed in me if they knew I had run away and pretended our marriage never happened.'

She thought about the effect his boyish excuses and evasion had had on her young life and wished she could go back in time and give him a very large slice of tongue pie, but there was little point now and there were more important things to worry about. 'I have known some curs with the most gentlemanly of souls,' she still said with a pointed look to make clear he was not one of them.

'Very well, then, I was worse than a cur. I was so wrapped up in my own ills I took no account of yours and I am very sorry for it now.'

Not then or at any time after I got to India, or even yesterday or earlier today, when I set out to finally rid myself of you for good, Rosalind. But now...now I am finally sorry.

She silently put the words into his mouth and found they fitted it too well. She argued silently that was not good enough and he shrugged as if he knew what she was thinking and she was right.

'I cannot go back and put any of it right now, it happened too long ago,' he admitted out loud.

'I hid as far away from Edenhope and your family as I could get once I realised I was with child. And it turns out that I could have gone to live in the next town for all the difference it would have made to them. I was even glad when I found out your grandfather was dead and I no longer had to fear every passing stranger was sent here to rescue his great-grandchild from my clutches. That memory makes me ashamed, for I expect he was only trying to do his best for his family.'

'Aye, he was, he would have welcomed you at Edenhope and felt sorry for you for being tangled up by his idiot grandson. It is my fault you and my child have been living in poverty and she has no idea about her heritage. He would be the first one to tell me so if he was still alive.'

His critical gaze was stern on the jumble of oddments they used here on a day-to-day basis and Rosalind had to see it through his eyes. What seemed cheerful and cosy until he came looked scraped together and poverty-stricken. If this was how it felt to see with a duchess's gaze she wasn't sure she liked it. 'I am proud of our home. Jenny loves to pick out memories when Joan makes those rag rugs out of odds and ends,' she told him, since he was staring at the latest example with a frown.

'What?' he said as if lost in completely different thoughts. 'Oh, yes, I can see how she would.'

'Money isn't everything,' she added.

'Weighed against over seven years of my daughter's life it seems very close to nothing right now, but I still have it and you are still a duchess.'

'Then let me go, Ash; leave us be.'

'Don't you see how impossible that is? With my daughter to protect and me still wanting you like the very devil,' he said, voice rasped by the fire and hot need in his eyes now he had turned them full on her.

'You do?' she asked, shocked when she thought she was the only one struggling against the fiery passions that had always hummed between them whenever they were together in the old days. Now those needs and wants were screaming for everything they had been denied while they were apart and apparently he was torn by them as well.

Chapter Five

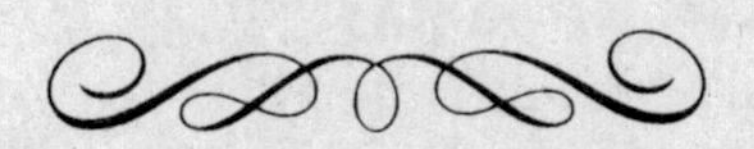

'How would *you* feel if I really was first mate of a merchantman come back to you after all these years, Mrs Rose Meadows?' he asked as if her answer was important to him.

How much simpler their lives would be if he was, but it was a fantasy she could not afford. 'I would feel deeply relieved you were still alive,' she said tightly.

'And that's all?'

'As you are not Mr Meadows what does it matter?'

'Maybe I would prefer myself that way as well, my Rosalind.'

'Not yours, Ash. Not any more.'

'Ah, Ros, we made such a mess of things, didn't we?' he said as if he truly regretted it and she was still too cautious to be convinced.

'You look like a successful man to me, Your Grace,' she said, but he went on staring into the fire as if searching for answers to far bigger questions. 'We have both done well enough,' she added. 'You in your way and I in mine.'

'Aye, I thought I was rich until I came here and found out what I lacked.'

Rosalind was tempted to breach the gulf between them and say she and Jenny would fill the spaces in his life he seemed to have only just found out about, but this was far too important to be mended with easy words and generous impulses. This decision he was almost asking her to make would affect the rest of her life, and perhaps define Jenny's as well. 'You are tired and cold and probably feel like a stranger in your own land,' she told him instead and even to her the words sounded trite.

'Don't mother me,' he argued, turning his brooding gaze on her again and letting her see the very grown-up need in his smoky eyes. He looked so familiar and yet so different from the boy she once knew as he stared back at her in the firelight.

'Perish the thought,' she muttered and looked away.

He moved so fast he had pulled her out of her chair and into his arms before she drew breath. Her body clung to his as if it was home after eight years in the wilderness. Her world had shrunk to arms that felt like steel sheathed in muscle and the instant familiarity of his body against hers. There was a moment of getting used to the fit of him and her, then here they were again; her body plastered against his masculine one and purring like a cat. He was ten times stronger than last time he held her so close and more emphatically male, but he still felt dear and familiar and it was appallingly alluring. He met her mesmerised gaze with the devilment, the old wild spirit and stubbornness of her young husband in his hot grey gaze and a new helping of Ash, the Duke, to add a steadier flame to the mix.

Her humble kitchen faded away as they stepped out of the everyday world and could have been anywhere. His lips teased hers and she gave a faint little moan of encouragement instead of the demand to let her go her last traces of good sense had been working on until he kissed her. He dipped a butterfly kiss on her half-open mouth and what point was there pretending she didn't want him when it was like a force of nature raging to be unleashed inside her? Next he opened his wickedly persuasive mouth on hers, let his tongue slide in with a leisurely flick that made her insides flip over in hot and heady anticipation. The aching memory of their only night of love was sultry and yearning, a goad to do it all again, right now. He must know her tongue would dart out to meet his, but he withdrew from the full ardent contact of lovers before she got there. One last gentle, lover's nip at her lower lip and he raised his head again. She felt tears sting and blinked them away. It would never do to let him see her cry and she seemed to have been holding back a whole river of tears since she set eyes on him again.

If only, oh, if only... The old besotted Rosalind almost betrayed her by whispering it out loud.

That part of her was distraught at the terrible waste of all they could have been together, if he had not turned into her stern judge when they had been so young and dangerously in love it was almost certain to end in tears. The rest of her was a lot more cautious and tried to read his reaction to the kiss she had returned with so much interest. She even did her best to douse the sweet fire inside and gazed back coolly.

'I wish you hadn't done that,' she managed to murmur huskily at last.

'Why?'

'Because what went wrong between us can't be put right with a few kisses and a pat on the head, then back to where we left off eight years ago.'

'How can we make it better, then?'

A good question. 'With honesty and good will, I suppose,' was the only answer she could come up with and she read the cynical look in his eyes that said her dishonesty did for them last time, so she knew they were still a very long way from mending a broken marriage. If it was even possible to do so.

'Joan will be back soon,' she reminded them both.

'We had best not fall on one another like wild beasts again until bedtime, then,' he said as if he had said and done all he needed.

'Oh, no, you are not staying here.' Moments ago she had been longing for her bed and freedom to slake whatever was left between them now the love was gone. The idea of him cynically climbing the narrow stairs to a bed she had only ever shared with her daughter when Jenny could not sleep in her own felt unthinkable. She needed more than lust and his urgent need of an heir to risk so much of herself with him after he had hurt her so much last time.

'Come to my room at the inn, then,' he urged as if he thought it was only fear of Jenny or Joan bursting in and interrupting that kept her from eagerly agreeing to be his devoted slave. 'It seemed comfortable enough and at least the whole place is spotless. I told them I was Mr Meadows as well so it will be perfectly respectable.'

'You have a very strange idea of not causing scandal in a small village, especially one about to be shut down by a snowstorm so we cannot escape watching eyes and wagging tongues.'

'How can they make up warm stories about us? We are married.'

'Because I have been living here without you for seven and a half years and you don't look like any merchant seaman I ever saw. I am not adding fuel to the fire by strolling through the inn to your bedchamber.'

'If they are going to gossip anyway, why not give them something to gossip about?'

'No, you're not getting round me by turning the truth inside out. You always did have a smooth tongue when you cared to use it.'

'You have become very free with that *No* of yours since we last met, despite my not-very-persuasive powers.'

'If I had said it more in the past, we would not be glaring at one another across my humble kitchen now, Your Grace.'

'Would you have waited until you were of age to marry me, then?' he shocked her by asking as if he truly wanted to know.

'Yes, maybe it would have been better if I had. You might have lost interest in me altogether,' she said and saw him veil something like hurt pride as he stared at her as if he was still reluctantly fascinated. 'Or we could have got to know one another better and might have weathered the storm my old folly unleashed when I finally found the courage to tell you about it,' she added.

'I doubt your stepfather would have let you sit on the shelf for three years while we tested out our faithfulness.'

'True, but at least mine lasted better than yours.'

A hot flush of colour across his high cheekbones was all the answer she needed. Of course he would have kept a string of mistresses while he was away. Most noblemen had affairs with courtesans while playing the dutiful husband and father even when they were at home, so why would Ash resist them when he was so far from a wife he despised? Now he thought she would take him to her bed after one hot kiss and a click of his ducal fingers? She had never wanted to be one of a crowd and there was far more to marriage than passionate kisses, as she was in a very good position to know.

'And you were never tempted?' he asked as if her lack of interest was an insult. There really was no pleasing some husbands, was there?

'I am human, but I have a child. Ask Joan if you don't believe me, but I have no room in my life for a man.'

'She would lie for you,' he said, a bite of jealousy in his grey eyes she was fiercely glad to see. A lot more was roaring through her at the thought of all the lovers he must have had in eight years.

'She would not lower herself and she knows I would rather scrub floors than be at the mercy of a capricious lover again.'

'There will be plenty of floors in need of a good clean at Edenhope,' he said with an unforgivable, wolfish smile.

'And *you* are capricious beyond belief,' she told him crossly, trying not to smile as a picture of herself in a duchess's coronet and robes down on her knees scrubbing floors to keep her desire for him at bay flitted through her mind like a traitor. Her mind was a very busy street nowadays, thanks to the ridiculous emotions he was arousing in her and very uncomfortable it was, too.

'I was once. Now I am an industrious and steady sort of fellow and I dare say I will make a fine duke once I put my mind to it. Which is something I shall not be able to do properly if you are busy rearranging my dukedom but refusing to sleep in my bed.'

'We would need to get used to one another again first, if Jenny is not too shocked to find out you are her father, for us to travel and live together straight away.'

'And if there isn't an *r* in the month or snow on the ground or birds in the air?' he said as if she was the awkward one and he hadn't stormed off, then pretended he didn't even have a wife all this time.

She shrugged. 'Do you want me to endure life as your Duchess or not?' she asked haughtily.

'I do,' he said, suddenly very serious and what a difference having a daughter made to a duke, her inner cynic whispered.

'Do you intend to be faithful to me from now on?' she asked to get the contract clear before she agreed to it on even a trial basis.

'If you take me to your bed before I expire of frustration,' he qualified as if it would be a struggle to keep his hands off her and she didn't believe that for a moment. He had lived without her very easily for years and would have done so for the rest of his life if he had not chanced on Jenny up to her usual mischief at the village inn. It was probably just a warning not to expect a white marriage, as if she was that stupid when he so obviously needed an heir. Was she supposed to be grateful he was prepared to wrap that need up in a fantasy he wanted her so urgently then, when he had managed very well without her for so long?

'Should I take that as a no, then?' she asked coolly.

'If I had you in my bed, why would I want anyone else?' he said with a hot and hungry look that said she was still physically beautiful and she still wasn't sure if that was a curse or a blessing.

'I don't have the skills of a courtesan or the charm of a mistress and I have lived my own life for years. I am not a pretty plaything to pick up in idle moments and put down when you need a little variety.'

'I would not toy with you, Ros,' he told her so seriously she might have to believe him if she wasn't careful. 'One day, if I am a very good duke, and you are my Duchess again in more than name only, maybe we can build on our mutual need and make something better than we had last time. Our kisses proved we still want one another urgently and we won't have stepfathers and grandfathers trying to frustrate us at every turn this time.'

'They had very little to do with what went wrong between us last time. I would like to believe we could have something better than a marriage of convenience in time as well, but we have been apart for years, Ash. We are very different people and can hardly have known each other even when we eloped, since we parted so soon afterwards.'

'At least we can never make the same mistakes again.'

'Just different ones,' she said cynically.

Perhaps it was as well Joan came in then, with a great show of stamping snow off her boots and shuffling about in the little hallway to warn them she was home. 'You haven't broken my kitchen china, then?' she said with a look around to see if shards of it were lying in a dark corner.

'Not yet,' Rosalind replied.

'Better if we had perhaps,' Ash said satirically. Rosalind blushed at the scene of unrestrained passion he was obviously playing out in his head.

'For you maybe, young man, but we have to live here until the snow melts and I don't enjoy eating straight out of the pot,' Joan told him with one of her best disapproving looks. 'Speaking of eating, it's time I was busy cooking and more than time you two got out of my kitchen.'

'We could all eat at the Duck and Feathers,' Ash offered.

'You go, we are quite used to eating stew or a pie,

but you must be used to the captain's table.' Rosalind hoped the thought of humble fare would make him leave them in peace tonight. They were hardly going to steal off into the snowy darkness without Jenny and she needed time to think.

'And very tedious it was after a few weeks at sea,' he replied a bit too seriously for her taste. 'And we still have a great deal to discuss.'

'I disagree,' she said, all they had already talked about rattling about in her head.

'Go and argue in the parlour, then, and light the fire while you're about it,' Joan said impatiently, then lit them a tallow candle and shooed them out of her domain.

'I thought she was a lady's maid,' Ash muttered as he shivered in the chill on the other side of the kitchen door.

'She was my mother's maid and then mine, as I am sure you know.'

'Aye, but she was never quite convinced I was good enough for you even before we left her behind when we eloped.'

'She was right then, wasn't she?'

'Yes, but I thought we were beyond sniping at one another like this.'

'We are,' Rosalind agreed with a sigh. 'We have to be,' she added and reached for a spill from the jar on the mantelpiece.

'I should do that,' he said as he reached it far more easily and held out the spill in front of him as if wondering what to do with it.

'You lit a lot of fires while you were in India, then, did you?'

'Not exactly,' he replied and she twitched the thin sliver of wood from his loose grip and held it to the candle flame.

'Best leave it to those of us who have, then,' she said and it would have been a fine put-down if only giving him such a wide berth did not make the lit spill flicker and die.

'You were saying?' he mocked, stretching out a hand for another.

'I would do a lot better if you would only get out of my way.'

'As you have been telling me since I got here.'

'Quite right, too,' she muttered as she snatched the next spill from him and this time picked up the candle so she could take it with her to the fire.

'Clever,' he observed as the spill caught and she held it to the wood shavings and kindling with an almost steady hand.

'Necessary. I thought you were cold.'

'I am; I haven't been properly warm since we passed Africa and hit the Bay of Biscay.'

'It must have been rough at this time of the year,' she said, carefully keeping her back to him as she blew gently on the beginnings of the fire and watched the fragile flame.

'It was,' he said grimly and she wondered how rough it really was.

'You should have waited for spring.'

'Apparently it can be even worse then and time was

a-wasting. My cousin Charles was always writing to me about the parlous state of his houses and estates. Grandfather was ill for a long time before he died and then there was Charlie's minority. He had no power to do very much about any of it until he was five and twenty and fully of age as far as the Hartfield trusts are concerned, but he never got that far. He was still a year away from taking control of his inheritance when he died.'

Ash's deep voice sounded full of regret for the lively young cousin Rosalind only vaguely remembered. The endearing young man she had once met in Ash and his elder brother Jasper's company in the Park could only have been a year or so younger than she, but he had seemed such a boy. She sighed and hoped he managed to have some fun before he died.

She sat back on her heels and pretended to give all her attention to the flourishing fire. Ash carried a heavy load of sorrow for a man not yet out of his twenties though, didn't he? Perhaps it was no wonder he let distrust of his mother and grief for his little sister eat away at his trust of any woman who did not fit his ideal of angelic purity. She had only wanted to love him when she was eighteen and he was one and twenty, but his love had been so easily lost. His mother did sound incapable of loving anyone but herself and Rosalind supposed a boy who grew up with such a large blank in his life had some excuse for reacting to her belated confession as if he had been stung by a serpent. How hard it was to be fair when she was the girl he had called a liar then refused to listen to all the way back to London. The past still stung—how could it not when she had loved him so much and he obviously only saw her as a pretty possession? He would never have left her so easily if he truly loved her. The fact remained she loved their daughter and would do almost anything to see Jenny grow up happy and secure, so she never made the sort of mistakes her mother did when she was so desperate to be loved she could not tell lust from the real thing.

'Your cousin must have been fidgeting to be fully of age and get on with things,' she said carefully as she leaned forward to take a log from the basket and add it to the fire.

'Even I can stoke a fire once it has been safely lit,' he said impatiently and took it off her and placed it, as if he thought she might break if she didn't take care.

'I am not a weak little ninny used to having everything done for me, Ash. I shall go mad if I do come with you to Edenhope and you insist on treating me like one.'

'No need to snap at me for trying to act the gentleman for once,' he said mildly. 'I suppose you don't want to know you have soot on your hands and now on your face as well, considering you are such a rough-handed woman-of-all-work nowadays.'

'I do *not* have rough hands,' she protested, and sped out of the room to find soap and water and a square of mirror to at least get rid of the soot, even if her hands might take a little more work with one of Joan's softening lotions and a stern resolution to wear gloves to protect them whenever she was digging the garden or sowing and planting from now on.

Hold up, though, Rosalind; there can be no more of any of that for the Duchess of Cherwell.

She supposed she ought to be glad, so it was a pity she felt as if she would even miss the exertion, and satisfaction, of digging her vegetable beds and all the planning of what should go where this year. She would miss her home as well and would have to turn the vast, empty Edenhope Place into a home somehow, if she went there with her husband. It seemed almost impossible when she realised her whole house would probably fit once or twice into the entrance hall of Ash's famously grand mansion.

Chapter Six

Ash fastidiously wiped his own hands on a snowy handkerchief, put it back in his pocket and wished he was warm again. It would be rude to go and fetch his greatcoat to wear inside the house, but he would rather not die of an inflammation of the lungs now he knew he had a daughter. Shock at the complete turnaround his life had undergone since he rode towards Livesey, met Rosalind on the heath, then looked up into that hayloft and met his daughter, shook him all over again as he huddled close to the fire. He had never known how much he longed for a daughter of his own until he saw one staring back at him fully formed. She was so very real his Jenny, so much herself, even if she was also the living image of his little sister Amanda. Jenny Meadows, he reminded himself with a smile—it had a nice ring to it, even if it wasn't quite his family name to make it clear she was his. He had to give Rosalind her due, though; it was a version of it. 'Trust my clever wife to turn her fields and meadows around and leave off the heart bit,' he murmured.

If not for the snow, he would get them all on the road as soon as he could hire a coach and organise their journey. Charlie's worries about his lands and property had weighed on his mind all the way from Calcutta and the long voyage meant even more damage would have been done by the time he got home to start putting it right. It felt like a sacred trust now Charlie would never have full control of his own estates and fortune. His daughter was an even greater responsibility than any Ash had ever dreamed awaited him in England, though, and she must come first. Charlie would understand if he was still alive. Having been brought up by his grandfather after Ash's Uncle Edward, Marquess of Asham, died, his cousin valued the relatives he had left so dearly he even managed to love their prickly and eccentric Great-Aunt Brilliana and that took a lot more tolerance and dedication than Ash had had when he was a boy. Charlie used to follow Ash and Jasper about like an eager puppy and always swore he would have an enormous family of Hartfields as soon as he came across the right Duchess to have them with. 'Some achieve duchesses, some have duchesses thrust upon them,' he misquoted under his breath and decided he had to stop it before his wife came back and heard him.

Was she such an imposition, though? His cautious mind whispered, *maybe*, but his body had no doubts at all how it felt about the former Miss Feldon. It longed for her with a feral passion it never seemed to have quite got over after that one night of unmatched pleasure in Rosalind's arms. Even the thought of her naked and eager and as heartbreakingly lovely as she had been that night when she gave everything she was to her silly young husband was enough to make him very glad she wasn't in the room—given the embargo she had put on lovemaking. So, no, she was not an imposition at all. But this was a very different future to the one he had planned when he had come to find out if this was really Rosalind and make it very clear to her that their marriage was over. He had been prepared to be generous with her, he recalled guiltily. As long as she really had agreed to be divorced as quietly as the ridiculous fuss only a rich man could stir up to end a marriage allowed. Instead he was looking at a very different future now he knew they had a child and did he truly regret it? He didn't think he would miss his milk-and-water second Duchess. He contrasted his sensual longing at first sight of his estranged wife up on the wintry heath and felt guilty about the girl he had promised himself he would keep in a duchess-shaped box while she got on with providing him with heirs. He would have made sure it was a comfortable space, with all the luxuries a girl could dream of at her feet and her noble husband's respect to make it tolerable, but he never had any intention of loving her or even wanting her more urgently than it took him to make those sons with her. The poor girl would have had a cold life, perhaps loving her children, but denied the true relationship he had grown up promising himself with his one-day wife. His marriage was not going to be like his parents'—a thing of convenience and dynastic duty that barely even held together after his own birth and what his mother saw as the end of her obligation to provide spare heirs for her husband's father. He wasn't going to be caught in that trap—with Charlie and Jas between him and the dukedom Ash would find a woman he could love and enjoy and live with as a man should truly live with his wife. Look where that notion got him and Rosalind.

So here he was, back to the real here and now; waiting to persuade his wife a cool, cynical marriage where they both got what they wanted was better than the alternative of divorce and her living without their child. Not much of a choice, though, was it? He sighed and wondered what that hot-tempered young man would make of his older self. Not a lot, he realised; but just look at the damage the young Ash had done with his dream of true love. The boy had made the mess his older and wiser self was trying to clear up with this offer of exactly the sort of marriage he once despised.

The reason they had eloped was to stop Ros being nagged into a marriage of convenience with a middle-aged lord by her stepfather while Ash was far away. He thought of coming back to England after leaving it as her desperate and disappointed former suitor instead of her estranged husband and felt his hands clench again. Would he have experienced the same hot mist of desire at first sight of her again after so many years apart? What a disaster to want Lord Somebody Or Other's convenient wife so hotly and deeply. Or perhaps she would have settled for being her husband's lovely and adored wife and been happy enough without him? Appalling thought, he decided, and forced his imagination away from futures that would never happen to work on the one he had. He only wanted a convenient wife in a different form, he told himself uneasily, as he recalled that haze of hot need on first seeing his wife after so long away from her unique allure that it punched him in the gut.

And why be ashamed he could now offer her so little of himself? She lied eight years ago and had carried on lying ever since. He could hardly claim she knew about the baby when he left England because he didn't give her enough time to find out before he left, but she had kept her pregnancy and the birth of his child a secret all these years. And hidden her tracks so well his lawyer admitted it took him six months to find her, when he eventually made the effort. Ash felt his fingers tighten yet again as he realised how much that lawyer cost him. Never mind the little fortune he thought he secured on his wife, the man lost him seven years of his daughter's life. He would have sailed right back to England if a letter from his lawyer had come by the next ship to say his brief night of marriage had led to more than the collapse of his hopes and dreams of a happily passionate marriage. He imagined getting back home in time to see his baby walk and talk, even if he would have been too late for the birth. He recalled helping to foal his favourite mare when he was a boy and the effort and fear and joy of it all. Being deprived of the pitfalls and glory of birth with his own child made him feel so furious with a hasty youth who ran away from the mess he had made of his life he had to get up and pace or release it by punching a hole in the wall. Since he could only stand up properly at the centre of the room where his head did not brush the beams holding up the room above, it did not take him long to stop.

'Confound this rabbit hutch,' he barked.

'You are very welcome to go back to the Duck and Feathers and rail about their timbers instead,' Rosalind told him huffily from the doorway.

'Later,' he snapped.

'If you are going to storm about the place complaining I would far rather it was now,' she said sharply.

'Lord knows how you can claim to be humble when you sound like an offended princess when someone crosses you.'

'I don't have to pretend it, I am,' she said as if it was true.

'But you must have got your air of touch-me-not royalty from your father, since I cannot recall ever noticing it in your mother.'

'You remember her?' she said, warmth in her blue eyes that made him envy a good woman dead for nearly a decade.

'Of course, she was one of the most famous beauties of her day.'

'She was, wasn't she?' Ros said wistfully and threatened to make a fatal hole in his defences. Here was the Ros he first knew, a vulnerable and sometimes needy half woman, half girl. She had felled him with one look, then walked straight into his heart with the second one as if to say, 'What, you mean *me*?' when he had stared back at her like a mooncalf.

'And a kindly soul with rather simple tastes under the fine clothes and exquisite society manners she was, too. She was very kind to my little cousin and even had patience to play a game or two with my brother and me when she came to stay at Edenhope with your stepfather. I suppose you were deemed too young to travel with them at the time.'

'Probably. And the Earl was always afraid one of us would make a mistake and reveal what he considered to be our humble background, so he kept me out of the way. He even made Mama take lessons in etiquette after they were married, in case she disgraced him by not knowing how deeply to curtsy to a prince or when to look down her nose at a mere mister. She was a lady to her very bones and he had the impudence to think he had married beneath him, because my father was only a poor scholar, then a teacher.'

'I am beginning to see why you dislike Lord Lackbourne so much,' he joked to try to relax the frown almost knitting her slender brows together.

'As if she needed anything of the sort,' she carried on darkly. 'Mama was a lady. He begged her to marry him even though Grandfather Whitbourne was a cathedral canon the Earl consulted about an obscure point of ecclesiastical law for one of the churches on the Lackbourne estate. He could hardly claim Mama was anything but a lady even if she did wed my father and live a simple life with him until he died.'

'And so are you, wherever you were born.'

'Apparently not,' she replied shortly.

The Earl of Lackbourne had done such a good job

convincing his stepchild her birth was inferior that Ash would have a deal to say to him next time they met.

'Aren't you warm yet?' she said like a scolding wife.

He knew a change of subject when he heard one, but even so it felt more of a blessing than a curse to be nagged for his own good again. His grand house in Calcutta had been full of willing servants and busy clerks ran round at his bidding. Then there was the succession of willing beauties kept in luxury to supply feminine company and sensuality when he needed it. They had left him with some fond memories and slightly lighter pockets, but he had never loved one of them.

Just as well—you are done with love, remember?

Ah, yes... This Ash took the reminder from the old, bitter one and turned a more cynical eye on his wife. *How could I forget?*

'I have come from a hot and verdant country to midwinter,' he said.

'I think you had best go back again if you dislike it so much, then. I hear Yorkshire has even colder winters and at least we have the south westerlies here to keep us warm.'

'Not noticeably.'

'It will be far colder at Edenhope,' she pointed out.

'How would *you* cope with rougher winters and later springs?' he asked. He still loved the place, despite years away and always knowing it was going to be Charlie's one day, but Rosalind had never even set eyes on it, so he wondered how she and their daughter would cope with the severe weather.

'I would manage, but you are softer than I am so we might have to come back south for the winter.'

'Perhaps,' he said moodily, because it seemed a sign of weakness to admit he felt as if he would never adjust to the cold after all those years in a hotter climate. And that *we* of hers sounded tempting and intimate; he wanted to be tempted and intimate with her all the way up her crooked staircase and into her bed right now and she was not persuaded their rematch would be a good idea yet. The longer he spent in her company, the more he wanted everything and the less likely she would ever give it to him. 'Is dinner nearly ready?' he asked, an image of this far more acerbic Rosalind loving him despite his sins still beckoning.

'If you are so very hungry, Mrs Paxton at the Duck and Feathers is accounted a very fine cook.'

He had laid himself open to that one, hadn't he? 'I shall try to be patient.'

'I can see what an effort it will be,' she mocked him and he turned to watch her with all he really wanted in his eyes and hoped it would warn her to stop teasing before his self-control broke completely.

Rosalind had to take that hot and explicit glare of Ash's and force food past the lump it put in her throat then pretend she didn't know he wanted her for the rest of the evening.

'How did a lady's maid learn to be such an excellent cook?' Ash asked as the two of them sat at the little gate-legged table and Joan waited on them as if the line between mistress and servant had grown back the moment he walked through the door.

'Because she had to,' Joan said gruffly.

At least she wasn't going to respect Ash without a lot more effort on his part, so some of the certainties in Rosalind's life had not melted away. 'I tried,' Rosalind said. She had to smile at Joan's wry expression. 'When we first came here I could not work and Joan used to do fine sewing in order to earn some money until Jenny was born, then be old enough to be left for a few hours so I could work. We were both relieved when I could earn more by teaching ladylike accomplishments to reluctant young ladies while Joan took over the house and cared for Jenny when I was out. She is a far better cook than I am. I could not seem to keep my attention on food and the fire and managed to burn most things I tried to cook.'

'So it was learn to cook or starve?' Ash guessed.

'Most things are better than that,' Joan said dourly and left the room with his empty dinner plate and Rosalind's half-finished food.

'Was there ever a danger of it?' Ash queried sharply.

'Not really, I would have sold the watch if things got that bad, but we had to be careful until I was fit to work.'

'The fat scoundrel who pocketed the money I meant for you had better get out of town before I get back,' he snapped. Rosalind wondered if he could light fires without a flint by simply staring at them long enough with such scorching fury in his eyes.

'We survived, Ash. No, we thrived and he probably

did us a favour. You would have stormed back if you knew I was having a baby and accused me of cuckolding you while your back was turned.'

'I might not have done,' he said, but she could see the truth in his quickly averted eyes and slight, giveaway flush.

'You might have learned to hide your feelings from business rivals, Ash, but it doesn't work with me.'

'No, confound it,' he muttered into his cider mug and downed the rest unwarily.

'There, there,' she said not very sympathetically and got up to thump him on the back as the strength of it caught at his throat. 'I dare say you will soon learn to take your liquor again.'

'I am accounted to have a very hard head.'

'Not something I would be proud of, but there is no accounting for masculine vanity.'

'Or the feminine superiority,' he countered grumpily.

'Are you two quarrelling again? What sort of example is that to Miss Jenny when she gets back in the morning?' Joan asked as she came back in with apple pie and the cream jug. 'There's some rum left over from the Figgy Pudding or a piece of Twelfth Night Cake they sent round from the vicarage if you don't fancy the pie, Your Grace,' she added, with a stern look at Ash to say if His Dukeliness did not like any of those alternatives he could go without.

'Apple pie will do very well and I developed a taste for rum at sea.'

'Let's hope you're better at it than Dorset cider,

then,' Rosalind muttered into her own small helping of apple pie and wondered why sniping at him was so irresistible.

'For your sake if not my own,' he replied smoothly.

That was enough of a warning to make her hope he really did have the hard head he was boasting about. He must have, because after an awkward half-hour sitting opposite each other while she drank tea and he brooded, he informed her it was high time he went back to the inn.

'No doubt you have been up since before the nearest cockerel thought about crowing and I have had all the shocks one man can stand in one day to mull over before I can stand any chance of getting to sleep.'

'It has been a long day,' she said and what an understatement that was.

'You had a walk that would tire an elephant,' he added with another of the frowns she had a feeling she was going to have to get used to. 'You must have run most of the way back down that hill as well and it's a wonder you didn't break your neck, Ros.'

Ros was Ash's name for her during their secret, thrilling courtship and it called back a side of her she wanted to forget. 'I am used to rough country. I never really was a delicate society miss.'

'No, you always had an adventurous spirit under the society manners and faux obedience to Lackbourne's orders.'

'I certainly wasn't very obedient about you.'

'No, but you would have been married off to a

nabob if you were that well behaved, so thank goodness you were not.'

'You are a nabob now, are you not?' she said.

'Oh, yes, my Duchess, I most certainly am. And you are definitely my Duchess.'

'Not until I agree to be and we leave here. And we still have yet to tell Jenny who she really is.'

'The sooner the better,' he said dourly and she had to hope there was some of the old devil may care Ash left under all the ducal frowns to get them through the next few days or they would have a hard time explaining themselves to their daughter and living with the past.

Chapter Seven

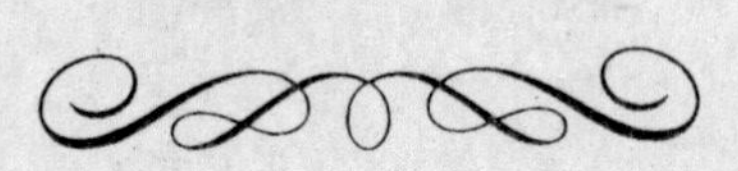

Joan had made herself scarce again and Rosalind could hear pots being vigorously washed in the scullery when they passed the half-open kitchen door on Ash's way out. 'Here, you will need a lantern,' she told Ash and grabbed one, then led him to the back door. She refused to struggle with the heavy bolts and unused timbers of the front one on such a damp night and the sight and sound of him shouldering it open would have tongues wagging even harder than they must be already. Even with the rush light to lighten the darkness it felt too intimate in the gloom and enough heat had escaped to warm the little hallway so they did not have to shudder from cold. Yet there was still a fine tremor in her hand when she reached for the lantern's candle and put it to the rush light so he could leave safely. She wanted to pretend it was from the cold, but it wasn't and the waver in the light must have told him about her disturbed feelings because when she tried to pass him the lighted lantern he stared down at her as if fascinated by the play of candlelight on her unruly golden hair. She should have found time to take it down, tame it and re-do the knot that held most of it in place or, better still, put on the concealing cap so he could not look into her eyes like this or glance at her slightly parted lips as if he was starving for a taste of them.

'Thank you,' he said and stared at it almost as if he had forgotten what a lantern was for. 'I would rather stay,' he told her huskily.

'It is too soon,' she said after she had cleared her throat to force the words past the lump in it at saying no to him when she had every right to be wary of him. She still had this stupid urge to step aside and invite him right into her home as if he really was the lost wanderer miraculously returned.

'Not for me it's not,' he told her in a sensual murmur that added fire to the fine shiver of need already afflicting her. He sounded wistful about her wild zest for his rangy body last time they were this close to a bedroom and he wasn't accusing her of being a foul liar. She made herself step back and eye him warily, despite the tension of wanting and needing so alive now how could she ever have thought it was comfortably dead and done with? Obviously it was only sleeping until he stood before her even more potent and promising as a lover.

'If you really want me to be your Duchess, it will take more than you have said or done so far to get me to share your bed again, my lord Duke. I am certainly not jumping back into it the very day you ride back into my life after years away and everything you said before you left.'

'I will persuade you to want me again somehow,' he said with a silky challenge in his deep voice that did unfair things to the whole of her body and even made her fingers and toes tingle.

No need for persuasion she decided ruefully. Not when this longing for him whispered temptations she had tried so hard to forget about during her years without him. Look what passion had done to her last time, though, and he certainly didn't love her now. She stiffened her backbone and opened the back door, silently inviting him to leave. Instead he lingered in the tiny add-on she was surprised they both managed to fit inside without one of the doors open to the inside or outside to make enough space and they were far too close again.

'Now I am supposed to walk into the local taproom and admit my wife threw me out after all these years apart?'

'I only said you were missing because I had no husband and a baby on the way. What did you expect me to say?'

'I don't know,' he said with a sigh. 'I admit you have sailed as close to the truth as you dared.'

'Good for me,' she said with bitter irony. 'I will not change my mind about letting you stay because you don't want to cross the taproom of the local inn, Ash,' Rosalind managed to tell him calmly, although her insides were threatening to turn cartwheels and her heartbeat was so loud in her ears she wondered he could not hear it. The very thought of a night of unrestrained passion in his newly mighty arms made her knees go weak, but she wasn't going to let him know it.

'I wager you will let me into your bed soon,' he murmured softly.

'You don't wager, remember?'

'For you I could make an exception.'

'No, I won't be a bet you have to win.'

'Now I think we would both win,' he said so softly she told herself that was why she was standing on tiptoe and staring up at him as if he had put a spell on her.

It sounded more of a promise than a threat when he kissed her in the close confines of the porch she never thought had a romantic plank in it until now. How could she let him do this to her? And what was so special about him that she still wanted him so ridiculously when she ought to push him away and slam the back door? His kiss was hungry and, for a long, giddy moment, she felt sweet fire stir again deep inside. Eagerness hardened her nipples as memories of her wild young lover tore at her certainty she did not want this. She heard herself moan with need when he pulled her inside his heavy coat and ran a wicked hand over her tightly fitted bodice to find the fullness of her ridiculously aroused breasts. He must be gloating over the frustrated needs she could not hide and his heavy-lidded eyes told her he knew about the sweetest of tortures at her secret feminine core as well. Despite all her layers of wool and cotton and flannel he had still managed to spread havoc through her body like wildfire and he knew it, the smug wretch.

Ash deepened his hotly drugging kiss and explored her mouth as if he was starving for her. Rosalind reminded herself how she had to birth their daughter alone before she discovered real, heart-and-soul and bone-deep love. The innocence of her baby—a perfect, fiercely loved little being who would never have been if not for their driven desire—was what saved her from loneliness and despair. She would never regret marrying Ash, because he had given her Jenny, but she would never let him hurt her that much again.

'I said no, Ash,' she finally managed to say and found the strength to push back against his arms.

He dropped his hold on her and backed away as far as he could get in this small space, which was not far. The scent of him, the fact of him, tore away at her resolutions so she was glad when he gave a heavy sigh and seemed to accept her no at face value. 'Coward,' he mocked softly all the same.

She still saw something new and almost regretful in his eyes as he let her go. 'Heavens above, it really has been snowing,' she gasped as he finally took up his lantern and forced the door on to the outside world open against a hindrance of snow. A lot more time must have passed than she realised while they were eating and arguing.

'And I really must get back into the warm before I freeze on your doorstep, my Duchess,' he said with a very visible shudder as his booted feet sank into the snow.

'I am not a duchess.'

'Oh, I don't know,' he told her with a long, intimately assessing look that made her blush, 'you have a way of looking down your nose that would not be out of place on a queen, let alone a duchess.'

'How flattering,' she said blankly.

'Never mind, you will soon be dressed as befits your station again,' he said as if her never knowingly fashionable countrywoman's clothes were far more of a worry to her than he was.

'I am perfectly happy as I am,' she said impatiently, refusing to think of wearing fine velvets and satins, with softest lawn next to her skin instead of her usual practical gowns with their sensible underpinnings. She lived a practical and useful life and being decked out in the finest Bond Street had to offer would please him far more than it would her, wouldn't it?

'No, you are covered up and warm. Trying to fade into the background will never work when you could look spectacular in a sack.'

'Thank you for that fulsome compliment, Your Grace, and goodnight,' she said firmly, and shut the door in his infuriating face, so he would not know how very tempted she was to tell him she had changed her mind. She kicked the solid old door instead and instantly regretted it.

'Goodnight, Sweet Princess.' His deep voice managed to penetrate even that barrier and she was certain there was a chuckle in his voice, despite the snow and cold.

'He's gone, then,' Joan said when Rosalind walked back into the house proper and went to stand in front of the still-glowing kitchen fire to warm up. She was racked by shivers and at least half of them were due to the cold.

'Of course,' she said, dignity offended by the suggestion she was not strong-minded enough to throw her husband out into the snow.

'No "of course" about it—he is your husband.' Joan sounded as if she was not very much in favour of the breed either. Rosalind considered her mother's often-strained second marriage and her own very short one, until today, and could hardly blame her maid for being sceptical of aristocratic alliances.

'I can't shrug my shoulders and let him back into my bed as if he has never been away,' she answered defensively.

'Some would not wait for a yes or no, Miss Rosalind,' Joan said as if trying to be fair. 'And after all those weeks at sea he did listen to you.'

'Are you playing devil's advocate?'

'Probably, but he is your husband.'

'As he has been all these years, with never a word to his wife.'

'Would you have known if he did seek you out?'

'I read the papers after the Duck and Feathers have done with them. He could have advertised if he wanted to find me. He had no interest in where I was until he needed to divorce me, Joan. He would still be doing so if not for him finding out about Jenny.'

'Oh, my dear girl, he hurt you so much, how can we be sure he isn't going to do it again?' her friend burst out, her real anxiety finally coming out as she looked about to cry.

'I won't let him break me, Joan. I am not an eighteen-year-old mouse scared of her own shadow now and I will not let my daughter grow up seeing her mother ruled and humiliated by her husband as I was forced to. My mother may have felt she had to endure Lord Lackbourne's slights and petty rules for my sake, but I will not be dominated by my husband, you can be very sure of that, and he is not as chilly as the Earl even now.'

'A husband has all the power in a marriage,' Joan said bleakly. 'I believe Lord Lackbourne loved her, but longed for a son so much it bent him out of shape.'

'Ash is no Lord Lackbourne, even if he is a duke, Joaney,' Rosalind said, 'and this is not going to be a love-match on either side this time.'

'You can't undo the past and you loved him far too much once upon a time.'

'And now I know better,' Rosalind said lightly, but she still crossed her fingers behind her back because she really had loved him so dearly back then. *Never again*, she promised herself as the thought of what she might have done if not for the little life growing inside her when he left her made her shudder away from the little fool she had once been for love. She did know better, she had to. It was too much of a risk to let the impulsive, needy young Rosalind out of her closet and let her yearning to be loved rule her again. 'And I don't know about you, but I have found all these shocks quite exhausting,' she added as if she thought she would get even a wink of sleep.

They went about the reassuring routines of bedtime: making up fires and placing guards in front of them; laying out plates, cups and knives ready for breakfast and making sure doors were locked and bolted. Satisfied at last, Joan went to her bedroom by the little staircase that wound around the kitchen fireplace to the little bedroom above it and Rosalind went the other way to the not-very-grand main bedchamber to toss and turn for most of the night. Jenny was not in her familiar little slip of a bright room tonight and nothing was as it should be. The bed felt empty and that yearning Rosalind felt was a lot more substantial tonight than it ought to be. The girl who had loved Ash enough to walk to the ends of the earth for his sake kept prodding her with all sorts of inconvenient memories she would really rather forget and get some sleep. She didn't trust the feelings he provoked in her, but he seemed very different in some ways from the boy she once knew. He had matured well, in body and mind, but what about the Ash underneath, the boy with all that hurt and grief boiling inside him the day he had denounced her as a liar, then walked out of her life and kept on walking? Could she ever trust him again with the true inner Rosalind who had loved him so much she felt torn apart when he left?

It snowed again in the night and Rosalind woke to the odd light of sun reflecting off snow. After not being able to eat much last night and her long walk yesterday she was hungry and ate her toast and even the egg Joan insisted she needed to keep her strength up. Rosalind was pouring a second cup of tea from the fat brown pot when a knock came on the back door and she knew it was Ash. Her heart was pounding when Joan stood aside to let him in, his tall, greatcoated figure almost blocking the light. He had found an extra scarlet muffler from somewhere and what looked like another pair of gloves under his riding gauntlets. He might look funny if she felt like being amused, but he was far too real and intimidating to laugh at.

He rid himself of outer garments before entering the parlour. 'I had breakfast at the inn, I thank you,' he said to Joan, who was watching from the little hallway. 'And I wiped my boots before I came in, like a good duke,' he added drily.

'I never said you didn't and now you're here again I must get hold of some extra provisions,' Joan said with another stern look before going back to the kitchen.

'I doubt she will get anyone to kill a fatted calf for me,' Ash said ruefully.

'Never mind, I expect they will do that when you get to Edenhope,' Rosalind said, imagining a small army of inside and outside staff startled to see their new Duke with an unexpected Duchess, and the sinking feeling in her stomach made her wish she hadn't eaten that egg after all.

'Aye, but they would be pleased to see anyone who will have the roof mended and chimneys rebuilt so the place is warmer than the Arctic again so I will try not to let it go to my head.'

'It is really that cold there?'

'Charlie always said so, but let's not talk about it now. I might decide to stay here until it's high summer and I doubt you or your maid would like that.'

'Nor would you if you had to stay at a country inn for months on end.'

'You need a few weeks to get used to me before we are husband and wife again, but don't expect more, Ros. I am only human.'

'Yet you have been without me for so long,' she said coolly.

'Which doesn't mean—' He stopped speaking and froze in the act of adding a new log to the dying fire as the back door opened abruptly.

Feeling a bit frozen herself, Rosalind listened to Jenny chatter excitedly to Joan about her night with her friends and all they had got up to already this morning while she was handing over her coat, hat, gloves and scarf, then being whisked into the kitchen to take off her wet boots and stockings by the fire. They could hear Joan's half-hearted scolding through the slightly open door as she insisted Jenny put on the dry stockings and the indoor shoes warming by the fire before she let her charge out of her sight again.

Ash stoked the fire and stood up, looking as if willpower was stopping him rushing into that kitchen and seizing his startled daughter in his arms now he finally knew he had one. It felt almost as hard for Rosalind to sit and wait for Jenny to be dry and warm again as it must be for Ash not to pace and curse while he struggled to contain his emotions.

'Just look at your toes, Miss Jenny, they're nigh blue with cold,' Joan's muffled voice exclaimed and Rosalind strained her ears for her daughter's usual protests as they were rubbed with a rough towel until she was warm and dry again. When her stepfather was not about Rosalind, her mother used to argue about such little things as wet feet and the time it took to dry them when there was so much for a young girl to do. Would a duchess be permitted to fuss over her child with so much stateliness to keep up on her husband's behalf? Probably not—she was sitting here now while Joan did it for her and there would be nannies and nursery maids and governesses galore for Lady Imogen Hartfield and any future brothers and sisters she might have.

Inside the parlour the old mantel clock ticked solemnly on and the log Ash had added to the fire shifted, then sank into the heart of it to give out an extra glow of heat. They both listened for any word they could catch as Jenny told Joan about her day so far and Ash waited, tense as a racehorse ready for the off. Rosalind felt slightly sick when she realised Jenny must have had enough of being fussed over at last and was heading for the parlour to tell her mother about her latest adventure.

'Oh,' Jenny said as she stared at the tall stranger looming over the low-ceilinged room. Rosalind guessed Ash had been struck dumb and motionless by this second look at his surprise child and she was about to intervene when her daughter added, 'You're the man from the stables at the Duck', before shooting Rosalind a guilty look.

'I hate to think what you were doing there yesterday,' she scolded mildly. 'And where are your manners, young lady?'

'I beg your pardon. Good morning, sir,' Jenny said with a long-suffering sigh and even managed a wobbly curtsy.

'Good morning. Mistress Jenny Meadows, I presume?' Ash replied rather hoarsely.

'My real name is Imogen,' Jenny corrected him gravely.

'My apologies, Miss Imogen.'

'You were not to know,' she said kindly, 'but who are *you*?'

'Jenny...' Rosalind's rebuke wound down as her daughter frowned and shook her head at her as if to say, *If a complete stranger uses my proper name, why can't you?* 'Oh, very well, then. Imogen, if you insist. Whatever name you want to go by this week, you know it is shockingly rude to ask such direct questions of a grown-up.' Rosalind shook her head as if Jenny's lack of company manners made her very sad indeed.

'She has a right to know,' Ash argued.

'Why?' Jenny asked and Rosalind held up her hands in mock despair.

'It doesn't matter if she has forgotten to be seen and not heard just this once,' Ash argued again, as if he was impatient of such things at the best of times and this was not one of them.

'It might not if she had ever learnt it in the first place,' Rosalind muttered, but watched him with wary eyes and decided it was time she recalled her own manners and introduced him to his own daughter, before he could not contain himself any longer and blurted it out. Her nerve almost failed her as they both watched her with smoke-grey Hartfield eyes. What if Jenny never forgave her for the lies she had told since her daughter was old enough to ask where her papa was? 'You remember I told you Papa had to go to India before I knew I was expecting you and I never heard from him again so we had to believe he was dead, Jenny love?'

'Of course I do,' Jenny said with a puzzled frown as if to say, *Why bring that up now?*

'Well, as it turns out he is not dead at all.'

'Have you brought us a message from him, then, sir?' Jenny faced Ash with her eager question. Rosalind searched for her last drop of courage to tell her more, but Ash took the start she had given him and ran on with it.

'No, I do not need to send messages to you or your mother now I am home at last and longing to meet you properly.'

'What do you mean?'

'I *am* your papa, Jenny,' he said gruffly and there was so much hope in his eyes, such love, Rosalind held her breath while they waited for Jenny's reaction.

'You can't be,' Jenny told him with a fierce frown Ash ought to recognise as a mirror of his own.

'I am, I promise you. I had to go away and do a lot of things before I could come back home to you both,' he tried to explain that impossible gap of years and whatever Rosalind thought of his feelings for her she could see how important his daughter was to him. His hand shook as he held it out to his child almost beseechingly, then noted the fact and tucked it behind his back as if he thought she ought not to be burdened with his feelings and had his wretched mother taught him that? His emotions were right and true for his own child and she cursed Lady John Hartfield even if she was long in her grave for teaching her children a parent should not actually have any feelings for their offspring, or that they must be concealed if they did exist.

'You never wrote to us and you never sent any presents,' Jenny said in a hard little voice that made Rosalind's heart twist for the tears knotted up in them. She felt as if she had failed her daughter by letting Ash slip through her fingers before she was born. 'And Ally and Hal and me are sure my papa is dead because Mama gets tears in her eyes when I ask about him.'

That revelation earned Rosalind a thoughtful look from Ash, but he was too preoccupied with his child to spare much more than that right now. 'I really am your father and certainly not dead, Imogen. I have been in India and it is a very long way away,' Ash said carefully. 'And I did not know your mother was expecting you when I left. If I had known that, I would never have gone, but even your mother did not know about you back then. She decided not to tell me she was expecting you after I had sailed. She thought it would make me feel even worse about being so far away that I could not come back until I had made my fortune and could afford to buy a passage home.'

He bent the truth a little and shot Rosalind a pleading look as if to say *Please let me get away with this version of us for now? She is too little to know what you and I really did back then.*

She met his eyes and shrugged, then watched her daughter's face to gauge what she made of his gentled-down version of the past.

'Did you make one, then?' Jenny asked artlessly and Rosalind smiled despite her anxiety about the huge changes about to overtake her daughter's previously very settled young life. No doubt a long list of toys, games, finery and ponies were lining up to be spent good money on if Ash was rash enough to admit his new riches.

'Yes, but it took me far too long,' Ash said and softened his story with a few more white lies. 'In the end I had made enough money never to need to worry about keeping you and your mama in fine style ever again so it was time I came home.'

'Good, because Mama needs new gowns and a smart hat and coat all matching, like the ones she and Joan made me for Christmas.'

'Oh, Jenny, my love,' Rosalind said before she had to stop so she would not cry. 'Thank you, darling,' she added gruffly and hugged her wonderful child despite Jenny's martyred expression. Rosalind even managed a wobbly smile at Ash, as if to say *Isn't our girl a marvel?*

'You ought to have told him about me, Mama, and *you* should have written to ask how she was, even if you didn't know about me. If you were very sad about not being able to get home, you could still have written so we would know you were not dead,' Jenny challenged Ash.

'I wrote to your mother so many times, but somehow I never sent the letters and I could not write to a daughter I did not even know existed,' he excused himself with a manly shrug.

At least he was not treating Jenny as if she was witless, like some adults who lacked experience with young children were inclined to. Rosalind had longed for a letter after he left, though, and his lie felt hard to swallow. Any letter would have done, sent from any port along the way, or even full of his new life without her once he got there. None came while she waited at Lackbourne House, pretending to be the still-marriageable Miss Feldon until she was quite sure she was carrying his child. She did not believe Ash had sent any after she left the place of her own accord either, before she began to show and even her stepfather would notice she was pregnant.

'Why didn't you write to Papa and tell him to come home, Mama?' Jenny asked with her usual merciless logic.

'Your mother knew I could not come back until I had made enough money and she had no idea where to send her letters,' Ash said before Rosalind could reply. She let him speak for her just this once—but it had better not become a habit.

'Oh,' Jenny said as if she saw the sense in what he said.

Rosalind supposed, from a child's point of view,

it had a ring of truth, although she *could* have sent a letter via the Governor General's Office, with a covering one asking them to send it on to her husband. It might have found its way to Ash, sooner or later, and told the world he was nowhere near as free and single as he appeared. Or she could have sent one to the Hartfield family solicitor, since the then Duke of Cherwell and Lord Lackbourne used the same one. They could have forwarded it to him, with a startled demand for an explanation or a thundering ducal scold to go with it.

'When *did* you find out about me, then?' Jenny asked Ash.

'When I saw you in the hayloft at the Duck and Feathers yesterday afternoon,' he told her truthfully.

Jenny obviously did not want Rosalind to find out what she had been up to, so some things had not changed since this time yesterday. 'How did you know I was me?' she asked and Rosalind had to admire her distraction technique if not her grammar, or the way her daughter kept her promise to be good for the senior members of the Belstone family and their governess.

'I had a little sister once. She looked and acted very much like you do, being a naughty little imp, forever looking out for her next lot of mischief. I thought you were her for a moment when I first set eyes on you.'

'Is that why you looked so strange?'

'Yes, I really could not believe my eyes,' Ash agreed.

Rosalind pictured him both then and on the night he furiously described his agony at not being able to save his little sister's life to his distraught young wife.

She understood his actions that night a little better now she had a child of her own, and his mother's when she found out what had happened to her daughter even less. Maybe shortly after that revelation all those years ago Ash had an excuse for leaving his new wife to stumble into her clothes and join him for a long, silent journey back to town. While his hurt and anger still burned and blinded him to the way things really were, perhaps he had had a good reason to treat her with silent contempt, but not all the way to London, then on to Calcutta. She had kept that awful night when she was sixteen secret even when they raced to Gretna to marry each other, there was no denying that. But back then he had managed to ignore the differences between his chilly-hearted and selfish mother and his young and yearning wife and that *was* beyond her. He had simply painted Rosalind the same colour as Lady John Hartfield, filed her away in a sealed box marked *Unwanted Wife*, then carried on with his life as if she no longer existed as far as he was concerned. When he had got to his destination he must have acted as if he had never met and dazzled Rosalind Feldon into marrying him as well and she found that very hard to forgive. But any further questions about that night and his implacable fury afterwards must wait, she decided, and even managed not to glare reproachfully at him while her daughter was trying to puzzle out the gaps between their stories.

'Have I got an aunt, then?' Jenny said after a short silence. She was always eager for any sign of a relative and Rosalind felt guilty for not providing any. Lord

Lackbourne had cut contact between his stepdaughter and her real father's family, if he had any, and her mother had been a late and only child.

'I fear not; my little sister Amanda died when she was a child and I miss her sorely to this day,' Ash told his daughter.

'You have me now, so you don't have to be lonely any more,' Jenny said, as if it was her task to comfort *him*. 'And Mama as well, of course.'

Rosalind wasn't sure if Ash thought of her as a shield against grief and loneliness, more as a means to an end and mother to this wonderful, naughty, precocious child he probably did not deserve. A child who clearly thought they had dealt with this subject now and it was time to get back to the urgent realities of everyday life.

'Mrs Belstone said I would have to come and ask if I could have my luncheon with them and go sledging afterwards, Mama,' Jenny asked. 'So can I? Please, say I can.'

Perhaps her return to more urgent matters was a tribute to their determination to make Ash's return sound normal and even a little bit mundane. Whatever it was, Jenny was now more concerned about her next adventure with her friends than the surprise return of a father she hadn't known she had until today. Rosalind thought Jenny's young mind was simply finding a way to cope with such a massive change by pretending it was not that big after all. Time would tell, she decided and postponed that worry until they got to it.

'Why don't we all go?' Ash said and of course it

would be far better to spend time with his daughter and her friends than stay shut inside with his wife brooding over the future and how soon they could get out of here and start the next, and very surprising, chapter in their lives.

'Maybe we could,' Rosalind said cautiously.

They had the time it would take for the weather to change and a thaw to stop turning the roads into quagmires to get through yet, so the more of it they spent in company the better. That way there was less risk she would succumb to his brusque masculine charms and give in to his urging to truly be his wife again. Less chance of falling under his spell and trusting him to love her back when that could never happen again as well.

'I think you had better stay and have luncheon with us, then we can all meet the Belstones afterwards,' she said. 'We need a snowman in the garden as well as the one you must have been building with Hal and Alison before you came home, if the state of you when you got in is anything to go by. I am sure Papa would like to help you, if you ask him nicely, while I go and tell Mrs Belstone about our change of plan and ask if we can still join them later.'

'Thank you,' Ash said sincerely and she felt a little bit guilty about her sneaky feeling getting him very cold while Jenny was busy instructing him in the art of snowman construction might send him back to the inn for a warm bath and had there been room for another change of clothes in his saddlebags? He might have to stay there until these were dry, since yesterday's travel-stained outfit could hardly be ready for him yet.

Best not think of him striding about his room wearing nothing much, Rosalind. That sort of fantasy will land you under his thumb faster than you can say knife.

'Seth Paxton is nearly as large as you are, Ash. I dare say he would lend you some of his old clothes to get wet if you ask him nicely,' she told him to soothe her conscience. Of course the prospect of seeing a duke in an innkeeper's cast-offs was wickedly appealing as well.

'I dare say,' he said a little bit less gratefully, but he managed to shake off his ducal dignity long enough to stroll back to the inn with an overexcited Jenny in tow, so she could plague Mrs Paxton with tales of her new papa while he changed into any warm clothing Seth could spare him.

Chapter Eight

It turned into a far better day than Rosalind dreaded when the snow trapped them all in Livesey last night. Of course she had to confess to Judith Belstone, her best friend apart from Joan, that her husband was home hale and hearty *and* had come back to her rich and a duke, even if he was currently masquerading as the not-very-humble Mr Meadows. Judith was speechless for a few moments, when she was finally persuaded to believe Rosalind was not joking.

'Best not tell Ben that bit if you want your husband's rank to stay a secret until you are all ready to leave for Edenhope. He is a vicar and very stern about lying, even though he is such a dreamer in other ways.'

Rosalind shuddered at the thought Ben Belstone had a great deal in common with Ash already. 'I would rather not be the sensation of the village,' she admitted with a grimace of distaste.

'You will be anyway. Your husband is alive after being missing for years, so how can you not be?'

'We did not part friends,' Rosalind warned and that was as much of the past as she wanted to drag up with anyone but Ash.

'I had already thought that one out for myself,' her friend said drily, then went on to exclaim about Rosalind really being the chatelaine of such a vast and famous mansion. 'And a grand house in Grosvenor Square as well I recall from some eulogy on it from an ancient maiden aunt of mine who once met a rake there and had her heart broken far too easily if you ask me. There are probably half-a-dozen other estates and fine houses and who would have thought it, what with you living in a cottage ever since I have known you? You will be spoilt for choice of places to live and when I think of you managing on nothing much a year for so long I am not sure I am going to like your Duke, Rosalind.'

'He only inherited it all when his young cousin died last year. Until then Ash had no property at all in this country,' Rosalind heard herself defend him when he really didn't deserve it. He obviously had plenty of money now and at least one fine house in his adopted land. He probably would not have left it for another couple of decades either, if not for the Cherwell inheritance. Jenny could have been quite grown up and maybe even with a child of her own by the time her father came back to England with his vast fortune and maybe even a by-blow or two to displace her in his affections.

'But he did have a wife and child,' Judith replied rather sternly.

'Only a wife as far as he knew,' Rosalind objected and why on earth was she defending him?

'Ah, yes, I had forgotten about that bit of your story. Why did you decide to cut him out of your life as if he was truly dead instead of half a world away, then, Rosalind Whatever-You-Call-Yourself-Now?' Judith said sternly, as if she was beginning to agree with her husband about lies.

'Because he did the same to me,' Rosalind said rather sadly and shook her head to tell her friend the subject was best left alone. It was best left that way even between her and Ash. If they were going to make any sort of future together she supposed they must always skirt around the past.

Rosalind got back to Furze Cottage to see her family out in the snow admiring their handiwork. Even Joan had left the warmth of her kitchen and her self-imposed domestic tasks to supervise the placement of Rosalind's old and disreputable gardening hat on top of the vast snowman and pass Jenny the carrot nose and coal eyes Ash had to lift his daughter up to push them in and make a face, since their handiwork was taller than Jenny.

'We rolled our snowball halfway around the village, Mama,' Jenny told her excitedly as soon as she spotted Rosalind looking on with bewildered wonder at their joint enterprise. 'I was afraid we wouldn't get it back through the gate, but it just about fitted and then we rolled it about a bit inside and around the house as well to make it even bigger.'

'I can see that,' Rosalind said. 'It is the largest snowman I ever saw.'

'People will come from miles around to look and we can charge them a farthing,' her mercenary daughter announced happily.

'They can't get here from miles around and why pay when they can see it from the road?'

'Never mind, Jenny,' her father said, then gave Rosalind an almost sheepish grin to admit he had enjoyed himself hugely. 'You have the makings of a fine business woman, even if you didn't think your enterprise through properly this time.'

'Then I suppose next time we must make it further away,' Jenny conceded and Rosalind didn't disillusion her, because leaving the only home she had ever known would be difficult enough for her daughter when the time came without her mother constantly pointing it out before it could happen.

The afternoon was taken up with sledging and snowball fights and in between they all crowded around the brazier the Vicar had brought out to keep them all warm. Even Rosalind was relaxed enough to tease Ash about clinging to the heat and only joining in the fun between warming his hands and stamping his feet as if he would never get used to his native climate again. 'Call yourself a Yorkshire man,' she taunted him, then had to duck when he threw a snowball at her and she was half-enchanted by the boyish grin he gave her before they joined battle.

So at least they were all tired and hungry. Ash went

off to the Duck and Feathers, resigned if not actually happy about his exile, once he had carried Jenny up to her room after she fell asleep at the dinner table, so that was one day to cross off the list of the ones they would have to spend here as the dramatically reunited Meadows family. Almost reunited, Rosalind qualified that statement as she watched Ash lope off to the inn as fast as he could so he was not quite frozen to the bone by the time he got there. She would not feel guilty. It was far too soon to let him kiss and sweet talk her up the stairs she was plodding her weary way up on the way to her lonely bed.

It was ten days before the coach and four Ash had managed to hire in Dorchester as soon as the roads were fit to ride set out for London. The wind had changed to a mild southwesterly the day after Ash and Jenny built their snowman. Their magnificent creation dwindled to a couple of dirty-looking snowballs as mud took over from snow and disappeared altogether when it rained one night and washed even the last of the snow away from the gullies and folds in the heath where it had been hanging on. By the time their carriage pulled out of Livesey at the start of a very different life for all of them Furze Cottage looked very forlorn and empty with no smoke issuing from its chimneys and a shuttered and abandoned feel to it that made Rosalind feel guilty about deserting the place that had been her sanctuary for so long.

The changes about to take over her life had finally begun to sink in for Jenny as Rosalind and Ash discussed them in front of her, so they would not come as such a surprise when they happened. Jenny had never questioned this was her home and it had come as a shock that she was going to be removed from it. She tested the limits of Ash's patience as well as her mother's as the day they were to leave got closer and Rosalind waited for Ash's temper to snap. She knew he had a fine one from bitter experience, but he kept it under strict control for Jenny. He tried to reason her out of her sulks and backed up Rosalind's discipline rather than stamping off in a fine Hartfield fury. He *had* been restless and preoccupied at times, though, and Rosalind was glad when he could ride his fine horse out every day and get some of his fidgets out of his system, but otherwise he pretended to be the wanderer miraculously returned with such ease nobody could have accused him of being above his company.

Now they were finally setting out it was a relief to get on with this new life, even if it was daunting. Joan insisted she was looking forward to getting back to being a lady's maid again and forgetting how to cook and clean, but Rosalind had her doubts. However close a duchess was to her personal attendant, they could never work as closely together for Jenny's comfort and happiness again now Ash was back. Perhaps Joan would accept Rosalind's offer of Furze Cottage, once she was satisfied the Duke and Duchess of Cherwell and Lady Imogen Hartfield had settled into their new life and could manage without her. *So many perhapses, Rosalind*, she told herself rather wistfully as Livesey faded behind them and not even

Hal and Ally's frantically waving little figures were visible any more.

Apparently they would be staying at Cherwell House for a week or two when they finally got to London and Rosalind reminded Jenny of that exotic treat as she wiped tears from her daughter's cheeks. They would have to wait for enough new clothes to be made so they could arrive at Edenhope without looking as if they had come out of the ragbag. The rest of their fine new clothes could be delivered later, but the seamstresses would have some work in the quiet time after Christmas when the *ton* resorted to country houses and hunting boxes and had not thought about coming to town for the spring Season yet. Jenny imagined being dressed so finely would be sheer pleasure, but she didn't know how many hours it took to stand and be pinned into this and that while they were fitted to the satisfaction of a fine London dressmaker and Rosalind didn't want to disillusion her yet.

She had already begun to worry Jenny would pine for her two best friends and their settled old life, until the novelty of the road and very different countryside and new towns they passed through distracted her. Ash added tall tales of his adventures in India to keep her amused, when he was not riding his fine grey out in the fresh air, and Jenny seemed to enjoy herself once her excitement blotted out the worst of her sorrow at being parted from the Belstones.

By the time they got to the outskirts of the capital city at long last Rosalind was almost desperate to be free of the tedium and intimacy of travel for a few blessed weeks. Secretly straining for every glimpse she could get of Ash's fine and manly form riding in front of them, or trying hard to pretend she was indifferent to the long stretch of his muscular legs so close to her own when he did share the carriage with them for a while was winding her into such a tight knot of longing she sometimes felt as if she was in danger of exploding like an artillery shell. It was eight long years since she made love with him, for just one night of passionately intense fulfilment.

You would have thought your body would have forgotten how it felt to yearn and sing and welcome a lover by now, but it hasn't, has it, Rosalind?

No, especially not with that lover constantly under her nose, but flitting about like a will-o'-the-wisp and frustratingly never settling long enough to be told he would be welcome in his Duchess's bed, now she could let herself recall what a fine lover he was again. Her fear he would take her daughter from her had abated and even the lingering fury left over from the past seemed like a useless sort of armour to fight this wretched attraction in now they were on the way to a new life.

Every night along the way she had secretly longed for Ash to inform them he would be sharing the largest bedroom with her. And every night Jenny took up most of that big bed by sprawling across it at her mother's side and Ash slept in the little room that the courier he sent ahead of them must have booked for their daughter. Rosalind could not get the image of herself and Ash making sweet, driven love together out of her head even when she did manage to snatch sleep at her restless daughter's side in dream-haunted packages. She was a fool, she informed herself, as the mud-splattered coach and its latest team of weary horses finally pulled up in front of Cherwell House and she had forgotten how grand London town houses could be as she stared up at such baroque splendour it didn't look like a home at all.

'Is that all one house?' Jenny asked as if she wasn't sure whether to be awed or overwhelmed.

'Yes,' Ash said as he handed her down as if she was a princess.

'Is it *your* house?' she asked with a second look at her mud-splattered and windblown father as if it hardly seemed possible he could own so much.

'It is ours now,' he admitted and Rosalind was glad now they had told Jenny who he really was, before they got here and it came as a terrible shock to her.

'And you really are a duke?'

'Yes, although I don't suppose I look much like one right now.'

'And I am really Lady Imogen because I am your daughter?'

Rosalind met Ash's rueful look over their daughter's head and he smiled—it reminded her sharply of their old warmth and complicity as young lovers for a brief moment—before he nodded and shrugged back to being a travel-worn duke as servants began spilling out of the grand front door to welcome him home again.

'Ah, Snigsby, good to see you,' he said to a butler who looked far more stately than his employer at the moment.

'Thank you, Your Grace.'

'My dear, Snigsby here has known me since I was a scrubby brat and is sure to be delighted my Duchess is finally willing to take up residence here when she is in London, now I am home again at long last.'

'Indeed, Your Grace,' the man intoned solemnly and Rosalind was very glad that courier had been sent ahead to warn his household the new Duke of Cherwell was on his way with a wife and daughter nobody had any idea he had until now. The man still looked so shocked he forgot himself long enough to raise his eyebrows as he finally took a proper look at the daughter part of his employer's surprise. Jenny's likeness to Ash's little sister must be startling to account for a London butler losing his serenity even for a moment.

'I am Lady Imogen Hartfield,' Jenny informed him regally and Rosalind wasn't sure if she was proud of her or worried this was all going to her head.

'So I see, my lady,' the butler said, perfect composure restored.

'And I am *very* hungry.'

'That is hardly to be wondered at after such a long journey, my lady,' the man said and Rosalind was sure she saw his lips twitch as if he was hiding a grin and warmed to the man, although he would probably be far less human with a secretive duchess than he was with a duke's secret child.

'And *I* need a bath,' Ash announced to chivvy them all inside before a crowd gathered to gawp.

'We all do,' Joan muttered as she followed them up the steps as if she was used to making such a grand entrance and of course she was, although this time her mistress was a duchess instead of a countess, so perhaps it ought to be an even grander entrance than it had been in the old days. Rosalind felt as if she was letting the whole household and her family down by being so countrified and plain and not looking as a duchess should.

'Welcome home, Your Grace,' Snigsby said solemnly once they were inside the grand marble entrance hall with the doors closed against a sneaky east wind.

Rosalind glanced round to see where Ash was, then felt him gently push her forward so she finally realised the butler was talking to her. If she went around forgetting who she was in her husband's own house, what would she be like when she reluctantly joined the *ton* again at his side? She thanked the man for his welcome and was very glad when Ash cut short any attempt to introduce her to the rest of the household.

'Later,' he said with an expressive gesture at his own travel-stained person and a nod in the direction of the stairs. 'Direct my wife's dresser to her room and have the luggage brought in, there's a good butler,' he ordered genially and offered Rosalind his arm up the stairs.

Jenny suddenly looked forlorn and grabbed Joan's skirts as if she was afraid of losing her in such a vast space. She would be safe with Joan and Rosalind must not turn into an over-protective mother because she would like to cling to the familiar as well.

'Heavens above,' she gasped when Ash led her into a vast baroque bedchamber with so many gilded cherubs and cupids and bows and swags around the state bed she would feel as if she was never alone in here for a moment.

'Monstrous isn't it?'

'Yes,' she said with a huge sigh of relief because he didn't like it either.

'If you think this is bad, you must see mine,' he added and opened a connecting door on crimson-brocade-lined walls and enough heavy scarlet-velvet draperies on the gilded bed to give anyone nightmares.

'Even worse,' she exclaimed, then shot back to her own echoing room when a door to what must be his dressing room opened and a thin man who looked like a valet ghosted through it with a snowy white towel over his arm. 'I shall leave you to your ablutions, Husband,' she said hastily and shut the door.

She would have to get used to the intimacy and strangeness of having a husband again, although their marriage over the anvil had been so brief she had never had much practice at it and now he was a duke as well. She wandered around the over-decorated fantasy room the Duchess of Cherwell was supposed to sleep in and felt even less at home when she caught sight of her own reflection in a myriad of mirrors. She didn't look or feel much like a duchess. Perhaps she resembled a country wife who had been dragged through a hedge backwards, but definitely not a grand lady. Luckily a housemaid soon arrived with a hasty knock to say her bath was ready in the dressing room, so Rosalind was soon a clean country wife again and that was a relief.

Chapter Nine

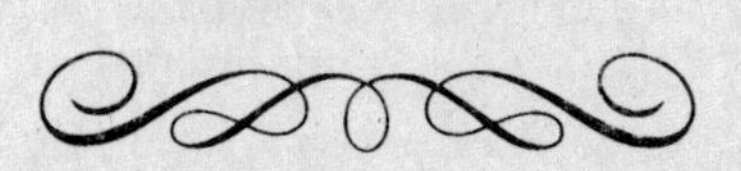

Jenny had been given one of the smaller guest suite with Joan. Rosalind blessed whoever decided her daughter did not need to endure an echoing nursery at the top of this vast old house that probably had not been used in decades.

'That's better,' Ash said as he strolled in with an approving look around to say he had ordered it.

'Almost cosy,' Rosalind confirmed absently.

He was wearing immaculate white linen, a well-tailored coat and a pair of cream trousers that emphasised his long and muscular legs. It was not formal evening wear and she should bless him for being considerate when he knew she had nothing fashionable to wear, except she felt ridiculously shy and at a disadvantage. He really was handsome though, wasn't he? With dark gold hair lightened by the sun and an unfashionable suntan highlighting his direct grey gaze, he was a mature and powerful man.

'Mama and I are going to eat our dinner in the Small Dining Room. We would have preferred to share your supper, of course, but it doesn't look as if there is much of it left,' he told Jenny as she tried to pretend she was not tired and certainly did not need her bed.

'Come back up and kiss me goodnight,' she demanded past a mighty yawn.

'We had best do that now,' Rosalind said before he agreed to wake her up because he couldn't deny his little girl anything now he had found her.

That done, Ash crooked his elbow as if Rosalind was dressed in Bond Street's finest. He had treated her with respect all the way here and now they were in his ducal London home Rosalind felt depressed by the time she had sampled bites of all sorts of delicacies his cook must have set out to impress them with. They could be two strangers settling down to while away an hour or two of stately boredom instead of husband and wife. Was this what a polite marriage felt like? Would he make an appointment to bed her once a week once they had finally reached an agreement and embarked on the project of producing his heirs? She didn't think she could be coolly obliging when he knocked on that communicating door to signal his intentions to trouble her with his masculine attentions that night. Maybe he would take a mistress to satisfy his lustier urges and make sweet love to another woman. He had told her he intended to be faithful, but inside such a boring arranged marriage he would soon be restless and ready for a silken seductress to lure him away from dutiful couplings with a woman he had so easily managed without for many years.

'We could retire to separate rooms for port and

tea,' Ash said when they had both shaken their heads at Snigsby's offer of yet more food. 'Or would you prefer to retire for the night and avoid me altogether?'

'Is there anywhere truly small we could retire to in this vast house?' she said, looking around the huge 'Small Dining Room' and feeling she had suddenly shrunk to Lilliput-like proportions. So far she disliked the pompous state of his hereditary town house and wished they were back in her cosy parlour or one of the comfortable coffee rooms in any of the inns where they had spent the night on the way here. She felt like a kitchen maid pretending to be a duchess rather than the real thing and all her insecurities were lining up to tell her she would never make him a creditable duchess, in bed or out of it.

'Not really. Would you like to see the rest of it though, anyway? We might find a room comfortable enough to want to sit in for more than a couple of minutes if we look hard enough.'

'I suppose so, but do we really have to live in such state whenever we are in town, Ash?'

'Not necessarily,' he said, looking very thoughtful as he waited for her to precede him through double doors heavy with the usual carving and gilding. 'Charlie and Jas and I always hated the place when we were young and strictly forbidden to sully the public rooms with our grubby presence. The first Duke seems to have had a very high opinion of his own importance and political ambitions. Thank goodness he spent most of his time in London, or Edenhope would be covered in gold leaf and self-importance as well.'

'I am sure it was much admired at the time, but I prefer less splendour and more comfort.'

'And warmth,' he agreed with a shiver. 'This place would do very well for a palace, but for ordinary mortals like us it is a burden I could happily do without.'

'Do we need to economise?'

'No, but we already have one daughter to provide for and I never did subscribe to the view an eldest son should inherit everything, so it will be a drain on ours and I don't think you like it any more than I do.'

'Not so far,' she admitted, his casual mention of the son they had not done a thing to bring to being yet making her insides flutter and her nerves jump even more. 'I thought we might make some improvements and perhaps divide up some of these vast rooms and redecorate, but if you would rather begin again that would be much simpler.'

He seized a branch of candles from a heavily gilded side table so he could show her the not-very-intimate details of the rest of the staterooms.

'Isn't it entailed, though?' she asked as they briefly viewed the first few feet of the cavernous State Dining Room and exchanged rueful glances at looming splendour wrapped up in so many covers it looked more like a ghostly lumberyard.

'No, I think my great-great-grandfather thought it so splendid none of his descendants would ever want to sell it,' he said. He was so careful not to touch her as they continued down the enfilade the awkwardness of their situation only made her feel more out of place and disorientated than ever. She was supposed to be mistress of all this, she told herself hollowly as they moved on to glance at the State Saloon, the Duchess's Drawing Room, the Duke's Sitting Room and all the rest until they got to the Library at the least important end of the long sweep of wonders, most of them wrapped up and only used for a few days of the year and probably not even that since the old Duke died.

'I doubt your ancestors were great readers,' she said as they surveyed yet more gilding and not very many books and the sound of their breathing and an occasional spit and flare from the fine wax candles in one of the draughts that teased past shuttered windows and brocade curtains. This room was a little smaller and less intimidating and Rosalind felt the familiar prickle of awareness making her skin feel hot and yet shivering, oversensitive, so she hid her hands behind her back and clasped them fiercely together to stop herself reaching for him—for comfort if nothing more intimate was on offer, but they were not that sort of man and wife, were they? And she was nothing like the Duchess he had promised himself on his way back to England and told her about that first time on the heath, before he knew about Jenny. He was showing her all this out of duty. Their whole life together, if they ever actually began to have one, would be founded on his duty to his duchy and his child. He was not the wild young lover she eloped with because the thought of spending the rest of her life without him was unthinkable. He was the Duke of Cherwell and a much more sober and mature man than that young man had dreamed of becoming in his wildest nightmares.

'They must have been too busy entertaining,' he said and she searched her memory for what they had been talking about before she got diverted by silly fantasies, then slammed up against stern reality.

Books, she recalled as she faced his interrogating look and managed a weak smile of agreement, or something polite and agreeable *á la* convenient Duchess. Now she was trying to be someone she could never truly be and she shot him a sidelong look in an attempt to read his thoughts. No, they were a complete mystery to her. Either he was as conscious of her every move as she was of his, or Ash did not feel this aching attraction she was struggling to resist. She puzzled over his feelings until he coughed and quirked an eyebrow at her as if he was inviting her to share her thoughts with him. Absolutely not. She shook her head and decided it was intimate and dangerous in here in the half-dark, surrounded by their little circle of candlelight and all but alone in the silence of too much space.

'Are all the other bedchambers as bad as our rooms?' she asked more or less at random.

'There are one or two smaller ones like Jenny's, but I think the first Duke wanted everyone who stayed here to be overawed.'

'I really don't feel the need to impress anyone that much.'

'Nor do I. Shall we do it, then, Ros? I could easily live without this much splendour in my life and I can imagine Charlie cheering us on and Jas as well. And we had best get on with it since it could take decades to find someone who wants to live in this sort of state and Jenny will be making her debut before we can get it off our hands if we're not careful. We will need to make our family a comfortable home here before all that fuss and flummery begins.'

Rosalind stared at the spines of the books in front of her as if she could read their gilded titles in the fitful light as his implication they would have a tribe of children by the time Jenny was old enough to make her debut sank in. The idea of bearing his child, with him here to wait and hope with her this time, felt more than a price to pay for staying in Jenny's life and only made this silly yearning for the physical closeness with him she had missed for so long feel even worse.

'You think it could take so long to be rid of the place, then?' she asked the nearest shelf of not-very-worn volumes.

'At worst, but we don't have to stay here very much until then, do we?'

'No, I dare say if it was only for a week or two at a time we could endure it until it can be sold.'

'We are agreed, then?'

'No need to sound so surprised.' Except she was surprised he had consulted her before he sold it anyway; surprised it felt as if they were both trying to build a real marriage instead of the chilly contract he laid out when he realised Jenny was his and decided he did not want a divorce after all. But she was not surprised when he lit their way up the stairs and along the chilly corridor to the Duke and Duchess's private suites, then left her outside the gilded double doors to hers with a polite goodnight and not even a ducal peck on the cheek.

Ash stirred in his sleep and suppressed a groan as he came sharply back to his senses and felt far too wide awake, but it was the middle of the night. He tried to relax in the vast old bed. It had felt like being laid out in a museum when he returned from his travels, but now Ros was next door. The thought of her in the same house was enough to keep him awake, even in the most comfortable bed in London. Only one fragile door away, she was the most exquisite temptation he could imagine. He cursed his wretched body as the very thought of her on the other side of that door made his sex go hard, again. If only Ros was here with him, this would be the finest bed in London and never mind his ancestor's questionable taste. Fantasising about her lying next to him, sated and limp with loving, was not going to calm his wretched body, so he tried to imagine he was marooned on a lonely Arctic ice floe yet again, before he woke her up to beg.

Contrarily he longed for the comfort and intimacy of her cottage, if only she would have let him share it with her, but that was firmly in the past now. When he had first stepped inside the place it felt small and cramped and he wondered how she endured it, but now his whole body cried out for the luxury of being Mrs Meadows's long-lost husband and lying next to her exhausted and thoroughly pleasured warmth instead of lying in the lonely and frustrated Duke of Cherwell's lofty state bed.

He heard movement next door and felt guiltily relieved Ros was restless as well. At least he would not wake her when he got up to feed the fire. Then he heard a muffled scream and was out of his stately bed before he had time to look around for a weapon or more than the silk wrap from a warmer life. On the alert for an intruder, he cracked open the door to hear a distressed little snuffle of protest before Rosalind gasped in the distance of this ridiculous room and had him almost running to her side. By the light of the candle left burning by the bed he saw that her eyes were closed, but her body was writhing under the bedclothes as if she was fighting them, or trying to run away in her sleep. She must be in the grip of a nightmare and did not look to be in mortal danger after all.

His panicked heartbeat slowed a little as he stood by the bed and wondered about the best way to wake a dreaming person without scaring them half to death. 'Rosalind, Ros,' he said softly to try to wake her gently. 'It's only a dream, you can wake up now. I am here.' As if that would help, he thought on a sigh, but she did stir and open her eyes before squeezing them tightly closed again as if she wasn't sure he was real. She must still be half-asleep, since she reached out a hand to him as if to reassure herself he was really there. Fully awake, she would have locked her thoughts away from him and he was beginning to think that was the worst punishment he could be given for his sins.

'Ash?' she murmured sleepily. 'All those nights I woke up and you were not here.'

He wasn't sure if it was good or bad that he was real tonight. 'I am here now,' he said as neutrally as he could and shivered. 'I'll see if I can get the fire going again,' he said to divert himself from freezing half to death or diving into that wide bed with her and kissing them both warm and very thoroughly awake so they could make love and scare her dreams away with heat and passion and— No, that was quite enough of that.

'You are more like to put it out,' she said and that sounded much more like his unconventional Duchess.

'At least I know you're properly awake now you're scolding me again.'

'I am *not* a scold.'

'Of course not, you are a quiet and obedient wife.'

'Pah,' she said gruffly.

'Lucky I never wanted one of those, then.'

'Yes; my mother was both and look where it got her.'

'Married to an earl?'

'Owned by one, body and soul.'

'But I never wanted that sort of marriage,' he protested.

'Just as well; I could not endure it.'

'I think you would endure anything for our daughter's sake.'

'Not that. Watching Mama feel inadequate because *he* could not sire children did me no good at all.'

He met her shadowed eyes as steadily as he could. 'Since Jenny is living proof I can father a child, I don't think that will be a problem for us.' When they finally got to share the same bed, of course, and he was not going to force that issue until she was as ready—even if he had been from the moment he set eyes on her again and was very definitely ready right now, so he had better turn away from her somehow or another or she would see that for herself in very short order.

'And if you don't stop looming over me like a quaking pudding you'll freeze to death soon and we might never have any more children. Here, you can have this; I didn't want it,' she said brusquely, pushing the padded and embroidered bedcover at him as she jumped out of bed in her plain cotton nightgown to see to the fire and suddenly he didn't feel cold at all.

She probably didn't know her nightgown was as transparent as fine gauze as she stood in front of even a dying fire and Ash wasn't going to tell her. He obviously enjoyed torturing himself with wanting her as he saw the newly rich curves of her breasts and hips as well as that tiny waist and the long and lovely line of her legs outlined by a far duller fire than the one scorching him. Luckily he had the warmth and cover of her quilt and could watch her coax the fire back to life, then sit back on her heels to stare at her handiwork and he did his best to endure it like a man. He wondered what she was thinking and wanted her so much, but at least this boiling hot frustration was stopping his shivers.

'What were you dreaming about?' he asked huskily. Silence felt far more dangerous than words. Even this echoing old museum of a bedchamber suddenly felt almost intimate and made only for them.

'A time when Jenny was ill and you were half a world away,' she said tersely and without turning her head.

'I wish I had been there then,' he said, heart hammering at the idea his child was once so ill the memory of it still gave Ros nightmares. 'When?'

'She was three and had a fever that seemed to get worse and worse until I thought she was sure to die of it.'

'I should have known.'

'Why?'

'Because she is my daughter as well—did you think it wouldn't matter to me if she died before I even knew she existed?'

'You left me because of what your mother did, or rather what she did *not* do, when your sister was ill. Why wouldn't you have blamed me if our child had died?'

'You were there, though, weren't you? You didn't leave her for whoever was around at the time to raise and look after when she was sick.'

'No, I slept in a chair by her bed and ate there when Joan forced me to. They were the worst days of my life, even worse than when you turned on me as if you hated me. I sat watching her delirious and so small and pale with your tale of your sister's death haunting me as we tried everything we could to bring her fever down.'

'I'm so sorry I left you alone to cope with all that

fear and worry, Ros, and that I put such fear into your head with my sad little tale about Amanda's death.'

His heartfelt apology seemed to spark her temper into fierce life for some reason, since she jumped to her feet to glare at him and he wasn't sure if he was glad or sorry here was the real Ros again under all that protective cover. 'Oh, good, the Duke is sorry. Well, that makes everything all right then, doesn't it? And what were *you* doing four years ago, Your Grace? Who was the lover you had put in my place that year? Did you ever spare a single thought for what I might be doing after you left me? No, you obviously did not, since it never occurred to you that you could have left your eighteen-year-old wife with a lot more than a broken heart.'

'You are so beautiful I thought you could have any man who took your fancy,' he confessed recklessly.

'From the moment I married you to this very moment *I* have been faithful to my marriage vows. What about you, Asher Hartfield?' There was a furious pause in her tirade and of course he couldn't offer up the same amount of loyalty. 'Well? Did you wrap up your fiercest desires in cotton wool and pack them away until you got home to your wife as well then, *Husband*?' she demanded relentlessly.

'No,' he admitted.

'Then there we are, you are a self-confessed adulterer and I once told a lie. What a monstrous pair we are.'

'More than one, Mrs Meadows,' he reminded her of her cover for the last eight years and felt like a worm for doing it even as those defensive, self-serving words came out of his mouth to counter her accusations with nothing much at all. 'But however bad I am, we did agree to stay together for Jenny's sake. I promise on my honour that I will be faithful to you from now on.'

'How very noble of you,' she said scornfully, then seemed to think a little harder about what their marriage had become. 'Is that all we shall ever have now, Ash?' she said bleakly, backing away from the full heat of the fire now the room was almost warm again.

'No. Even when I didn't know we had her it was more than that.'

'Yes, it was hatred,' she said flatly. 'It could only have been that to make you go so far and stop away for so long, Ash,' she added bleakly.

'I could only think of— No, that's not right. The truth is I didn't think at all after we parted because I knew I would be dangerous. I wanted to stay and wrench every last iota of passion out of you—prove it was me you had always wanted and not your lover. What we were before we were married defeated me every time we stopped on that wretched journey back to London, though. I could not put passion where I was so sure love had been before we were married. By the time we got back here I was wound so tight the only way to keep my hands off you was to take my grandfather's offer of a new life away from my wild friends and leave you behind until I was sane again. Maybe I never truly was. I turned you into someone you never were on that long and lonely voyage out. I invented a harpy out of my bitter hurt and frustration and a fit of boyish temper. Because of my folly and immaturity I let you carry and bring up our child alone and that was unforgivable.'

She drew breath to argue.

'No, let me admit it, Rosalind, please?'

'Why not? After our wedding night you refused to let me tell you a single word of love. I thought you set the stars in the sky back then. I loved you as truly as ever, almost as if it was impossible to stop doing it and you still left me, as if I was nothing—as if I didn't matter.'

She doesn't sound as if she loves you now, though, does she, Ash? whispered a bleak voice in his head.

'I would have cried,' he admitted gruffly.

'Do you really expect me to believe it took you eight years to be able to tell me you don't love me without weeping, Ash?'

'I don't expect anything,' he said, genuinely ashamed of the idiot who had walked in his shoes for so long.

'Well. I do,' she surprised him by saying forcefully and she really had changed from the shy girl he fell in love with that first night at Lady Somebody-Or-Other's ball, hadn't she? And from the tightly contained version of herself he had had to get used to over the last few days since they set out from Livesey and the life she had made for herself and her child there. '*You* have had as many lovers as you fancied taking for eight years,' she raged on and he was fiercely glad his Ros was still there under the armour and the hurt he inflicted on her all those years ago, even if persuading her to let him back into her life would be even more of a challenge now she was truly awake again. '*You* gave me one mean little night of passionate lovemaking, then abandoned me, Asher Hartfield. *You* made me a woman on our wedding night, then left me to struggle with all those wants and needs alone as well as raise our child without you.'

'You mean—?' He let his voice trail away as he contemplated the incredible and hardly dared believe it. His sex leapt with hope and desperation, but he still thought he was man enough to take it back to his dismal bedchamber if she didn't really mean that at all.

'I have not had a man in my bed for eight years, you great fool. How do you think that feels for a healthy married woman of six and twenty?'

'Very much like it feels for me right now, I should imagine. Would you like me to beg though, Rosalind? Because I will if that makes you feel better.'

'Yes, I rather think I would,' she said softly, wicked mischief in her eyes as she stood over him with her body outlined by the fire and her beautiful face fierce as a pagan goddess's. She was a challenge he longed to meet, a fantasy he had been struggling with ever since he left England all those years ago and all the more so since he met her again.

'Please will you take me to your bed, then, Duchess Rosalind? Let me adore every inch of you kiss by kiss and touch by touch,' he whispered and although he had meant to be gallant and let her set the pace he was only a man and not a saint.

'That's not begging, it's provocation.'

'Is it working?' he asked hopefully, teasingly, feeling as if the humour and warmth and happiness of them when they were young lovers with the world at their feet was waking up again after a long sleep.

'It may do. Tell me more,' she said throatily, eyes a hot blue and a witchy smile on her beautiful face that made him feel as if he was about to fall to pieces if he did not have her *yes* very soon.

'Not right now,' he said and dragged in a great breath to force himself to stay where he was and keep this as her choice and not his demand. 'Say no to me now and mean it, Ros, because I will have to go outside and lie on a cold marble floor for the rest of the night to distract myself from yearning for you if you don't want me here and now.' He leant forward until his mouth was all but touching hers. He could nearly taste her on his hungry lips and this balance between heaven and hell felt like agony as she thought about it and him. 'Yes or no, Rosalind?' he murmured gruffly. Every inch of him screamed for *yes* but a small part said he must get out of here now if it was to be *no.*

'Yes,' Rosalind whispered. 'Yes, I have wanted you so badly and for so long, of course I want you,' she said and he felt his heart crack at the sound of it in her husky voice and let out a huge sigh of relief even as clever words deserted him and he couldn't seem to tell her about it.

Chapter Ten

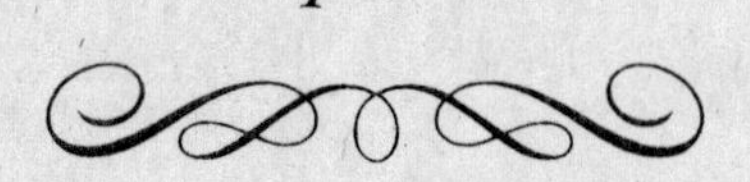

Rosalind slicked her tongue over suddenly dry lips and felt the echo of her own words as if she had shouted them out loud. Fool to let that haunted longing out when he didn't need to know she had wanted him mercilessly after he had gone. He would not notice her slip, she reassured herself, and let a little bit of her be amused that the Duke and Duchess of Cherwell were about to do just what the clumsy symbolism in this over-decorated room demanded of them with all its cherubs and cornucopia and lover's knots.

'We look ridiculous,' she whispered as she caught sight of them in one of those many mirrors. He was wrapped in her bedcover and she had her practical nightdress on and she was the one who was shivering now, but not from the cold.

'I do, you couldn't be if you tried,' he argued with what looked almost looked like awe in his hotly smoky eyes.

He tugged at the ribbon that held her heavy plait

in place and wound his fingers through it until her wildly curling hair sprang free from restraint, as if she had been keeping it prisoner. He gazed at the heavy weight of it lying all down her back and even covering the cheeks of her backside as if he had never seen the like. It had been cropped the last time they met to frame her face with guinea-gold curls. Now he was staring at it as if he wasn't quite sure where it had all come from and he seemed quite fascinated by all she had been hiding from him until now.

'Joan keeps offering to cut it,' she said self-consciously.

'No, it's lovely,' he said huskily and lifted a heavy tress as if it was a wonder to him. 'My task is to convince you to keep it as our private golden fleece,' he argued. 'No, not a task, a pleasure,' he added and let the bedcover drop at last.

His exotic bedgown did not give him much more cover than her thin cotton nightgown did her, so no wonder he was shivering when he dashed to rescue her from nightmares. At least his arms were finally around her and the heat coming off her was enough for two. Surely he could feel her heartbeat race as she felt the changes in him with her own body and marvelled at this new them as they finally embraced, this Rosalind and this Ash, and learned to live in the now?

'Did you walk, run and row your way around India on whatever business you were too busy doing to come home until now?' she asked as she leant a little back from him to test the steel of his muscular arms and knew he would never physically hurt her.

'I had to do something to make myself stay there.'

'Ah, don't, Ash. Don't make me the reason you went away and stopped there. Make it because you wanted to prove you could make your own money or be your own man, but please don't make it because you hated me.'

'Does it feel as if I hate you?' he said seriously and it didn't at all, but there was so much that was unsayable between them, so many places they could not walk it made her physically shake for the risks they would have to take if they ever got past just wanting each other and tiptoed on to more dangerous ground.

'It felt as if you did back then,' she whispered huskily as caution reminded her not to get so wrapped up in wanting him she let out a syllable of love when none was permitted between a duke and his convenient Duchess.

'Then I never wanted you desperately? Never fought not to take you for our mutual pleasure night after night all the way to Gretna? You think I didn't want this until I was deaf, dumb and blind to the rest of the world, lost to everyone but you when we were on our way to be wed?'

Not for long, her inner doubter whispered, but she pushed her into a corner and watched him mean it now.

His kisses up on the heath and at Furze Cottage had been like sips of water after far too long in a desert, but at least his desperation seemed as huge as hers was now. He shook under her urgent hands and she soothed him with a motherly pat. He raised his head to cock one eyebrow at her, as if to remind her he was a fully grown and mature male and there was too much proof eager against her body for her not to know it all too well and glory in it as well now they had finally got past the stiff awkwardness of being man and wife again for everyone's sake but their own, or at least that had been how it had felt until now. Now this felt like self-indulgence of the most luxurious kind to be lovers without boundaries and why ever not? Why not enjoy the duty of providing heirs for the Cherwell dukedom and worry about thornier problems like love and fidelity later?

'I am not the unmarked sylph I was last time we did this,' she warned him, cringing away from the thought he might be repulsed by the changes in her body after bearing a child.

'I like your breasts and hips womanly like this, Ros. Your curves will feel all the more wondrous when we are naked now, not that they don't feel delicious already.'

'I have marks on my body where it had to stretch around my baby and I didn't care enough to use oils to help it do so when Joan tried to persuade me I should,' she said, hoping he would not hear the reason why she did not care enough for herself in her voice as she recalled being that lonely and despairing girl growing bigger and bigger with her husband's child while he sailed away oblivious to her and began his life in a new world. 'You might not like me naked now,' she warned him as some of her insecurities crowded back in at the thought of being so despised by him he could not leave fast enough.

'How could I not love the marks having my baby left on your body?' he reassured her and there was fire in his eyes as if he might worship those silvery stretch marks and turn her into some sort of mother goddess if she let him. She wasn't having that—she was a very human woman and he was her husband and they had not been together like this for far too long. At least that look said one worry was crossed off her list and she could look forward to being a lover again without it holding her back.

'Why are we still talking, then? It has been eight years since I had a man in my bed and I am a very hungry woman,' she said and, catching him off balance, she pushed him backwards on to the bed. Despairing of him taking the lead for fear of making her feel pressured into this, she bent to take his mouth with a kiss so hard and needy it felt as if they were melting together for all time like hot wax. At least that seemed to snap him out of his chivalry and back into Ash the lover. He met her challenge so eagerly it was hard to tell which of them won, or perhaps they both did, she decided hazily as wildfire shot through her. Heat met heat as her body remembered all he had taught her to glory in on their wedding night and added years of frustrated longing to the mix. It was hard to know where his urgent pleasure in her ended and her hot need of him began, but somehow they managed to fit them together and make vibrant, urgent love to one another until *me* faded into *us* again and joined hands in infinite pleasure that shot through them like a huge force of nature and landed them back in one another's arms, gasping with passion and laughing like fools.

Refusing to discuss what they had done while the glorious heat and thunder of their lovemaking still echoed through her, Rosalind pretended she was already lost in sated dreams as she willed herself to go to sleep in Ash's arms. She wanted to rest here while they calmed into silent contentment together. He was holding her so close she could hear his heartbeat and feel his chest rise and fall with each breath he took. The very life of him was beating under her head while she felt him play with her long hair as if it fascinated him. This felt so intimate and certain it was best not to think that he didn't love her any more or of all the times she could have lost him in a far country or on a distant ocean. Best not to think at all, but drift like contented lovers as the only sound in the room was their steadying breathing and an occasional sizzle of burning sap from the glowing fire.

It felt like hours later when Rosalind stirred again. She felt Ash tense under her, as if he had been drifting in a daze of contented intimacy for most of the night as well. She longed to be back at Furze Cottage, waking up with him in the privacy of her own feather bed and without a whole great mansion outside this room waiting to break in on them again. She had to fight a heady urge to provoke him into doing what they did last night all over again, before anyone came to disturb them and make them a duke and duchess again.

'Breakfast,' she said sleepily instead. As if food was the only thing on her mind when it was really far more concerned with Ash's powerful body waking up in a very different way. Learning to be lovers again would make up for some of the gaps in their convenient marriage, she decided, with a contented little stretch against the fine linen sheets that made his smoke-grey eyes go even smokier, as if he was tempted by all the possibilities being in his Duchess's bed presented him with this morning as well.

'Do you have a comb?' he asked, eyeing the heavy and now knotted mass of her hair. 'We seem to have tangled you up rather badly and I think your personal maid is busy,' he added. There was a reminiscent glint in his eyes for how all that tangling happened that made her go heavy-eyed and dreamy all over again, but they needed to be up and doing and she didn't want her daughter to catch them making love if she burst in to find out what was keeping her mother lying abed of a morning.

'Luckily, yes, but you aren't coming anywhere near me with it. It will take ages for me to tease the knots out as it is. You had best comb your own hair before you go, though, lover, or everyone will know what we did last night,' she added with a longing glance at his dishevelled dark blonde locks she had helped make far more windswept than a fashionable hairdresser. She really was settling into her new role as an experienced wife and woman of the world rather nicely, in her opinion.

'They will anyway,' he said gruffly and she supposed she ought to stop trying to provoke him into losing control again. There must be a lock on one of those ridiculous doors somewhere, just in case they both lost it and forgot about the world outside them again before bedtime.

'I still don't want Jenny to see me looking far more dishevelled than she is used to of a morning.'

'We need to find her a nanny or a nursery governess.'

'We do, but not to keep her out of my bedroom at this time of day,' she said with a frown because she didn't want to be a remote mother who visited her child in her nursery every morning, then forgot her for the rest of the day.

'Not what I meant, Rosalind,' he said sternly and as if she had deliberately misunderstood him. That was the trouble with rearranged marriages like this one. There were still far too many prickly patches where misunderstanding could flourish between them. 'Keeping a child as lively as Jenny happy and amused all day is hard work. And you need a lady's maid as soon as your new clothes begin to arrive, if not before.'

'Speaking of clothes...'

'We must get up, you houri, so stop playing with fire,' he chided.

'As if I have been keeping you in bed rather than the other way about.'

'Ah, but we Dukes and Duchesses have duties to perform and only a couple of weeks in London to do them in.'

'I thought that was what we had been doing.'

'No, that wasn't duty, it was pleasure,' he argued and to punish her for that suggestion he kissed her until she could hardly remember her own name, then slipped out of her bed and went back to his monstrous red room without looking back. She knew it cost him every ounce of willpower he had because she had to use all of hers not to call him back and risk someone catching them making love after all.

It was actually a month before everything was finally ready for them to leave Cherwell House for the north. Rosalind and Jenny had the makings of a fine new wardrobe each by then and even Ash had added a few more layers of manly warmth to the ones he hastily ordered when he stopped at Cherwell House on his return from India. That was before everything changed, when he still meant to divorce her so he could start a new life with a very different woman. She knew it was foolish of her to harp on that other woman, now everything was so different between her and Ash, but Rosalind was still haunted by his other Duchess—and jealous, which felt even more stupid and self-defeating since the girl did not exist. It was not as if she wanted to be a debutante again, paraded for the likes of Ash to pick for a splendid marriage of convenience. Yet that girl would have been unmarked by life, an innocent page for Ash to write 'Duchess' upon. She left her fantasy rival behind with a sigh of relief when the new travelling carriage Ash had bought for the journey rolled smoothly out of London and the fine team of horses were soon bowling along in fine style on the open road.

'Do you think Joan minds being in the second carriage with Carrie and Miss Burrows?' Jenny asked.

'I think she will strive to endure all that blissful peace and quiet as best she can,' Rosalind teased.

'I am not *that* noisy, Mama,' Jenny protested indignantly.

'I expect Joan is enjoying telling Carrie exactly what you will eat and not eat and describing to Miss Burrows all the marvels of education Mama and the Belstones' long-suffering governess have managed to cram into you between them, my scamp,' Ash said.

His scamp looked wistful for a moment when reminded she used to have her lessons with her best friends, but he realised he had done that without meaning to and managed to convince her it would not be very long now before the Belstones kept their promises to visit Edenhope in the summer.

'What's it like, Papa?' Jenny asked and Rosalind thought it had become something of a game for the them: What Papa Remembers about his Grandfather's House As A Boy and What Jenny Would Like It To Be.

Rosalind was secretly delighted Ash had chosen to stay in the coach with them this time, rather than riding ahead. It was only partly because it was easier to keep their daughter amused with Ash's help and Jenny always seemed to be wondering where her father was and what he was doing or seeing without her when he was out of sight. Jenny adored her father and that was another thing Rosalind had to accustom herself to. She was glad they had become so close without either having to try very hard, of course she was, but sometimes it felt difficult being only Mama, who had always been there and always would be, whilst this was Papa, who was new and shiny and a duke into the bargain.

Jenny had longed for a father and Ash had a light touch with her. She did not know where their marriage was heading, but at least it was a true marriage now and he was a very present father. Not perfect, of course, he would be sickening and even more infuriating if he was, but he did try to understand the hopes and fears her bold little girl faced every day. The Duke and Duchess and Lady Imogen intended to take their journey north in short stages—as befitted such stately people. It could be an adventure this way and not the tedious, seemingly endless journey Rosalind and Ash remembered from their dash by mail coach from London to Scotland to get married. That was a longer journey and they were tense with nerves, but this was going to be different in every way. Rosalind stared out at the passing scene and told herself everything was different now and at least she had learned not to expect too much.

Even in February there were sights to see and fine old inns to stay in while they explored marvels along the way. And fine old inns meant fine old best bedchambers, where the Duke and Duchess of Cherwell could explore one another all over again. Every night they made passionate, satisfying love after Jenny was so fast asleep a regiment marching past her window with bugles at full blast would not wake her. And sometimes they even lasted until after dinner, when of course it was quite commonplace for a husband and wife to seek their bed after another not-very-weary day travelling or exploring less intimate sights than one another.

Making love with Ash on their leisurely journey north was almost as hungry and driven as it had been at Cherwell House when they had taken up every aspect of being married again with such enthusiasm. When they fell on one another with the ravenous hunger of all those years apart to make up for, it was always hotly wonderful as far as Rosalind was concerned. Sometimes it could even be leisurely; Ash could stretch out pleasure into a glorious climax that made every nerve and sinew in her body vibrate with sated contentment if she let him have enough time. He was a master craftsman when it came to making fiery love to his wife.

And how many other women had he done it with just as urgently and hotly since he left her? a snide little voice asked as Rosalind floated back down to earth in their latest comfortable bed for the night.

She still shook with echoes of the wild ecstasy that had convulsed her again and again as they found their own private Eden yet again, but there were snakes in Eden, weren't there? Her own particular snake was jealousy. Not of a present and hateable rival, but all the ones he had met and made fierce love to while he was away from her. Rosalind had never been able to give Ash naive innocence and trust, even on their wedding night. Not with another man vaguely remembered and the humiliation of realising what that rogue had done to her after he rode away laughing. That night had tainted her first night with her husband and made her fearful the first time they made sweet, driven love at Carlisle. Not the second or the third time they did so that night, of course. There may even have been more—she was in such a haze by then they could have done it again on that hotly enthusiastic wedding night.

Now Rosalind lay next to her husband as he slept and stared into the familiar darkness, wondering about the future. Ash had wanted a wife who would stay neatly inside the lines he marked out for his Duchess and instead he had got her. She was already the mother of his child and, since he seemed to want to be a proper father to Jenny, he could hardly get Rosalind with child every time he felt the need for another heir, then leave her in Yorkshire while he lived the carefree life of a not-quite-single duke in London. And he did make love to her with exquisite consideration. The Asher Hartfield she fell fathoms deep in love with at first glance had been left behind somewhere though, hadn't he? Maybe that Ash was still in India with the svelte and soft-skinned woman he whispered love words to after he found Rosalind so undeserving of them? She remembered the wonderful fizzing sense of absolute happiness from the day she first fell in love with the finest and most handsome young man ever born and wanted to weep, even after being made love to by the Ash of now as if he had spent eight years secretly yearning for her, which he most definitely had not or he would have been back long ago.

'What is it?' he asked rather gruffly and turned out to be awake after all.

'Nothing,' she answered as lightly as she could. 'I am not tired.'

'Me neither,' he admitted and got out of bed to stoke up the fire lest the whisper of a draught got past fast-closed shutters, drawn curtains and a firmly closed door. He had already done everything he could to seal any cold air out of the room and Rosalind wondered how he would manage in a draughty mansion in North Yorkshire. Maybe they could oust the scullery maid from her truckle bed and sleep next to the kitchen fire.

'Do you think you will ever get used to our climate?' she teased as he visibly shuddered in a room she thought a little too warm already.

'I hope so, or I will have to build my own private hothouse at Edenhope for when it's snowing outside or the wind comes in off the North Sea,' he said, his disgust plain at the thought of never growing used to his native land again.

'Maybe you stayed away too long,' she said before she caught the full sense of her own words. She had not meant to refer to the years they had lost, or at least it felt like it now.

'I did,' he admitted steadily. 'I acted like a whipped boy, Ros,' he added and looked weary at the thought of the old Ash she had loved so much.

'We were not much more than children,' she said with a shrug. 'We should have found out who we really were before we risked marrying each other.'

'Lord Lackbourne would have persuaded you to

wed some rich old man long before we had a chance to. It was either make a runaway match or watch you married off to a cold, old aristocrat with an empty nursery and deep pockets. I could not endure the thought of you caged up and sad inside such a marriage.'

'I have learnt a lot about real life in eight years, Ash,' she told him as he pushed back the covers and got into bed again. It felt glorious to have a long-limbed, rough-haired male in the bed next to her again, but maybe this was not the time to find any contact with his naked body quite so stimulating. 'And, as you were the one who taught me to need, you can hardly claim I do not enjoy your male body as deeply as you seem to enjoy my female one. You made me feel things I never thought a true lady could or should feel, Ash. And you have shown me a wild need most of them will never find out about.' She warmed up to her subject in more ways than one and began to feel that need stir as sharply as if they had never satisfied it so intensely not half an hour ago.

'Even if they love their husbands they will never know how fierce and fiery lovemaking can be and I pity them. This is your fault,' she told him triumphantly and laid back against the pillows, waving an airy gesture over her voluptuously naked figure with her desire-tight nipples crowning breasts that had gone fuller and tighter again far too soon for comfort and invited him to be wickedly abandoned with her all over again. His gaze followed the course of her hand over her naked body as if he was still as hungry for her as a starving wolf. When she lay back even further on the soft feather mattress and opened her legs to let him see how ready she was for him all over again, he could not keep his hands or the rest of him off her, since he was visibly in the same state when they both ought to be exhausted and fast asleep by now. Rosalind simply abandoned herself to being just that—abandoned, beyond shyness or guilt. By stoking their carnal desires so high there was nothing left but the absolute need to be pushed to the highest peak, then taken with the utmost pleasure by one another. She could stop them talking about anything wider or deeper they once thought they were going to have, until they got caught in this silken trap instead and, apart from her secret demon of jealousy, she was loving every moment of it.

Chapter Eleven

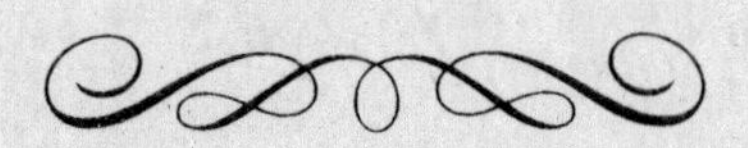

Rosalind knew Joan was worried Ash was making heirs instead of love with his wife as they made their very slow way to their new home. Her maid was the only one who had cared enough to pick up the broken pieces of her late mistress's daughter last time Ash had his way with her, then walked away, so of course Joan had a right to worry, but this time everything was different. Rosalind had seen concern in Joan's eyes whenever they bade each other goodnight, though, before Ash could endure the wait no longer and entered whatever bedchamber they had for the night whether she was ready or not. And what could she say to reassure her friend when she had no real idea how Ash really felt about her either? He made love to her so passionately he had to see her as something more than the Duchess who would give him little lords and ladies for his sadly depleted succession, but it was not quite the grand romance they thought when they sped north as fast as horses could get them there to be wed eight years ago.

'At least Ash and I agreed this would be a marriage of convenience from the outset this time, Joan. I went into it with eyes wide open and this is enough for me.' She paused. 'More than enough,' she added dreamily and already felt the heat building in her belly at the very thought of another night of driven love-making to come.

'No, it's not,' Joan argued as if she could not keep the words in any longer. 'He has no idea what you went through after he was gone. He wasn't the one left here to hold and try to comfort you while you sobbed your heart out for him as if you might break from sheer loneliness and sorrow. I was afraid you might even lose the baby because you didn't care enough about yourself to take care of you both. I remember all the times you needed him to be a husband to you and a father to your coming child and where was he? Why, he was sulking on the other side of the world, pretending you was nothing to do with him, no, nor that sweet babe neither,' Joan said, her Cockney origins showing far more now she was letting her emotions rip. 'And now I'm supposed to act like I'm that pleased he's come home I can hardly contain myself? Well, I ain't. I can't pretend that hard, Miss Rosalind. Send me away if you must and you know I love you and Miss Jenny so dearly it would fairly break me to go, especially since your poor mother begged me to take care of you when she knew she was dying. I'll not have him looking down his long nose at you again and calling you names. Not while I'm here to argue he's a fool, even if he is a duke. After what you went through birthing his child without a father, I ain't got it in me to pretend it don't matter that he's come back and decided he wants a wife after all.'

Rosalind hugged her good friend and wished she had not been quite so bound up in enjoying what she and Ash could do in a bed now they truly were husband and wife again. Of course Joan was concerned and she was grateful for it. Her maid was the only person who had offered her warmth and understanding when Ash was gone. Lord Lackbourne would never have understood she adored the thought of her coming child, disgraced and deserted by her husband as she was. If she had waited to show before she left of her own accord he would have made her feel less than she knew she could be. And with Joan's support she had been strong enough to be reckless for her baby's sake. Her maid had been her loyal friend and sole companion in a harsh world while they waited for her baby to be born and built a new life on the ashes of the old one.

'I could never turn my back on you, Joan, whatever you say or do. I worry as well, but I decided to live life as it is and simply enjoy being married again. I did miss him so and you know that better than anyone. But you were my family when I had nobody, Jenny's and mine once she was born, and you still are now. I will never be as alone as I was when he left me again though, not with Jenny and any children we have in the future to make it impossible to be so shattered again and he won't do it, Joan. He's different now. And even if he wasn't, how could I do anything but love you when you stayed with me through so much and are family anyway?'

'Aye, well, there's no need to get mawkish about it,' Joan replied with a suspiciously loud sniff and bustled about the bedchamber as if she had never let that outburst of anxiety out.

'I heard,' Ash said when he came into their bedchamber several minutes after Joan had left. 'I listened at the door, then crept away before either of you heard me.'

'They do say eavesdroppers seldom hear good news, don't they?'

'I always knew your maid was your stern protector, so why should she pretend I was good for you when I was young and wild and stupid,' he said with a shrug.

'Joan really is family to myself and Jenny,' she told Ash defensively and dared him to argue.

'I would never even try to dismiss her for showing too much loyalty to you, even if I had the power. Joan is in your employ, not mine.'

He had always treated the servants with an ease her stepfather had deplored and now he was passing Rosalind independence inside marriage. He was a fair man and a fair employer, but the old Ash had been easy with most people. She missed that genial young man for his own sake, not only as the ardent lover she used to steal away from Lackbourne House to meet wherever they could snatch a few moments of heaven in each other's arms. He had not been real though, had he? He had only lasted a single day of marriage, as if she had wed a shadow instead of a real man. She sighed and wished life was a lot less complicated as she eyed the man who had grown out of that boy and nobody could call him unreal, could they?

'Did you really miss me that badly?' he said as if he had only just realised how much he had hurt her.

'I had your baby in my belly. Of course I missed you, you great idiot. You hurt me more than I ever thought it possible to hurt until then, but I loved you so much, how could I not miss you?'

'Poor little girl,' he said, grey eyes heavy with shadows as he seemed to be looking for a girl who didn't exist any longer as well.

'Don't pity her; she's dead,' she said starkly. 'She had to die so I could be a fit and proper mother. Young Rosalind and young Ash both had to be dead for me to do that. If they were not, I would never have got over the loneliness, so I killed us both off when I went to live in Livesey as Mrs Meadows.'

'Oh, Ros,' he said as if the hardness behind those words hurt him far more than her softness that made her sit in that wretched carriage and weep all the way from Carlisle to London, since he was so intent on deserting her when they got there, had hurt her.

She managed a wry smile and made light of it. 'I am not sorry the old version of me is gone, Ash, she was such a watering pot I am well rid of her.'

'I suspect she's not quite as dead as you think,' he said as if he knew her better than she did herself. 'You always had a sense of humour under the vulnerability and strength under that. You were a complicated young woman and I was nowhere near clever enough to work you out the first time around, but I'm getting better at it, Duchess Rosalind. I might even be starting to know you better than you know yourself.'

'Don't flatter yourself,' she said disgustedly.

'There you are, you see? I knew you would react like that.'

'A lucky guess.'

'Spiky, outspoken, stubborn to a fault, quick tempered, impatient…'

'Stop right there. According to you I am such a virago I am surprised anyone is prepared to work for me, let alone live with me.'

'I had not finished. Now where was I? Ah, yes, impatient…'

'Don't be ridiculous; I am the soul of patience. I could not put up with you if I was half as hasty and bad-tempered as you say I am.'

'Impatient,' he continued with a look that told her there was all the proof he needed. 'Funny, brave, compassionate, strong, loving, kind—did I mention stubborn?'

'I believe you might have done,' she said and tried not to let that second list go straight to her silly, soft heart and persuade her she loved him all over again. He was right, confound him; young Rosalind wasn't dead at all. Best let the act of loving blot out the possibility of it taking her over ever again, she decided, and stood up on tiptoe to press a hot kiss on his mouth to silence him. Not that it worked for very long. He snatched a breath, held her slender waist in both hands to push her a little further away and look down at her with goodness knew what questions and emotions in his smoky gaze this time.

'And impatient, did I say that?' he said huskily.

'Three times,' she replied with a snap in her voice.

'There's nothing wrong with a little bit of impatience in the right place and at the right time,' he said and his hands moved round to her back so he could pull her closer. 'And I do believe this is both,' he added softly as he kissed her mouth with butterfly kisses that made her so impatient she raised herself on tiptoe and pushed her mouth hard against his to stop him promising so much and delivering too little.

After that there were no words big enough, only sighs for breath and guttural little lovers' noises as she revelled in their mutual impatience. She shook with haste and heat as he undid the tiny buttons of her new nightgown with a ridiculous amount of patience. At last there he was…oh, there…and there as well. His magician's hands were on her breasts again and it felt like bliss.

'Lush,' he murmured. Her nipples went as hard as pearls in the cooler air, longing for his mouth there. 'Plush,' he added admiringly as his wicked hands measured the richness of her mature figure. His approving hum was more seductive than a book full of poetry and he slid a teasing finger across them admiringly, wickedly arousing her as he withheld just enough of his touch to make her long for more. She actually felt her breasts go fuller and more eager under his gloating gaze and wriggled sensuously against him to push them closer to his hands and mouth.

'Hurry,' she urged and linked her hands behind his neck to urge him physically closer to the hotly tight nipples that needed him so badly it almost hurt. She bowed and moaned softly when he did as they both wanted him to and played his tongue teasingly across one and flicked it with such delicate provocation everything about her tightened and loosened at the same time as fiery need shot from there to the heart of her inner self and back again. Heat threatened to overwhelm her when he set up a merciless rhythm and she writhed and gasped while he held her torso steady despite her frantic wriggling and begging for more.

'Impatient,' he murmured as if his mouth had almost forgotten how to form words because he wanted her so much.

His self-control was still oceans ahead of hers, though, and she felt a hitch of insecurity before the pleasure of his hands and mouth and anything else he could get closer to her with washed it away again. Oh, but the heat of them, the power of him, the raking, velvet longing for him inside her was all that mattered right now. He had made her need like this, made her his that first night when they created Jenny between them. She parted her legs and ground her aching need against his aching need and he definitely, very obviously needed her. His turn to moan and raise his head from the feast he had made of her almost painfully aroused breasts; his turn to be hasty.

At last, here he was. She was so ready she needed

to fly past the usual stops on the scenic route he had planned for them and get straight to the heart of her hunger. She refused to let him gentle her, but set a merciless pace, her and him together as she got so close to taking fire it felt as if she would explode if she didn't burn out of control soon. They were so near to the achy, heady, wonderful, pleasure at the heart of all life in this world. Her Ash-damped nipples must have cried out for something even in the shadowy glow of firelight because his long, strong fingers played with her while she rode them both frantically, as if their very lives depended on reaching a climax before one of them broke.

'Ah, yes, there and there and there,' she found enough breath to gasp as the feel of him rampant inside her drove her up so fast she lost her way and he bucked eagerly under her until she snatched the reins back and there it was, the winning post, the glorious finishing line. She moaned with eager anticipation and triumph as it raced up to meet them and there; they were over it. Spasms of ecstasy shook her so hard she wondered if she was going to faint clean away with the power of this richness and release for a long heady moment as completion refined and claimed her. She spared Ash a greedy, lover's look as the ultimate pleasure rode him as well. His eyes had rolled back in his head and his mouth was open in a long, silent moan of release as his manhood jerked and drove hard inside her and her orgasm met his and clasped its hands. They spent each other—not His Grace seeding his Duchess, but Ash making love to Rosalind.

My love, she mouthed to the shadows as she bowed

backwards to send those words up to the ceiling where he could not read them, even when he was looking at the world again and not the fierce moment of completion that belonged only to them.

It wasn't safe to let him know this part of her still loved him and always would. This part could—the Rosalind who went wild in his arms every night she could get there—but the rest was not sure. That part still hurt too much to take such a huge risk so easily. She sank on to his heaving body with a great sigh and one last, powerful jerk of complete ecstasy as she wished ridiculously that their life was so different she could say anything to her lover and he could tell her all his secret hopes and dreams. *It's enough,* she told herself. *More than I ever dreamed of when we left Livesey.* Yet the Rosalind of all those years ago still stared into the firelit darkness while her lover slept and yearned for everything she was so sure she already had on her wedding night.

It was the middle of March by now and Rosalind saw the irony of the ducal entourage going one wa
up the Great North Road while a good many of th
ton would shortly be travelling down it to the capi
for the main social Season and all sorts of liaisons
making and breaking of young girls' dreams. Sh
membered her own certainty she would meet the
of her life on the dance floors of Mayfair and sh
been right, hadn't she? She had been sceptic
unconvinced by any of the beaux who had sv
around her because of her looks. At least her
ence of so-called love at sixteen had made

tious about anyone who claimed to love her purely because she had golden hair, blue eyes and a pleasing arrangement of features. Then she was finishing a dance with one of them when she looked up into a pair of smoky-grey eyes and saw Ash's wicked smile for the first time. The noisy ballroom had faded into silence, the inane chatter of her dance partner halted as he eyed Ash, then backed away as if he might be dangerous. 'Dance?' he asked as if that was all he could get out and she simply smiled brilliantly at him and said, 'Yes', and that was that.

Strange how life turned out when nothing about her youthful love affair had gone quite according to plan after the blissful beginning. Speaking of plans, which they were not, so very carefully not that Ash had not even mentioned the fact she had not seen her courses since the week they left Livesey. Had he forgotten wives had them? Not that she stood much chance of enduring many with him around to get her with child as soon as look at her. Rosalind had begun to suspect she was pregnant again by the time they set out from Cambridge on their long and meandering journey at the end of February, but now she was certain. She had decided to keep the news between her and Joan for the time being, because if she told Ash they would probably be marooned halfway between Yorkshire and London until the baby was safely born and he dared complete what felt almost like the bride journey they had never had. Far too romantic an idea for a duke and his convenient Duchess, especially with a daughter in tow, but it had been a lovely inter-

lude between grandiose Cherwell House and palatial Edenhope Place.

Now she was feeling sick as soon as she got out of bed in the morning and her nipples were tight and sensitive even when Ash was not around to encourage them to beg for his touch and drive the rest of her to distraction yet again.

She was able to delay another week before telling him her suspicions; since their journey had been so leisurely she wondered if he dreaded arriving at Edenhope even more than she did becoming its latest chatelaine. They were staying at the most comfortable hotel in Selby when she finally had to tell Ash he had proved himself as potent now as he was at one and twenty, or was she every bit as receptive to his rampant desire for his wife as she was at eighteen? Either way, she was pregnant again, but the Duke of Cherwell seemed less than delighted by the outcome he had bargained for when he discovered he already had a child and might as well keep the Duchess he already had to go with her.

'You truly believe you are with child again?' he said, sitting back down on the side of the bed he had just been trying to urge her out of so they could take an early morning ride she knew for certain would be a bad idea until she had finished feeling sick for the day, so she had finally had to tell him why she would not be up for some time.

'It does happen,' she said solemnly, glad she had not dared get out of bed yet, since she knew she would feel the room start to spin the moment she was upright again. He looked pale enough to faint even before she began her daily appointment with the pristine bowl in the adjoining dressing room Joan would have placed there in readiness. 'Especially to us,' she pointed out helpfully, in case he had not noticed it seemed almost as if he only had to look at her to get her pregnant.

'Not yet, though,' he said as if such things could be ordered one way or the other.

Rosalind was in a very good position to know Mother Nature had her own timetable as far as making babies was concerned. Apparently she and Ash were very good at it, almost too good. 'You are disappointed,' she said flatly, feeling as if the secret she had been keeping in case she was simply feeling a little queasy after so many upsets in her life since he came back into it, or it was too soon to tell and she lost the precious little life growing in her belly, had fallen very flat in the telling.

'Not that—never that, Rosalind. I just wanted you to myself a bit longer, that's all. We have had so little time together, I wanted—' He stopped himself from saying whatever it was he was fantasising over.

She looked away from his sternly handsome face, feeling a bit apprehensive about the whole business now she had finally plucked up the courage to share her hopes of another child with him. She had no idea if it was safe for them to carry on making love as if they had invented the act of it in all its infinite varieties either. He had not been here last time for her to worry about such important details and this might be his precious heir in her belly, so he would not want to take risks with it any more than she did. She would have to write a very private letter to her good friend Judith Belstone, mother of five children now little Rosalind was safely born, and where would their plans for this Rosalind to attend little Rose's christening as godmother end up now? Anyway, as soon as they were close enough to Edenhope for a reply to reach her as fast as it could be carried she really must write that letter and send it by messenger, who could wait for a reply.

'Maybe you should have been more careful how you spent your seed, then, Your Grace,' she said coldly as her news fell sadly flat and she wished she had kept it to herself all the way to Edenhope now.

She recalled this urge to cry for no reason from last time she was with child, so it could not be because Ash seemed less than delighted that his plans for putting his Duchess to work filling the ducal nurseries were turning out so perfectly they had not even got to Edenhope and she was already pregnant.

'I could not stop myself making love to you, Ros. I can't seem to keep my hands off you; I'm sorry,' he said.

She narrowed her eyes and argued silently with that statement as she felt her gorge rise even before she had got out of bed this morning. He had obviously had plenty of lovers under those magical, sensuous hands of his before he came back to her. Her mental picture of him in bed with another woman before he came home to her was too much for her. She dashed off to the dressing room just in time to retch into the bowl as if her poor stomach was being turned inside out.

He surprised her by appearing in the quaint old powdering room in this ancient inn despite her nausea and tears as she was repeatedly even more wretchedly ill than usual. This morning it was her husband who held her hair back from her face for her while she was horribly sick. Ash must have taken a quick lesson in what to do for her from Joan when he came back into the room a few moments later with a fresh bowl and a small jug and bowl. He washed her face with a cloth soaked in honey water, then folded her shivering body back against his strong one while they waited to see if her stomach had done cramping for the day. The blessed warmth and contact with him made her feel cherished as she sighed a great sigh and closed her eyes in relief because it felt as if her ordeal was finally over, for today.

'Dry toast and warm tea,' he told her with a nod as if he intended to be sure she had everything she needed to cope with this daily ordeal from now on, even if he had to make it himself.

'Joan will have ordered it by now,' she told him wearily.

'Is it like this all the time?' he asked. He had coped well today, but he was a man and they did so hate drama and illnesses.

'Not if this one is the same as Jenny, but I have no idea if it will be yet. I suppose we will just have to wait and see.'

'How long did you feel like this with her then?'

'Until the third month, then it was only now and again and once I felt her quicken in my womb I was never sick again until the day she was born.'

'I have only been back three months,' he said as if the thought of several more weeks or months of this might make *him* take to his bed every morning until she felt well enough to get up as well.

It might be a novel cure for morning sickness, but she would be willing to try if only Judith sent a swift reply to her questions about making love when you were with child. So now she knew what she would be doing while she waited for him to come back from his ride and supposed she ought to have written to Judith as soon as she suspected she was pregnant again. She had not, though, and they did not abstain from enjoying themselves in the meantime and it had done no harm, a thought that cheered her up quite wonderfully. 'But we have been very busy about my duchessly duty, Your Grace,' she joked.

'It never feels like a duty to me, Ros,' he said very seriously indeed and she twisted round to look up at his face now she was fairly certain she could do so without ending up back where they started.

'Nor me,' she agreed and that was as close as either of them got to admitting the endless need between them was more than lust and a duke's convenient desire for this outcome. It was enough, she told herself as they made an even more leisurely journey from Selby to Edenhope and Ash was as attentive as a doting husband could be until they had that letter from her friend to tell them if it was safe to make love with one's much-desired and desiring husband during pregnancy.

Chapter Twelve

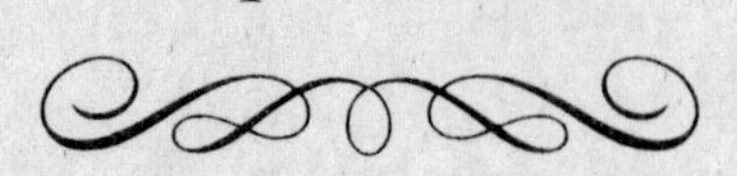

'Is this really where we are going to live, Papa?'

'Yes, my Lady Imogen. Don't worry though, Jenny—with a little bit of love and a lot of work it will make a very fine home for us all, I promise you,' Ash told his awestruck daughter. 'I loved visiting my grandfather as a boy. It is a beautiful place and there is so much to do even when it's raining.'

Rosalind's heart had been in her mouth ever since the coach turned in through the grand gateway between two Tudor lodges that looked more like small fortresses than a warm welcome to the Duke of Cherwell's grand country house. Now she watched the huge old house grow ever larger and more imposing on the horizon and wondered how this could ever be home. It was built to overpower anyone foolish enough to question the might of the Dukes of Cherwell on their own land. Yet although it looked very grand from afar it was weather-worn and close to down-at-heel. Many of the windows were shuttered, as if the house had its eyes closed in a long sleep, and some were even boarded up to keep out rain and wind.

'Your late cousin's trustees did a poor job of maintaining his house,' she murmured to Ash since Jenny was so fascinated by her palatial new home she was obviously not listening.

'Yes, Charlie was always writing to tell me how they disagreed over every little detail so nothing ever got done. I should have come home and made them attend to their duties instead of enjoying their battles so much they forgot what they were entrusted with. I failed my cousin as well as you, Ros.'

'Stop feeling guilty and put it right, then,' she said brusquely, because she refused to be a sore spot on his conscience. She was his wife and they had to live with what they had, not what might have been. 'And at least *you* are fully of age, even for a duke. Now those trustees must account for their neglect and you will be able to terrify them far more than your cousin would have been able to if he had only lived to take up the reins of this place.'

'Aye, he would have been five and twenty in July.'

'Then I cannot imagine why the whole place is not seething with workmen and covered in scaffolding. They could hardly have thought you would be pleased by all they have failed to do during your cousin's minority, even if they did not fear his fury. They had a legal duty of care for your cousin's inheritance, so you could always sue them for damages I suppose.'

'I am so glad to be shot of them I don't care what they do as long as they never come near the place again. I am astonished how much damage has been done in the five years since Grandfather died.'

'A place this old must take continuous maintenance and I doubt your grandfather was up to scrambling about on the roof or peering into drains and gutters during the last few years of his life.'

'Where were his agent and clerk of the works, then?'

'I have no idea,' she said with a raised eyebrow to warn him not to get any more furious over the state of his huge old house in front of Jenny.

'You're right,' he admitted. 'Confound it!' he snapped as the carriage wheels seemed to lurch along the edge of a huge pothole and they were almost thrown across the carriage. 'Are you all right?' Ash demanded, pale under his slightly fading suntan when he released her from the iron hold he had clamped around her to prevent a painful tumble.

'Yes, you were very quick. Thank you,' she said, her heartbeat settling after a few moments of panic at the thought of plunging headlong into the seat opposite and harming her baby.

'What about you, Jenny?' he said, letting her out from under his other arm and relaxing the long legs he had braced against the seat opposite to keep them all safe.

'I banged my elbow,' Jenny said a little bit tearfully, rubbing her sore place as she squirmed across him to get closer to Rosalind and it was quite wrong to feel almost relieved her child still wanted her comfort at times like this.

'Looks like you hit your funny bone, love, keep rubbing and the pain will fade in a few moments.'

'But it hurts, Mama.'

'I know, love. I never could work out why people call it a funny bone when there's nothing funny about it when you hit it.'

'It's a naughty bone,' Jenny said with a fierce frown at the place she had forgotten to keep rubbing so Rosalind concluded the pain must be fading already.

'Bradley!' Ash shouted up to the coachman. 'What the devil were you thinking of?'

'Sorry, Your Grace. I thought we was past the worst, then half the drive fell into a great hole the rains must have worn under the gravel.'

Ash took a long hard look at the runnel at the side of the drive and even from here Rosalind could see half the roadway had been undermined so the weight of a carriage and four made the rest collapse into the gap. 'It's a miracle he didn't upend us all,' she murmured, still shocked how close they had come to disaster.

'Not your fault,' Ash shouted back. 'Best stop here, though. We will be safer walking the rest of the way. I don't want to risk another pitfall with Her Grace and Lady Imogen aboard and neither should you,' he called up to the coachman, who was in a precarious position on the swaying box at the best of times. The poor man must have thought he would be thrown off as he struggled to guide his frightened team around such a sudden hazard.

'You did well not to overturn the whole carriage and do terrible damage to us or the horses, Bradley,'

Rosalind called past Ash's shoulder. 'I am very grateful, even if His Grace is still too shocked to thank you for preserving us at the moment.'

'Thank *you*, Your Grace,' the coachman said, sounding as if he thought his job might be safe after all if the Duchess thought he was competent.

Surprised to agree and thoughtful about her own influence on the husband she had thought about as easy to sway as a granite mountain at first sight up on that Dorset heath, Rosalind sat back in her seat and let herself be a little bit shocked by their near miss.

'Aye, well done, man. Unharness the team now and have them led to the stables rather than risk their legs and yours on another pothole.'

Ash drew his head back in and waited grimly for the team to calm after that unnerving collapse, then jumped down. 'I will have someone's head for this,' he murmured to Rosalind as he glared at the evidence of damage done by heavy rain and nothing done to mend it. She could hardly argue it was not dangerous and if the baby was harmed she might never forgive them either.

'Powerful though you may be here, my lord Duke, I really don't think such summary justice would be approved of,' she managed to say lightly. If they dwelt on what might have been she would never leave the house again until this child was safely delivered.

'Just their job, then,' Ash said grimly and Rosalind did not protest because they had come all the way from London without encountering a trap like that and someone had been criminally neglectful.

'I like it better from the ground. Poor old house,' Jenny said when Ash had lifted her from the stranded vehicle. Rosalind felt the easy power in his broad shoulders as she grabbed them when his hands closed around her still-slim waist and she was airborne before she knew it. At least being flustered by his strength took her mind off the baby and how easily they could have lost it, but for Bradley's skill and Ash's quick thinking in bracing his legs and grabbing a wife and a daughter under each arm. There was always the looming task of becoming the Duchess in power to divert her from fantasising about his rather magnificent body, but she wasn't sure she wanted diverting that badly.

Now she was down and already forgetting her bruise Jenny reached out a hand to each of them in silent demand. The new Duke and Duchess of Cherwell jumped their daughter over the lesser pitfalls on their way to their new home and Rosalind decided this was exactly how they should be—the three of them hand in hand as they walked towards their new home and never mind stateliness and protocol. She shook her head at Ash to tell him not to fuss, the baby was fine and she was enjoying the walk after being cooped up in a carriage for hours. She was a healthy and still fairly young woman and had seen far too much of real life in Livesey Village to cosset herself for the next six or seven months just to make her ducal husband feel better.

'You are quite right, Jenny, the house looks much nicer from here,' she said as the sun came out at the very moment the vast door creaked open, as if even

Mother Nature wanted to make them feel welcome. The indoor staff must have realised their new Duke and his family really were walking up the drive like ordinary folk. As many as were in sight of the windows or in earshot of those who were came piling out of the house to bid them welcome, but it was not the vast army of servants Rosalind had been dreading—more a gaggle than a regiment. Another sign of the neglect now so obvious in weed-strewn flower beds and unkempt lawns.

'We had best hurry up,' she said with a wry grimace at Ash over Jenny's dark head. 'The servants will catch their deaths in this sharp breeze and I really don't want to have to get down on my knees and scrub your splendid floors if they are all laid up,' she said, their joke about those floors before he had his wicked way with her again back in London so warm this sharp breeze only felt chilly around the edges of her splendid new travelling gown and fine pelisse.

The servants were so delighted to see Ash and his ready-made family they made them welcome with only a hint of scepticism, as if to say, *We're glad to see you again, lad, but you'd best make a good fist of things here or we'll soon change our minds.*

'The second carriage is not far behind,' Ash said as a depleted trickle of outdoor staff began scurrying from stables and gardens to get in on the act. 'A shilling for any lad who warns them the main drive is unsafe.'

'Tell them the road down from the North Gate ain't too bad and show them where it is,' one of the grooms called after the eager stable boy now racing the gardener's boy to the South Gate.

'Who is going to explain to me why there is a hole in the main drive you could lose a plough horse in?' Ash added with a chilly look around the group scattered over the shallow stone steps.

'Mr Grange told us to mend it, so Sir Henry said we was not to,' a middle-aged man finally stepped forward to say dourly.

'I remember you—Dawkins, isn't it?'

The man nodded and looked almost gratified.

'Why would anyone ask stable hands to do work estate workers are supposed to be here for?' Ash asked him with a puzzled frown.

Dawkins shrugged. 'Nowt makes much sense here since the old Duke died, Master Ash,' he said and Rosalind tried not to smile and ruin Ash's 'Grand Duke' act. 'I mean, Your Grace,' Dawkins added after a hasty elbow in the side from a minion.

'Sense or not, is there enough hardcore and hoggin on the estate to fill the holes and make good?'

'Aye.'

'Then why the devil hasn't someone got on and done it?'

'Good question, Your Grace.'

'The rest of our luggage should arrive in a couple of days and I won't have any visitors who come to pay their respects to my Duchess upended on their way to the house either. I hope you weren't trying to break our necks before we got here?'

That caused a flood of denials and a few furious accusations about folk who did as they were told rather than what any fool could see needed doing. Rosalind decided Ash had done enough to make the staff they did have eager to obey while he hammered his house and estates into good order again.

'All very well, Husband,' she said not very loudly so those trying to explain all at the same time had to stop or risk drowning out their new Duchess, 'but Lady Imogen and I would like to see the inside of your grand mansion before we freeze on the steps like Lot's wife and daughter.'

'I didn't know he had a frozen daughter,' Ash said, his usual humour reviving as he smiled at them both and shrugged to admit he still felt as if his fur had been rubbed the wrong way after their near miss.

'Of course not, Papa, but you might have soon if we don't get in the warm soon,' Jenny said with a theatrical shudder.

'Very well, back inside everyone who belongs inside. You can show us what hasn't been done in there instead,' Ash said and took Jenny and Rosalind's hands so they entered the vast marble hall together, the inside staff following them like very well-trained sheep.

'I don't think we will linger in here,' Ash said with a shiver.

Rosalind hoped this barn-like entrance hall was only used on state occasions or they would spend half Ash's fortune on coal, or whole trees if that was what they burned to warm this huge space when the Duke of Cherwell was officially at home.

'Most of these rooms have been shut up since the

old Duke died, Your Grace,' a flustered-looking housemaid informed them.

Rosalind was relieved to see far less fuss and gilding than there was at Cherwell House, although she did glimpse ornate plasterwork ceilings and venerable oak panelling as Ash loped along beside her as if he could hardly bear to look.

'Where is Mrs Porter?' he asked at last.

'Dead, Your Grace. A year or so after the old Duke died,' the most forward of the following pack said breathlessly.

'And Whipple?' he asked, seeming to realise he was going at a gallop and slowing down with an apologetic look at Rosalind.

'He retired, Your Grace. He can't manage stairs no more with his rheumatics. The last Duke said he was to have the North Lodge rent free because it ain't got no stairs and there was to be no arguments, for once.'

'Quite right, too,' Ash said, half a smile breaking through the clouds as if he could hear his late cousin's voice behind her words.

Rosalind wished she had known the lad better. She had hardly even noticed him hanging on Ash's every word when he was in town when they were all so young it seemed painful to think of now. Charles Hartfield, Lord Asham, had seemed such a boy then, but he was barely a year younger than she was. Best not think that if he had lived Ash would not have come home and none of them would be standing here now ready to begin a new life as the Duke and Duchess of Cherwell and their much-loved daughter.

'Just as well that Mr Snigsby is due to make his way north as soon as Cherwell House is properly closed up then, Husband,' she said to remind Ash one superior servant was on his way to make sense of his ramshackle house. They had wondered what on earth they were to do with him until the ancient Whipple was ready to admit he should retire, so at least that was one worry they could forget about.

'Best write and tell him to bring anyone else who is prepared to live in the chilly north as well, since we are clearly going to need them,' he said with a pained look at the intricately patterned, but dust-and-smoke-dulled ceiling above their heads.

'It ain't that cold here,' she thought she heard someone in the following pack mutter and she was glad these servants were human beings, rather than the well-trained automata she dreaded.

'First I will find out if anyone local would like to work here,' she argued with Ash's pronouncement. She privately thought it was that cold and not many London servants would want to leave the bustle of the town for this lovely but isolated countryside even if it wasn't.

And how silly that she didn't know what to call her husband in front of the servants—*Your Grace* seemed chilly between man and wife, *Ash* was too familiar and *My Lord Duke* made him sound one step down from a king. Such grandeur was best discouraged—he could be arrogant enough already without his wife treating him like a prince of the blood.

'Are there any rooms not shrouded with holland

covers here?' she asked the housemaid who seemed to have been elected spokeswoman.

'The new wing was done up for Lord Charles before the old Duke died. He said his lordship needed space of his own, since he must live with an old man the rest of the time. It seemed as if the old Duke never thought he would die, Your Grace, if you don't mind me saying.'

That remark was directed at Ash who shook his head and looked sad. 'No, it's true—he was too stubborn to admit he might be as human as the rest of us. But if that wing is in a better state you had best take us there before Her Grace and Lady Imogen decide to give up on Edenhope altogether.'

'Right you are, Your Grace. We lit fires and took off the covers in the new wing when we heard you was coming. There ain't enough of us to clean the whole house so we did the best we could in there.'

'Well done,' Rosalind said. 'What became of all the staff it must have taken to run this huge old place?'

'A lot retired when the old Duke died, Your Grace. They only stayed on because of him.' The girl shook her head as if there was no accounting for taste. 'Cook left when the young Duke died and you was gone so long we began to wonder if you was ever going to come home, Your Grace,' she told Ash apologetically. 'Cook said she might as well go where she got paid for her trouble.'

'You have not had your wages, then?' Ash snapped as if his much-tried temper was back on a hair-trigger again.

'Trustees said they was done paying out, you being older and not needing them. Yet they keep coming round so they can say the opposite of the other and make us all chase our tails.'

'How annoying,' Rosalind managed to say with a straight face. She ought to be nearly as irate as Ash about the sad state of the place, except it felt more of a home and less a stiff palace in the Dales this way. This girl was a delight; she must find her a position where she could use her quick mind. 'What is your name?' she asked.

The girl looked flustered, as if it was a faux pas to have been quite so outspoken and drawn attention to herself. 'Ruth Mathers, Your Grace,' the girl said and bobbed a curtsy.

'Good afternoon, then, Ruth, and at least I will know who to ask for when I need to know who is who here now.'

'I know most of folk, Your Grace, what with my pa being the village blacksmith while I was growing up.'

'Please carry on organising things as best you can for the time being for me, Ruth. We will talk again when I have a better idea of what needs doing here.'

'Yes, Your Grace, thank you,' Ruth said, curtsied again and left them at the highly polished mahogany door to the New Wing.

'You already have at least one supporter here,' Ash said once he and Rosalind and Jenny were inside and he had shut the door on the main house.

'I will need a small army of them if we are ever to get this place in good order again, but this is much better than the rest,' Rosalind said, looking at the swept and polished floors and sparklingly clean windows.

'It's so light in here,' Jenny exclaimed.

Large modern windows lined the corridor and more light flooded in from the half-open doors of rooms leading off it. Rosalind could smell wax furniture polish and the scent of lavender drifted from a bowl of the dried flower heads left on a side table. She blessed Ruth for organising her troops well enough to keep this part of the house relatively untouched by the neglect so obvious elsewhere. Sunlight showed up the rich grain and superb craftsmanship of the nearest door before Ash pushed it further open to reveal pale green walls and delicately scrolled plasterwork picked out in white. The furnishings were modern and light and there was none of the heavy stateliness she had dreaded after seeing so much of it at Cherwell House.

'What a beautiful room,' she said, gazing around at restrained luxury with just enough decoration to make it special. There were two long south-facing windows to frame the distant hills and whoever had this wing built loved light as well as the glorious view. She wondered if Ash longed for the light and heat of India every time he cursed the British climate and wrapped his greatcoat tightly round his shivering body, but maybe in here he would feel more at home. He looked impassive and, for the first time in weeks, she felt like an outsider as he brooded on the general state of his new home and who was about to feel the rough side of his tongue for it.

'Is this ours as well?' Jenny whispered as she gazed

round the *objets d'art* and fine furnishings as if she found that idea truly awesome.

'Yes, along with the rest,' Ash said with a wry grimace as he cast off his gloom and seemed to recall he had a wife and child to introduce to his stately domain.

'Well, I think we should live in here.'

'Let's see the rest before we decide, Jenny love,' he said, but Rosalind saw his braced shoulders relax.

'This one is nearly as nice,' Jenny said with an approving nod for a smaller room with one long window and a real collection of books crammed into the bookshelves built all around the walls. 'Ooh, billiards,' she said at the next doorway. 'Will you teach me to play, Papa?'

'Perhaps, when you are bit older and can reach better,' Ash said with an effort at lightness Rosalind did not quite believe. 'Jas and I used to spend hours in here with Charlie when we were young,' he said softly.

'You are not exactly ancient now,' she told him briskly, then tugged him away to stop him brooding on all he had lost since he was here last. There was a smaller sitting room and a dining room the right size for a family, but not half the county. The rooms were all elegant but intimate and not at all what she would have expected of a bachelor's suite in an ancient mansion.

'Come on,' Jenny urged, 'I want to see where we will sleep.'

'We will have to find a nice windy attic to stow you in if you carry on dashing about making enough noise for half a dozen, Jenny Hartfield,' Rosalind told her with pretend sternness. She hoped overexcitement would not give Jenny nightmares when it was bedtime.

'Even if Papa let you put me in one, Joan would rescue me,' Jenny said with the confidence of a well-loved child, but Rosalind would be pleased when the second carriage arrived with Jenny's new entourage and they could begin a new routine. Children needed order to feel secure and Jenny had not had it for too long now.

'Then we had best find out if there is a room fit for a budding young lady on the top floor,' she said casually and Jenny bounced up the stairs at a pace Rosalind almost envied.

'My grandparents were given this wing when they first married,' Ash told her. 'There are proper nurseries on the third floor as well as five or six fairly modest bedchambers in between. Only the nanny and nursery maid out of all their servants slept in this part of the house so my grandparents must have liked their privacy and the illusion they were living in a modest manor house. There is a separate stairwell leading up from the kitchens and the basement you would not even know was there from here as the doors are cleverly hidden on our side all the way up to the roof.'

Jenny had already run ahead to explore the nursery Rosalind suspected would be far more suitable than the one at Cherwell House. She approved of the wide enough stairs and practical elegance of this mansion in miniature. It felt like the sort of modestly big enough family home she had dreamt of as soon as she was old enough to dream of having a house and a hero of her own one day. After growing up in the chilly Palladian elegance of Lackbourne House, she had always been happier with the idea of comfort rather than luxury or splendour.

'I am sure we can be happy here until the rest of the house is ready, Ash, but what are we going to eat tonight? There is no cook and I doubt there will be much left in the way of stores since the staff have not been paid for so long and they had to eat something. Even a gardener and boy can grow quite a lot of food so maybe it's no wonder the pleasure gardens are so neglected.'

Ash frowned and looked grim again about the ridiculous state of affairs here, then seemed glad to concentrate on one thing he could put right easily enough. 'I will ride to Hartley Village for bread and cheese and a couple of pies from the local inn. Meanwhile Dawkins can fetch milk and butter from the Home Farm and you and the maids can order supplies in the morning.'

'Then you had best get off if you are to be home before dark,' Rosalind said and of course it was foolish to want to cling to him, wasn't it?

'I will be happier if you stay in this part of the house where the roof is sound and floors and windows intact, Ros,' he said as they listened to the sound of Jenny dashing about upstairs.

'I will tell her it is our duty to make sure everything is ready for Joan and the others when they get here. She will enjoy playing lady of the manor with rooms to allocate and the rest of this wing to explore.'

'Aye, far more than her mama, I suspect,' he said with a wry look.

'This bit is lovely, but the rest is vast and not exactly homely, Ash.'

'I suppose not, but you get so used to it in the end you don't notice the size of the place,' he said and chuckled when she looked sceptical.

'Is that what all you Dukes say?' she asked and he leaned close and kissed her only on the lips in case they forgot their daughter was upstairs.

'Only to our Duchesses,' he told her with a smile and a long, regretful look as he eyed her parted lips, then turned and ran downstairs before he changed his mind.

Chapter Thirteen

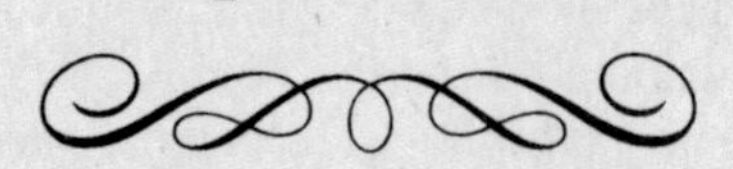

The kitchen in the basement was modest by Edenhope standards, but it had clearly been updated when the rest of this wing was redecorated. It was as light and airy as it could be made—the windows even had areas dug outside to let in more daylight and fresh air in summer. The Butler's Pantry and modest Servants' Hall took up the south side and shared at least part of the view she had wondered at from the Green Drawing Room above. It made sense for the kitchen and storerooms to face the other way so they were darker, but not gloomy. The kitchen would always be warm from cooking and never mind the cooler aspect and there was even a closed stove instead of an open fire. Joan would envy the next cook to rule this kitchen with such a modern convenience after the primitive cooking arrangements she had struggled so gallantly with at Furze Cottage.

'It's very big, Mama,' Jenny said, seeming intimidated by the echoing space. It did feel odd with the place empty when the whole basement would once have bustled with activity at this time of day.

'By our standards, perhaps,' Rosalind said absently, doing her best to work out how many staff they would need to run even a modest household until the rest of Edenhope was ready for occupation. She wondered why the remaining staff did not use these rooms instead of the vast and antiquated ones in the main house. Perhaps they slept on pallets by the fire in the main kitchens for warmth and company. She could hardly blame them if they flocked together to keep out the cold and the eerie sounds of a grand old house with too many uncared-for spaces in it. She would have chosen to flock down here if she had to walk in their shoes, but maybe they were more familiar with the vast ducal kitchens there must be somewhere at the back of Edenhope's grand Tudor splendour.

Rosalind opened doors on to largely empty storerooms and wondered where the keys to the wine cellar and strongroom were. Suddenly she realised it was even quieter down here and Jenny was not pattering in her footsteps and trying to pretend she wasn't a little overawed by her new home. 'Jenny?' she called out, the echo of her own voice coming back to her and no other sound but the faint stir of the wind in the slender apple tree outside the back door. 'Jenny darling, please come out now. I promise to pay attention to you and stop looking at boring, empty rooms.'

Silence. She called her daughter's name more sharply, but only her own voice echoed back. Panic started to scream potential disasters in Rosalind's ears while Ash's warnings about the state of the roof and some of the floors in the main house came back to haunt her. Jenny had been far too good for too long, now she came to think about it, and her daughter could be headstrong and careless of adult authority. With all that pent-up energy and such quick little feet to run silently when she chose to, Jenny could be almost anywhere in the house by now. It might take hours to find her in this vast barn of a house with so few people here to search it. Jenny could be in far more trouble than she knew before they managed to track her down.

'Think,' Rosalind ordered herself as her heart galloped as pictures of all the disasters that could overtake her child in this place flitted past her mind's eye. When had she last seen her? Jenny had followed her out of the kitchen, but empty storerooms and deserted servants' halls had little interest for a lively young girl. She should never have let herself be distracted by worries about her new role and details of how they could get this relatively small part of her new empire back in working order as soon as possible Rosalind scolded herself and tried hard not to panic.

Ash returned from his mission with half the food from the local inn's kitchen attached to his saddle so Pegasus jigged and snorted every now and again in protest as bags shifted, however tightly they were tied on. Ash was made so welcome it was hard to get away and now he felt guilty about how hungry Ros and Jenny must be. Sunset was painting the sky amber, rose and orange—surely the other carriage would have arrived by now?

'I hope your mission was successful?' he said to Dawkins after he had dismounted, despite the bounty the landlady had insisted was needed to stop his family starving before morning.

'Aye, Your Grace. Nobody in the New Wing so I left the pail on the kitchen table,' the taciturn groom told him.

Ash frowned. 'I told them not to go exploring,' he said, but the noise of the very much-delayed second coach rolling down the North Drive towards them interrupted them. Ash strode towards the kitchen door of the New Wing, disturbed to see no glow of candlelight from any of the windows. Ros had sent the few maids they had away while they explored their new quarters in private, so they would not come until summoned. Perhaps they should fit a church bell to toll when they needed assistance, he thought to divert himself from increasing worry about Ros and Jenny as he marched to the shadowy kitchen and dropped bags of food on the table without much thought for the contents.

Dawkins was right, he decided as he dashed up the kitchen stairs to the main floor and there was still no light or sound. It even felt empty up here and he wasn't surprised his bellow of Ros's name, then Jenny's, was met by profound silence.

'Think,' he ordered himself in an unconscious echo of Rosalind when she realised Jenny had disappeared into a vast old house. He ran up the front stairs of the New Wing to the next floor, bellowing their names as he went, but still hearing nothing back, not even an echo in these carpeted bedroom corridors. Up to the top floor, then, and still no answer to his shouts. Terror stalked him as he turned on his heel and dashed back downstairs even faster. He had lost so many of his family he refused to even let himself think how it would feel if he ever had to do without Ros and their daughter as well. Horror opened up in front of his hurrying feet as he realised they were his whole world. He might go on, might even function as lord of all this pomp and responsibility and the bearer of this ridiculous title, but he would be empty inside. No, he wasn't going to think about that. They could be out in the gardens but what would they see in the ever-increasing darkness? And Ros would have heard him or Dawkins coming and sent Jenny to say they were peering around for early flowers and that didn't seem very likely, did it?

'Your Grace?' Joan's voice asked from the front door, the new governess and Jenny's maid huddled behind her.

'I can't find my wife or Jenny,' he told her, trying to clear baffled horror from his mind and work out how to get all the remaining staff looking for them.

'I told you the little demon was being too good to be true, didn't I?' Joan told her companions.

'Been fretting about it all the way here she has,' Carrie the nursery maid confirmed glumly.

'Especially after one of the leaders cast a shoe and we had to wait for the smith to come home before it was replaced,' the Burrows girl said wearily.

'I will go and fetch Dawkins and his lads and anyone else he can find to help search, you three light candles and have a good look in all the rooms here one by one, just in case Lady Jenny was hiding and got trapped.'

'And Duchess Rosalind managed to get in there as well? I doubt it, lad,' Joan said and she was right; he would end up chasing his own tail if he didn't calm down and do this rationally. 'Light those candles, then see if you can rouse anyone else while I search here,' Joan ordered her companions.

'The staff will be in the kitchens in the old house at this time of day. Go outside and in through the back door or you will get lost,' Ash said even as his mind reeled with all sorts of paralysing fears. He tore out of the back door to meet the taciturn groom and send him for as many minions as he could find.

'Right old rabbit warren,' Dawkins said gloomily.

'The Duchess said they would only explore the New Wing,' Ash said with a puzzled frown.

'Best begin there, then, Your Grace.'

The man was right; there was one connecting door to the main house and even Jenny probably wasn't bold enough to dare the spiders and ghosts in looming darkness. So where the devil was she and why hadn't Ros answered his desperate calls as he dashed through the house roaring like a madman?

'Did you hear that?' he demanded as the faintest of faint whimpers whispered down to him through the gloom. 'The Lookout', he realised, terror increasing tenfold as he made himself look up and try to see through twilight by willpower alone.

At the top of the bay window tower a platform had been made to take advantage of the even better view than could be had from the drawing room a couple of rooms down the bay. It was the perfect place for a picnic on the leads and he and Jas and Charlie used to sneak up there and pretend to smoke one of Grandfather's cigarillos and choke on sips of brandy from a forgotten flask as boys. Later they would watch the sun fade from the valley and exchange hopes and dreams before Jas went back to war, Charlie to school and Ash to Oxford.

But the Lookout was safe enough, as long as you didn't peer over the edge and feel the earth spin when you realised how far away the ground was. Surrounded by a stone balustrade, your legs would hold you long enough to turn away and get your land legs back, but he recalled that pothole in the drive and the boarded-up windows and felt his heart race at the hazards there could be anywhere in this neglected house that had not been properly maintained far too long.

Maybe his face looking up was clearer than the faintest movement he could see silhouetted against the sky, but he had heard another faint cry. 'Pa—pa…' came very faintly through the dusk so at least she had heard his frantic cries and knew he was looking for her. Back inside the New Wing with Dawkins on his heels, Ash groped for the hidden door on to the back stairs from this ground-floor level only someone who knew the house well should be able to find. Unless

Jenny began it down in the kitchen. Of course, the servants' side of the house was purely functional. The back stairs were hidden from view by cleverly disguised doors on this side, but it was easy to find from down there. Someone in the family must have had an obsession with servants being not seen and not heard when this part of the house was built and Jenny could have found the start of the spiral back stairs leading up from the kitchens easily enough. He should never have left his wife and child alone here. He blamed himself for forgetting the devilment in Jenny's eyes the day he first saw her in that stable loft. His delight in having such a child made the mischief Rosalind and Joan were always on the lookout for seem exaggerated to him. Now he found the jib door, left it open behind him and raced up the back stairs, yelling at Dawkins to fetch ropes and light, and scolding himself for not listening to them.

Ash's legs were wobbly with effort and fear after he ran up three flights of narrow stone steps to the hutch-like exit on to the roof. He had to get his breath back before he could be any good in whatever trouble Jenny had got into while his back was turned.

'Over here,' he heard Ros murmur as soon as he was outside.

Ash sucked in another breath of cool Yorkshire air and crept carefully on to the leads lest he blunder into her. Unsure where he was treading, he even got down on his hands and knees so he did not fall over her.

'Papa?' he heard Jenny's voice wobble and she sounded far too close to the Lookout and the edge of the roof for comfort. The little platform gave an awesome view on a summer day, but it was not meant for frosty evenings and he wondered why Ros did not simply pull her back from the edge and bundle her back inside with a severe scold to stop her doing it again.

'No!' he gasped once he was close enough to see a gap where the balustrade should be in the last glimmer of twilight. Jenny must have slipped on the slimy lead and fallen against it so the stonework gave way. Ros would have made a desperate grab for their child, but now her clutching hands were all that stood between Jenny and certain death as he followed the line of their hands and marvelled they had not both pitched over to their deaths.

'Shush,' Ros ordered as she tightened her grasp on Jenny's wrists as if she could only keep holding on to her by changing her grip now and again.

'It just...' Jenny said, but Ash saw the strain in Ros's shaking arms and managed to crawl past her.

'Save your breath, Jenny love,' he said gently when he reached that precious bridge of hands and wrapped his large one around Jenny's suddenly very tiny arm. 'Let go now, my darling,' he urged Ros and felt the effort it cost her to do as he said a finger at a time. He braced his knees and called on all his strength to get their daughter back on to the roof. 'I have you now,' he told her and shifted his grip as Ros wriggled backwards out of the way to give him enough room to rise to his feet, then brace them on the slippery leads. 'Trust me to hold on to you, Jenny love. Let your feet dangle,' he ordered steadily as he felt her resist any demand she let go of the foothold she had somehow managed to find on the smooth stone below the parapet. 'I'm strong enough to fell a giant, don't forget,' he joked and felt her almost laugh, then trust him to take all her weight. She was a headstrong little demon, but by God she was brave. He summoned every muscle he had into action and stood as steady as he could to pull her upwards, then safely back through the gap and over the jagged remains of this section of the balustrade. Her feet flailed for a grip on it by instinct and he heard them scrabble and leant back to pull her as far out of danger as he could get her up here. A great sigh of relief shook him as his little girl stumbled on numb legs, then clung on to one of his as if she could hardly believe she was safe either. Backing away from that yawning gap with a fast-beating heart, he wasn't sure he would believe it until they were at least another floor down with the door to this deathtrap safely locked.

This time he really would have someone's head. Every single stone of the balustrade on this roof should have been checked regularly, but it was obvious nobody had been up here for years. The gutters were blocked and ice must have cracked the stones once the iron rods inside rusted. Their near miss on the drive this afternoon and now this close shave still felt random, a sign of the carelessness and neglect Charlie had been raging about for years, but it would be very convenient for those who let it happen if the new Duke followed the last one to the family mausoleum within hours of getting home, wouldn't it? He wondered who the next in line for the dukedom was, if Ros did not bear him a boy this time, and resolved to find out. But it still felt like criminal neglect rather than malicious intent and he had a wife and child to thank God for preserving first.

'I was so scared,' Jenny confided in a shaky little whisper now he had found the strength and presence of mind to move them away from that horrible gap with her in his arms and neither of them wanting to let go.

She wriggled against his chest as if trying to climb inside his jacket for comfort. *Not much comfort to be had in there, my Jenny*, he silently argued as he felt the chill of the cold wind through a long rip caused by the effort of pulling her away from danger.

'Me, too,' he heard Ros murmur with so much shock and weariness in her husky voice he wanted to hold her as well. If he was horrified when he realised where his little girl was calling from, how must Ros have felt when Jenny almost toppled over the edge and only a mother's desperate grab stopped a fatal fall? At least instinct had got him up here and whispered what to do, because Ash the Father was still cowering in a corner somewhere with Ash the Husband; biting his nails and gibbering with terror.

'Hand Lady Imogen to me, Master Ash,' Dawkins said as he appeared out of the hutch-like turret with a lantern. He took in the frozen tableau they must have made and shook his grizzled head. 'Your missus looks as if she needs to get inside,' he said succinctly.

'Jenny love, you can let go now, you're safe,' Ash said, but she clung even harder and shook her head.

'Ash,' Ros said simply and crept all the way towards this absurd little turret on her hands and knees, then used her hands to climb up his shaking body, as if she only dared try to stand if he was her prop. A poor prop when he was never there when she needed him most, he decided as he shifted to accommodate the two of them as best he could.

'Oh, Ash.' Rosalind heard her voice shake and bit her lip to hold back the torrent of relief, and reproach, for not coming sooner.

'Hush now, love, let's get you both inside and warm again.'

'Jenny?' she gasped, wondering if she would ever dare let her daughter out of her sight again with the memory of her slipping on an icy puddle against the balustrade and it crumbling so her child was hurtling towards certain death even as Rosalind made a desperate grab for her arm. That terrible moment kept playing over and over in her head, as if it was a painting someone kept showing her although she kept begging them to stop.

'We have to trust her to Joan's troops, love,' he said as he shifted Jenny so he could hug Ros as if he never intended letting go of her either. Luckily he was soon barking terse orders and didn't seem to feel her jerk of surprise at that unwary word. It must have been his fear and relief talking—not the deep-down truth she wished for.

'See that door is nailed up tight, man,' he ordered Dawkins. 'I don't want anyone coming up here until there is scaffolding all around the house and enough stone masons to rebuild York Minster waiting to put things right. The jib door from the nursery corridor must be locked from now on and Lady Imogen will not sit down for a week if I ever catch her up on any of the roofs here ever again, girl or not,' he added with a severe glance down at his child. Jenny's only response was to burrow even closer into Ash's shoulder and Ros felt the mighty shiver that rocked him as he hugged them both even closer as if he didn't believe they were all still here either.

'Base of the stone is cracked clean through, Your Grace,' the man said, rather daringly in Rosalind's opinion. 'Nobody could have known.'

'Maybe not, but every single roof on this barrack will be inspected for such faults once a month from now on, whether I am here to see it is done or not. I never, ever want to be that terrified again,' Ash finally turned around to say that last sentence to her as if only she could truly understand how deep that terror was.

Rosalind could still see it in his eyes, even by the meagre light of Dawkins's lamp. Then one of the maids turned up with a lantern and at least they could see their way down the twisty stair now. It was getting very crowded inside the boxy little turret on the roof and most of their current staff seemed to be waiting in a shocked line down the roof stairs and out on to the nursery floor. Since Jenny was still clinging to her father like a limpet, Rosalind insisted on going down the narrow stair behind him despite her shaky legs and a bad attack of the shivers.

'Aye, and I'm tempted to have that one nailed up as well,' Ash said after he had ordered the maids through it ahead of them and never mind them using the wrong stairs for as long as they needed to. 'Bolt it from the inside, will you, Dawkins,' he ordered the man he seemed to have elected his deputy and pulled it shut before Dawkins could argue.

'Never mind that now, Your Grace, the little madam needs her bed and might even get supper if she's very lucky. She certainly don't deserve any after scaring us all half to death,' Joan stepped forward to chide and Jenny seemed to relax a little as her world began to settle back into its familiar order.

Ash carried his little girl through to her new bedroom and persuaded her to let him go, but Ros could only stand in the doorway clinging to the frame, still too shocked at such a narrow escape to bounce back like her daughter. She would love to slip away to the peace and quiet of the master suite, but it might as well be a mile away. Ash turned away from the bed and took in the sad state of his wife.

'You can cope here, can't you?' he asked Joan and picked Rosalind up as if she weighed not much more than Jenny before Joan could say 'of course'. He carried Rosalind down the stairs to the bedroom floor despite her protests and refused to put her down even when they got there and she could probably manage the rest.

'Jenny needs you and you'll do yourself a mischief,' she protested, but he marched to their bedroom before he gently set her down on the daybed with a sigh of relief.

'Oh, Ros—' he said shakily, then broke off whatever he had been going to say to her as a motley crew of grooms and the gardener's boy filed in with steaming cans of hot water and a slipper bath. 'What on earth is it now?' Ash barked.

Joan had left her precious charge with the new maid and governess to dash downstairs behind them and breathlessly ordered one of the boys to light the fire and another to bring up coal before he left.

'Bath night,' the eldest of the stable lads explained tersely to Rosalind as if she was the less terrifying of his new employers. 'Mrs Dawkins sent our hot water and we ain't that dirty,' he added and left with his fellow urchins.

Even Joan looked a bit lost. 'Miss Jenny doesn't deserve all of us fussing over her and pampering her after the dreadful shock she just gave us,' she said with the fury of huge relief as she unpacked Ros's night things, laid out fine soap and turned down the bedcovers instead.

'I think she gave herself one as well,' Rosalind said gently.

'Little devil,' Joan said on such a sigh Rosalind hoped Ash realised it was as well if she left the others to see to Jenny's bath and get her into bed so Joan didn't have to shake her precious charge for terrifying her so badly.

'I won't argue,' Rosalind said. 'And if I hurry up with this bath it will be warm enough for you, Ash. I heard your coat rip so you must be cold.'

'Hmmph,' Joan grumbled as she bent to get the fire to do as she wanted even if the rest of the world seemed out of kilter. 'I'll leave you two to get on,' she said tersely once it was behaving properly. 'Dinner won't cook itself.'

'It doesn't need cooking,' Ash argued, but didn't stop her. He made sure the door was properly closed, then undid Rosalind's neat spencer jacket and pushed it off her shoulders as if he didn't think she had the strength and he was probably right. He gently undid her laces without his usual sensuous intent. 'Are you all right?' he asked very softly. She read fear for her and his unborn child in his intent grey gaze, as well as something deeper that made her wonder if he might have decided to love her again after all. *Unlikely*, Rosalind the sceptic cautioned, considering their marriage of convenience.

'I think so,' she said. 'Luckily this Hartfield seems a tough customer.' She rubbed her flat belly and knew there was no point pretending she wasn't anxious for the tiny life growing inside her after she had stretched every nerve and sinew in her body to save the child she already had. 'I was so near the end of my strength, Ash,' she told him shakily. 'So very frightened I would get too tired and cold and lose my grip. I didn't quite have enough strength to pull her back in.'

'You were superb, Ros. I don't know how you managed to catch our child in time to prevent her falling, but I think the time between me realising where you both were and getting to you must have shaved a decade off my life.'

The thought of him spending less time on earth than her was enough to make her cry when he finally got her completely undressed and plopped her into the bath like a helpless infant. Unable to stop now the tears had begun, she felt forlorn and silly while he soaped her soothingly, then rinsed out the sponge to wipe her tears away tenderly as a parent with an overwrought child.

'I should go up to comfort Jenny, not sit here weeping,' she managed to say between sobs. 'She has had a terrible shock. Oh, Ash, our little girl could have died. How could I have taken my eyes off her for five seconds, knowing that she's forever falling into mischief when my back is turned?'

'She is too much of a daredevil for her own good, she proved that today and I should have listened harder to you and Joan. High time I came home to bring a little discipline into her life,' he said half-seriously.

'As if you are not as soft as butter with her,' she chided with a mighty sniff and even managed a wobbly smile at him through the tears.

'Let's get you out of there before you overflow the tub with your tears,' he teased, but still looked worried when he held up a large towel invitingly until she stood up and stepped out. He wrapped her in it like a swaddled baby, then lifted her up again to put her in the chair by the fire.

'I wish you would stop carrying me about and I

can't seem to stop crying,' she complained with a hiccup in her voice from all these dratted tears.

'You have had too many shocks of late, my Duchess,' he said gruffly. 'I suppose you must have bottled the tears up until they broke free of their own accord.'

'Like a lachrymose flood?'

'A release; it's good to be strong, and heaven knows you have had to be, but why wouldn't you cry after what you just went through, Ros? I nearly did when I finally realised our little terror was really safe.'

'She is not a terror, she is a unique and wonderful child,' Rosalind said stoutly, then recalled how near Jenny got to disaster and nodded. 'And such a handful I was sometimes at my wits' end until you came home.'

'I don't know if I will ever forgive myself for being such a damned fool,' he said and got into the bath after hastily throwing off his ruined clothes. As if he was glad to hide his thoughts from her, he made a great show of washing every bit of his large and powerful body as quickly as possible in the cooling water.

'If you mean for leaving in the first place, we were both too young to cope with a romance gone wrong,' she said with a reluctant glance into the past and a quick shake of the head to dismiss it. 'Let's concentrate on now though, Ash, there's no point raking up the past when nothing can change it.'

'That's enough of it for tonight anyway. Do you suppose anyone has remembered to bring up my traps?' he asked and reached for another bathsheet.

Since an argument seemed to have broken out between Joan and Dawkins and his troops, Rosalind suspected they had. She had to laugh when Ash swathed his lower half in a bathsheet, then draped another over his shoulder like a Roman toga, and at least her tears had finally stopped. 'You could tell them we are both decent,' she pointed out.

'And spoil their fun?'

'Probably, we have a deal to do tonight.'

'I might have, but you're not going anywhere. You will eat your supper in bed if I have to tie you to the bedposts and feed you myself.'

'Another time, maybe,' she said with a mock leer that startled him into a bark of masculine laughter, then a much better imitation of a rake it was a shame to waste, but they would have to. He was quite right; they must be careful for a day or two. 'Will you go up and see Jenny once you're dressed again?'

'Yes,' he said with a sigh. 'I don't want her to have nightmares or be terrified of heights, even if it might make our lives easier.'

'It's not us who matter.'

'No, and you have two of them to consider now, although it still hardly seems possible when there is no outward sign of my child on your body yet.'

'They get more and more real as they grow in your belly, Ash. Wait until this one starts to quicken and you can feel it move as well.'

'Not from the inside like you,' he argued as if he almost envied her such intimate knowledge of their baby before it was born.

'Well, no, but at least you don't have to give birth.'

'True,' he muttered and looked a little pale at the thought, but managed to smile reassuringly at her before he went out to put a stop to the argument Joan and Dawkins were enjoying on the other side of their bedroom door.

Chapter Fourteen

'Well, Lady Imogen; and what have you got to say for yourself this time?' Ash greeted his daughter sternly.

'I am sorry, Papa.'

'I truly hope so,' he told her. 'If your mother had not caught you, we would all be feeling a lot more than sorry right now.'

'I won't do it again,' she said, tears swimming in her grey eyes.

'How often have you said that to Mama, then done something just as foolish next time, Jenny?' he asked with a sorrowful shake of his head.

'I don't *mean* to be naughty,' she said woefully.

'But somehow you still are.'

'Weren't you naughty when you were my age, Papa?'

'I never threw myself into thin air and expected my mama to catch me, which was just as well since she was not often at home when my big brother Jasper and I were boys and I would have tumbled to my death.'

'I didn't know you even had a brother,' she replied and perhaps she was right to leave out the most terrifying bit of that sentence. He wanted her to be less reckless, but not frightened of her own shadow, and he realised what a tightrope a father must walk when he had a child as adventurous as this one.

'Jas is dead now, but he would have doted on you.'

'When did he die?' she asked suspiciously. She still seemed dubious about death being permanent since he had apparently been lost at sea and then come back to life again.

'Jasper was killed at the Battle of Waterloo; he was as brave as a lion.'

'So are you, Papa,' she said comfortingly and she truly was his little miracle, wasn't she?

'No, I am a coward,' he said rather bleakly, with his flight from marriage to Ros and his refusal to see himself as he really was until today making him feel like a worm as he confronted what he had done to his very young wife full on for the first time. Then he recalled Jenny was only seven and a half years old and unable to understand what he meant even if he wanted her to. 'Would you like to hear about my brother and the things we did as boys?'

'Yes, I wish I had known him.'

'I wish you had, too, he truly would have doted on you.'

'What does dote mean?'

'That my brother would have loved you, despite your bad habits and wicked ways, Lady Imogen Hartfield.'

'Was he a lord, too?'

'No, my father was Lord John Hartfield, because he was the second son of a duke, but Jas and I were plain misters.'

'I quite like being a lady.'

'It would be nice if it was in fact as well as name.'

'You said you would tell me about when you were little—did you sleep here when you came to stay?' she said as she picked out the bits of their conversation her ears wanted to hear.

He sighed and decided to let her. 'If I did, I don't remember it. I had a room in the older part of the house as soon as I was thought old enough to behave myself. My grandfather always said he preferred us boys under his nose rather than stuck up on a nursery floor where we could have got up to anything without him knowing about it.'

'I would have liked a grandfather,' Jenny said rather wistfully.

Ash thought about some of the gaps in both their lives and told her some of his milder adventures with his big brother as boys to divert her from them. Jenny's eyelids began to droop and he finally fell silent and stared at his sleeping daughter with such love and fear in his heart. The more you loved the more you feared losing, he realised, but at least he knew Ros and their child were the centre of his universe now. Terror of losing them was a terrible ache he wondered if he would ever get used to.

He was right about being a coward, though. He feared telling Ros how he felt and maybe he had always felt it under his boy's fury with the world and his mother. Yet why would Ros want to know he loved her after he had treated her so callously, simply because his own mother had lied as if it cost her nothing and always swore anything that happened to them was not her fault? Maybe Ros's secret past seemed like treachery and trickery to the silly boy he was back then, but what a bitter betrayal of a sixteen-year-old girl's trust her sad tale of supposed first love was. No wonder she had hesitated to tell him. His fists tightened at the thought of anyone doing such a thing to his daughter—he would hunt the brute to the ends of the earth and kill him with his bare hands. So why hadn't he thought of doing that for Ros? Instead he had gone off to India like a whipped cur when he ought to have brought that excuse for a man to account for his sins against that sixteen-year-old girl instead.

He recalled how Ros had flinched away from polite society and the very idea of being a part of it again when they were in London. Did she dread meeting the unscrupulous cur who once betrayed her at Almack's Club or in a glittering ballroom? Ash was disgusted at the thought of her having to fear that the rogue who had raped her might turn up in polite society as if he belonged when even the gutter wasn't low enough for him. Ash might not feel he could bother her with feelings she would never be able to truly believe in after what he did to her eight years ago, but he could make sure that piece of scum would never dare taunt her with a knowing leer across a crowded ballroom.

* * *

Next day Ash insisted the local doctor visit Rosalind and Jenny. He prescribed a day in bed for Lady Imogen, since she clearly deserved it, but Rosalind must stay in hers for a week to help heal the strain of holding on to Jenny until help came. Her mother's weary stay in the sunny south-facing bedchamber, propped up only to eat and lying flat the rest of the time, seemed to make Jenny think harder about her sins than a stern rebuke. Rosalind insisted she was not told about the baby until they were sure it would survive, though. She was not having her daughter weighed down with guilt over something she did without any intention of causing harm to herself or anyone else.

'I am perfectly well now,' she insisted to Ash when her week was finally up and the young doctor finally agreed with her.

'Two lucky escapes for this little fighter in one day though, Ros. It's a wonder I didn't turn grey overnight,' Ash told her as he laid a protective hand over her still-flat belly. 'When will it start to show?' he asked and of course he had no idea, he had never knowingly been a prospective father before.

'Four months for a few speculative looks and five for it to be obvious to most people who care to look. After that I will just get bigger and bigger,' she said ruefully. 'I must wear as many of my fashionable gowns as I can before I am too big to fit into them for months on end.'

'We can order more,' he said with a casual dismissal

of the cost that made her shiver at the thought of Mrs Meadows's economies.

'I do like wearing beautiful gowns and dressing up as a duchess now and again, but I want to run with the children and be busy or go for a walk without perpetually changing into this or that gown, Ash. Shall you mind if I am still just me most of the time?'

'You would look beautiful in a sack,' he told her, almost exasperated by her lack of self-confidence. 'As long as you are wherever I am for the rest of our lives you can wear one of those if you want.'

'Everywhere? Riding pillion on the back of your horse; interfering in every decision as a duke; watching out for local beauties who want to lure a handsome duke into their bed when his wife is not looking?'

'Perhaps not everywhere, then, and you know whose bed I want to be in,' he said with a long, brooding look that said Judith Belstone's reply to the letter Rosalind had dictated to him while she was lying flat on her back had better come soon or he might get very moody indeed. It must be good news, though. Married couples all over the world would have gone mad or fallen apart for the lack of lovemaking by now if it was sternly forbidden during pregnancy.

'It might be best if we wait another week, just to be sure all is well.'

'I thought so, too,' he said gloomily. 'And I will not be looking at any other women in the meantime, before you start any getting ridiculous ideas. They might as well be invisible as far as I am concerned.'

'I keep thinking about the beautiful mistresses you

must have had in India, though, Ash,' she admitted as the image of girls trained to pleasure a man in bed and out of it lined up to make her feel less than she ought to and compound this ridiculous lack of confidence in herself that growing up lonely and unwanted in her stepfather's house seemed to have left her with, despite Ash's fascination with her body and his sensual attention being focused on her and her alone these last few months.

'None of them was ever as beautiful as you and I never wanted them as I want you. You are like a fire under my skin and water in a desert, Ros.'

'That was almost poetic,' she said dreamily.

'Put it down to frustration,' he replied and left the room as if staying there with all that on his mind would cost too much effort.

By the time Rosalind's pregnancy began to show it was full summer and even Ash could not complain about being cold on clear sunlit days and he obviously loved the green abundance of his native land even in the rain. At first she had secretly yearned for Dorset and the familiarity of Furze Cottage, but now she was learning to love the tough and often breathtaking beauty of the Dales. She liked these hardworking people with their dour humour and forthright speech. Except for Ash's Great-Aunt Brilliana, of course, who still aired her opinions with brutal frankness and seemed determined to hate every change she and Ash wanted to make at Edenhope. It was beyond Rosalind why Ash's late cousin Charlie was said to have adored the peppery old lady. She often did battle with Lady Brilliana over her determination to banish the stately formality of the past. Lady Brilliana would sweep into the New Wing unannounced and give her blunt opinion of this change or that innovation she insisted would *never* have been tolerated in her father's day.

'Her father sounds like a rigid old martinet,' Rosalind said to Ash one day, as the echoes of the door slamming behind his great-aunt still rang through the sunny little parlour they had turned into a morning room.

'He looks as if he had far more humour than his daughter will admit to in his portraits.'

'So she is putting words in his mouth?'

'Something she seems very good at, don't you think?'

'Oh, yes,' she said grimly, remembering Brilliana's last official visit to the New Wing, which she openly called a miserable little hovel for a duke to live in when he had a palatial mansion next door.

Trailing an array of expensive cashmere shawls, although some of them were almost worn to rags, the old besom had eyed Rosalind's baby bump with a sharp shake of her elaborately dressed head. She had never abandoned the fashions of her youth, but at least her silvered locks saved a fortune in hair powder. 'You two will have to get married properly before that child is born,' she informed them by way of greeting.

'We are already married,' Rosalind said calmly, glad Jenny had agreed this was the wrong night to want any part in a grown-up dinner.

'Hah! A few words mumbled by a blacksmith? Ridiculous. An anvil is no substitute for a church service—lot of heathen nonsense if you ask me.'

'Luckily we did not,' Ash bellowed in Lady Brilliana's slightly less-deaf ear.

'You are a rogue, boy,' she told him fondly and turned her fire on Rosalind, as usual. 'Do you want your son to be challenged for his father's title one day, just because you were too slipshod to make sure you were properly wed to his father in the first place?' she demanded brusquely.

'Marriage by declaration is perfectly legal in Scotland,' Rosalind said, reminding herself it was bad for the baby to let the fearsome old woman goad her into a temper. 'We would only have to tell two witnesses we were man and wife for it to be a legal commitment for life.'

'Poppycock—told Plumstead you should get wed again and he agrees.'

'He would agree to anything you tell him to. His nerves are completely shot from decades at your beck and call,' Ash told her.

'High time he retired, then,' Lady Brilliana said.

'And I would have to ask my wife to wed me twice,' Ash said, turning a deaf ear on her for a change.

'There is that, of course, but don't you want to make an honest woman out of me?' Rosalind asked contrarily.

He had been silent for a long moment and Rosalind tensed as she watched him warm his coattails in front of the fire he insisted on even in July. 'You are already my wife; it would be a fuss about nothing.'

'Not as far as your wife and child are concerned,' Lady Brilliana said impatiently.

At least she had accepted Rosalind was Ash's Duchess then.

The next day poor Reverend Plumstead toiled his way up from the village to offer his services, so Brilliana was even more intent on getting her way than usual.

'Do you think we should marry again to make sure nobody can challenge the baby's claim to your throne one day, Ash?' she asked after the weary vicar of Hartley had gone home to recover.

'It might be a girl.'

'True, but what if it *is* a boy?'

'I will write to my London solicitors and see what they have to say about a possible legal challenge if you like, but I feel very married—what about you?'

'Oh, yes,' she said with a significant glance down at her rapidly vanishing waistline. 'Very much so.'

'Then I will write to them, but I don't want to see Brilliana proved right any more than you do.'

'Indeed, if she had ever learnt the art of subtlety the world would be a far more dangerous place for the rest of us. You had best hurry up and write, though—knowing what solicitors are like they might not find a sure enough reply before the baby is born if you delay.'

'True,' he said, then Jenny burst in with news the stable cat's kittens had opened their eyes at last and managed to tug her father out to see them so that was the end of that, even if Lady Brilliana still brought the subject up regularly.

* * *

Ash was fascinated by the baby growing in Rosalind's belly. He made love to her gently but with flattering regularity as soon as Judith Belstone's letter arrived to say it was all perfectly possible as long as they loved quietly, which was Judith's tactful way of saying do nothing wild or too adventurous. Despite Rosalind's fear her pregnancy would put him off her changing body, Ash seemed to find it enthralling. He would rub oil into her rounding belly and feel for the whispers of movement she reported when their baby quickened inside her with such awe she fell in love with him on yet another level she now had to keep quiet about as well. He gentled his hungry need of her and found new ways to enjoy themselves without hurting the baby. Finding a honeyed tenderness under all the heat felt new to both to them and she hoped he had never felt like this with other lovers.

It was far more than the marriage of convenience he had proposed to her in Livesey and she agreed to so reluctantly. Yet there was something held back even as their lives knitted together in so many ways. Rosalind knew his desire for her was leashed but strong. She could not say he was inattentive, or showed any sign of wanting younger or slimmer women now she was visibly with child, but there was something unsaid and held back between them. Some last shred of caution always seemed to step in and stop them being true lovers as well as a practical duke and duchess, busy with their new lives and growing family.

* * *

Ash was finding it hard to keep secrets from his wife. If she knew what he was up to, she would react as if he had stuck a knife in her back, then put her armour back on to fight the intimacy weaving their lives together. He knew it was reckless to risk so much, but he was stubborn and might as well try to change the rock Edenhope was built on as pretend it was easy to get an idea out of his head once it was in there. He rode to the top of Edendale to watch his land, so abundant with new life at this time of year, and argued with his own set-in-stone determination Ros's seducer must pay for what he did when she was so painfully young. He wished he had found her first, with her head still full of dreams and all those years ahead of them to watch her grow into the mature beauty she was now. His fault he had lost so many of those because he had lost his temper and decided she was just like his mother, for no sane reason, he decided now he looked back.

He realised she had tried to lock it away and forget and she had said at the time her mother told her never to tell anyone, especially not her future husband, and perhaps Lady Lackbourne had been right. If Ros had not found the courage to clear her conscience, they might have been together all these years instead of far apart. Except did he really want a marriage full of little pockets of lies and evasions to drag it down? No, and they had to live with what was instead of what might have been, but that cur came between them once and he was never going to do it again.

He broke the seal on the first missive that arrived yesterday she did not know about. This one was from his London lawyers. It had been locked in a drawer in his desk in the old part of the house. Sighing at his own stupidity, he muttered a few soothing words to his horse and let the reins slide while Pegasus grazed and he brooded. Ash smoothed the hot pressed paper and read his lawyers' judgement. Apparently the Church considered marriage by mutual consent, freely given in front of witnesses, truly binding. Excellent news as far as the Duke and Duchess of Cherwell were concerned, except Common Law had argued over the issue endlessly since the Marriage Act of 1753 forbade such marriages under English law, while they were still allowed by the Scottish legal system. The English courts had still not been able to decide if the children of such runaway marriages were truly legitimate. The transmission of property to such children *could* be challenged now or at some time in the future, if a precedent should be set at last or the arguing Law Lords finally made up their minds one way or the other. It was all hedged about with caveats and maybes, but the crux of it seemed to be Brilliana was right; in order to prevent any future uncertainty and legal challenges to his heir, he and Ros ought to marry again before the baby was born.

He did not look forward to sharing this learned opinion with his wife, but they could always wed in private, with Joan and some other close-mouthed and reliable witness to render it legal. The right to wed by special licence with no banns was a privilege of the peerage so they might as well take advantage of it. Now he was thinking about ways to stop Brilliana finding out she was right and crowing about it. Except they must keep it secret for Jenny; they needed a record of a second marriage lest their first was challenged, but not a public admission they thought they might not have been properly married to bastardise their little girl. His personal fortune could go wherever he chose to leave it, but to inherit his titles and Edenhope his son must be unimpeachably legitimate if he was not to be knotted up in Chancery if an opportunist distant relative decided to challenge him one day. It was entailed and even if it wasn't they could hardly carve the old place up and hand pieces to their children so the eldest boy needed to inherit the lands that kept it in good order as well as Ash's title.

A delayed visit from the Belstones could be the ideal chance to marry again without Brilliana finding out. Ash wondered if the Reverend Belstone would agree to marry them in another man's parish, but if he explained well enough he was sure the man could be persuaded. Ben Belstone was obviously fond of Jenny and his own two little demons thought of her almost as an extra sister. Now he came to think about it, Plumstead must be overdue to retire and, if he could persuade the Belstones Hartley was a fine parish with a large vicarage Ash was prepared to rebuild from the ground up if it got them to come here, Jenny would be ecstatic and Ros would have her good friends close by.

And now he had considered that knotty problem,

what about the next? He carefully pocketed the first letter and pulled the second out. He could forget he ever wrote it and put the past behind them. Except he could not let justice for the girl Ros once was slip through his hands as if she didn't matter, so he broke the seal and unfolded his second missive.

Chapter Fifteen

Rosalind had no idea Ash was gone until she came down to dinner one day to find he had left her a brief note to say he was called away at short notice and would be back soon. No loving goodbye, no hungry, regretful kisses to tell how much he was going to miss her. She glared at his letter saying business called him away, but he would be home shortly. She asked Snigsby, in charge here now Cherwell House was shut up with a skeleton staff to keep it safe, if he was aware that anyone had called on the Duke.

'I am not aware of any *messengers*, Your Grace,' Snigsby told her with the usual bland butler's manner she was beginning to see through now she was getting to know him better.

'How about letters?'

'Two communications came for His Grace the day before yesterday, Your Grace, marked for his personal attention,' Snigsby said almost helpfully.

'Thank you, Snigsby.'

'And dinner, Your Grace?'

'Is Cook aware my husband will not be here?'

'Apparently so, Your Grace,' the man said, and bless him for looking faintly disapproving that Ash had told Cook he would not be here, but not his wife.

Rosalind ate because she knew she ought to, but the fine food seemed tasteless. The sense of unease she had been struggling with for weeks was telling her this was important. Ash had been distracted for days. What if he was bored with domesticity and all the problems the old part of the house kept throwing up after being left untended for so long? From what she had managed to find out about his years in India, Ash was used to the constant challenges of trade and outwitting his rivals, so would restoring a crumbling mansion in Yorkshire and living with the realities of family life hold his interest for long? She told herself not to be a fool and accept they had more than the convenient marriage they agreed to for Jenny's sake. Yet after the closeness of their journey here and that appalling day when Jenny's life had literally hung in the balance, Ash seemed to want more out of their marriage than an heir and a ready-made family. This sense he had withdrawn part of his attention from them since that day had hurt her far more than it should.

And what would Ash say if she kept important matters from him? He would probably accuse her of lying again and disappear for another eight years. No, that was unfair, they were further on than that, or at least she had thought so until today. And even if he had left them where she could find them she could not open his letters—that would be far too intrusive and mistrustful.

* * *

After dinner she went up to kiss Jenny goodnight and there was another setback to her belief that she and Ash were now far closer than they'd set out to be when they agreed to be Duke and his Duchess.

'When will Papa be back?' her little girl asked forlornly and another layer of Rosalind's fragile trust she was special to him peeled away. Everybody seemed to know Ash was leaving but her. Of course he had told his daughter he would be away for a few days—she was important to him.

'Well, what did he tell you, my love?' she asked, feeling guilty for asking such a sly question.

'That he will be back before I can miss him and I promised him I would be good while he was away, Mama.'

'There you are, then; it doesn't sound as if he will be gone very long since he knows what a strain it will put on you to be so well behaved.'

'That's not nice of you, Mama.'

'Even if it is true?'

'Not all the time and I said I would miss him lots so he is sure to come home soon.'

'Promise me you will be good for Miss Burrows and Carrie if he is away for a few days more than you think he should be? I cannot run about rescuing you from adventures that go wrong now I am expecting your little brother or sister to be born in a few months' time.'

'Papa says I will have to set an example,' Jenny said with a worried look that made Rosalind want to laugh.

'True,' she said solemnly instead. 'The baby will

look up to you as soon as he or she is big enough to take notice.'

'I might like that and with it being so much smaller than me it will have a long way to look, won't it?'

'Yes, Jenny love,' Ros said and managed to kiss her and tell her to go to sleep like a very good big sister before she left the room and could let out a chuckle at Jenny's version of looking up to someone without offending her. Then she wanted to tell Ash about it and he wasn't here.

Ten days later Rosalind was annoyed with herself for missing Ash so painfully after the last few months of daily intimacy it felt as if half of her had been chopped away. Once again she had to force herself to eat for the sake of her unborn child and anyone would think she was pining for the wretched man, like a misguided spaniel when its master was away from home. She heard the serenely ticking clock softly telling out the silence and wanted to scream. Ash was not here to chivvy her into eating more, or enquiring about her plans for the day over the breakfast table. Didn't he value the life they had started to build at the heart of his ducal empire?

Obviously not, she answered her own question. All she thought they were building after that first night together in London looked like not much at all from where she was sitting now.

They had never said anything about love though, had they? At least, yes, he called her *love* the day she held on to Jenny for grim life until he came to save their little girl from hurtling down on to the stone slabs three storeys below. It must have been an excess of relief talking and he hadn't meant it at all. So that day, when she knew for certain she still loved him, he could not have meant it.

She knew now she had loved him from the moment she first laid eyes on him and, like that spaniel, she had never stopped doing it under her armour of pretend indifference. She had cried for him while she was carrying Jenny. Then dreamt of him afterwards, waking with tears wet on her cheeks and trying to fool even herself she didn't care. Oh, yes, she had loved him through eight years of silence, of absence, of him not admitting he had a wife at all. Yet he had gone away and stayed away for all those years and kept who knew how many other women for their mutual pleasure and entertainment. And now he had blithely left her sitting here in *his* lair without a single word of explanation and it hurt so much she wanted to scream. All those empty years of loving a shadow hurt. She had stayed faithful because anything else was unthinkable and now he had gone away as if he felt no need to explain himself to his convenient wife? Suddenly furious with him for his protracted absence, she threw her toast at the gilt mirror that was mockingly reflecting a flushed and furious duchess back at her—and the dratted woman was crying now as well.

She had endured enough and this was the final straw. She had come here and tried so hard to be a good enough duchess, despite her reservations about the stately role chance had landed on her shoulders.

She had put up with his distracted mood and brooding silences since that never-to-be-forgotten day they arrived and most other wives would have turned tail and refused to come anywhere near his tumbledown inheritance until it was glowing with polish and newness. Now she was sitting here, patient as some medieval martyr growing bigger with Ash's child every day and she didn't even know where he was. Maybe he would leave her alone for another eight years, or perhaps he would come back when she was due to give birth, just to see who they had produced between them this time. Well, they would see about that, she decided militantly and glared at the Duchess, who seemed to have finally stopped crying and was glaring back at her from the mirror. Part of her knew she was overreacting and there might even be a rational explanation for Ash's absence, but the rest had reached the end of her tether. What a stupid idea to hope they could learn to live warily together inside a marriage of convenience for the rest of their natural lives.

'Convenience be damned,' the Duchess of Cherwell told her flushed and tearstained reflection past that piece of cold toast slowly sliding down the mirror and she doubted she could do that again if she tried it every morning for the rest of her life. Best not do that, but that was the least of her worries and she really had had quite enough of sitting here, like patience on a monument waiting for her lord and master to come home and reclaim her.

'I beg your pardon, Your Grace?' Snigsby asked hesitantly from the doorway.

'What for?' she said with a flustered look at the mirror now in need of a clean and polish from someone with better things to do.

'I thought you called me.'

'No, but please will you tell Joan that I need her.'

'Very well, Your Grace,' the butler said impassively and retired before any more bits of breakfast flew around the room.

'Whatever is it, Miss Ros?' Joan said as she huffed into the room only a few minutes later so Snigsby must have told her it was urgent.

'It is hot and noisy here and I miss the sea. We will pay a visit to—' Rosalind thought frantically for a moment. 'Whitby, that's it. We will go there for a few days of fresh sea air and a respite from all the hammering and sawing and trying to keep Jenny out from under the builders' feet.'

'Just like that?'

'Yes, just like that. I am a duchess and what use is there in being one of those if I can't indulge in a whim every now and again.'

'What about Himself?'

'What about him?' Rosalind said with a haughty glare at the mirror and the Duchess there, with jam and butter slowly sliding down her regal face. 'What's sauce for the gander is sauce for the goose,' she announced and dared even Joan to argue with her furious need to get away from Ash's home without him in it.

Two days later Ash rode back up the beautifully kept drive of his grandest country house. The main house was busy with builders and glaziers and plumbers and masons and sundry other artisans called in to correct the years of neglect Charlie had railed about with such good reason. He got to the stable yard and handed the reins of his weary horse to Dawkins, then looked around the sleepy silence of the stable yard. 'What's to do?' he asked uneasily.

'You're home at last then, lad,' the man said as if he hadn't heard the question. 'About time,' he added.

'You are impertinent.'

'Aye, and the Duchess is at Whitby with your lass.'

'Is one of them ill?' Ash said, a sharp plunge of fear in his belly at the very idea.

'Not as I know of.'

'Then why has she gone away?'

'Happen she wanted a change of scene and a bit of peace,' Dawkins told him with little respect and Ash had a feeling the old groom thought he hadn't earned any lately.

'Why the devil didn't you go with her?' he barked.

'I did; she sent us back, said she'd send for the coach when she needed us and there was no point paying for stabling.'

'Then stall Peg until he's cooled down and had a good rest and turn him out for a day or two,' Ash told him abruptly, then strode across the lawns to the New Wing as if the devil was on his heels.

'Mr Snigsby and Miss Burton are with the Duchess, Your Grace,' a flustered Ruth told him between curtsies.

'Tell my valet to bring hot water to my bedchamber,

then pack for my next journey,' he ordered brusquely. 'Oh, and send someone to tell Dawkins I expect my curricle in half an hour,' he added as he headed for the library to see if Ros had left an explanation.

Her letter was addressed to *The Most Noble Duke of Cherwell* on the outside. Inside there was no greeting at all.

We have decided on a change of scene. I dare say we will be back in a few days. Jenny sends her love.

And that was that. He ran upstairs to the modest main bedroom of their temporary home while the grand chambers in the main house were restored. As usual, it was bathed in sunlight and looked neatly comfortable. Yet it felt as empty and joyless as his foolish ducal chamber at Cherwell House in London had been without Ros in it. He missed the delicate scent of her light perfume, the rustle of her gown or the shine of a silk scarf discarded across the back of a chair, glowing with colour as sunlight poured in from the long windows she refused to have shuttered to stop it fading the upholstery. Most of all he missed her; the vital presence of her that lit up a room for him now he had let himself realise how very much he loved her and always had under a boy's pettishness and stupidity.

He had allowed temper and distrust to blight eight years of their lives when they should have been together. He had spent nearly a fortnight away from her now and it felt more like a year. If he needed one, he had learnt a lesson about how much he wanted and needed Ros while he was away. He felt dull and only half-alive without her and perhaps he had had to go away to realise how completely his life was entwined with hers. With her here he loved the hard work and challenges of making this rambling old barn a home for their family and combined future. Without her it was empty and pointless. He could see why his grandfather let the old place slip out of his control during the last twenty years of his life he had to spend here without *his* Duchess.

All the way here Ash had counted days, then hours and minutes until he could see his wife again. Even an overnight stop along the way had been full of frustration and loneliness as he contrasted his lonely and their heady journey here this spring. At least he had left Peg at Selby on the way down so the last miles flew past with his own horse full of oats and eager for a brisk ride. It wasn't even midday yet so he could still track Ros and Jenny down and not waste another day without them. It was high time he caught up with his Duchess and begged her to understand why he had left. Then he could try to convince her to write Dear Ash and Love, Rosalind at the beginning and end of every letter she sent him if they ever had to be apart again. Dearest Ash and Your Loving Rosalind would be even better, but he had best learn to walk before he tried to run.

'The Duke of Cherwell is driving up the lane,' Joan said warily after she had run upstairs from getting the washing in to tell Rosalind Ash had arrived and looked as if she almost expected a new outbreak of baked missiles to come flying towards her at the very mention of his name.

'Really?' Rosalind wasn't sure whether to be glad or sorry she had let Jenny go out with her governess and maid to watch the fishing fleet come in and scour any shops or stalls for booty along the way.

'No mistaking him and there can't be two like him.'

'One would hope not.'

'Hmm, we'll see about that, but let me have a look at you. No time to redo your hair now, so I suppose you'll have to do.'

'Thank you, they say no man is a hero to his valet, but I shall never be a heroine to you, will I?'

'You're as close to my child as I ever got,' her friend and loyal supporter said gruffly and this was no time to dissolve into tears. 'There now, you blow your nose before his nibs thinks you've been crying over him. I should keep my thoughts to myself.'

'No, thank you for everything and thank you for coming with me—despite your new role at Edenhope.'

'I won't say I don't like being housekeeper and all the busyness and life of the place now it's coming awake again, but you and Miss Jenny come first, Miss Rosalind. But that's enough of that, here's your husband hammering on the door and that Snigsby is daft enough to let him in.'

'I don't see how he could keep his employer out,' Rosalind said absently, since her heart was beating like a drum and the baby was dancing about inside her as if it knew its father was back.

'I'll slip out the back and go and keep Miss Jenny busy a while longer,' Joan said as she left the room. 'Best for you two have some time alone.'

Chapter Sixteen

Rosalind was staring at the view from the first-floor sitting room as if she had no idea Ash had arrived, despite his impatient footsteps on the stairs as if he was in a tearing hurry to get to her and that had to be a lie. From the open sketchbook beside her with the views she had sketched and painted to distract herself over the last two days she hoped he would see that she was busy and not at all bored or fretful. It was high summer and there had been so much to do, finding shells and rock pools and paddling in the sea with their daughter when nobody was looking, so she had hardly had a moment to miss him. She still felt his intent gaze on her back as if he knew all about the fast beat of her heart and tried to pretend she didn't care if he was here or not.

'Rosalind,' he said after a pause to take in her silhouette against the azure sky outside.

'Asher,' she responded flatly and refused to turn around.

'Don't you want to know where I've been?'

'Why would I? I am always the last to know your whereabouts and intentions. I hear them from the servants, or my daughter. I suppose if I was to ask a passer-by in the street he might know as much about the Duke of Cherwell's comings and goings as his wife.'

'Are you ever going to look at me again, Ros?'

'Not today, and I would prefer it if you went away again.'

'No. Come home?'

'To be your convenient duchess? No, thank you.'

'Of course not, but my wife certainly and—'

But his calm tone was too much and she turned on him and snapped; 'Don't worry, your heir is safe.'

'I have already told you I don't care if you bear a tribe of daughters, Ros. Being a duke is not such a wonderful burden I am desperate to leave it to our son.'

'That's not what you said when you came to Livesey and found out about Jenny. You said you required an heir if I wanted to carry on as her mother.'

'I was a fool back then.'

'You don't show much sign of improvement now,' she told him and he shrugged, which sent her temper into the ether. 'How *dare* you, Ash? How can you even *think* it is all right for you to step in and out of my life as if I am a doll you can pick up and put down at will?'

He was silent and she recognised his set look from their first go at marriage. He felt justified. She disagreed with him in every bone of her body and wanted to hit him for being such an obstinate great ox.

'All I wanted from you was a future with our family, but you thought you could dash off to wherever you have been and forget you even had one.'

'I had good reason and if I told you what it was you would have argued and fretted all the time I was gone.'

As if she hadn't anyway. 'What was it then, this wonderful reason?' She turned to watch him instead of the sea, but could see he still felt justified and how she disagreed. 'I am your wife, Ash. Only a convenient one, but entitled to know when you go who knows where for days on end all the same.'

'I had to clear your way,' he said as if she would understand and she felt more puzzled than ever.

'My way to what?'

'Back into the world we will have to spend time in now and again for the sake of our daughter, if not to meet friends and enjoy ourselves away from Edenhope on our own account.'

'Oh, you mean the polite world and not the real one, I suppose?' she said flatly and felt an old apprehension tighten her constricted stomach.

'Yes, but one we have to be real in every once in a while.'

'Why?'

'Because we need to exercise the power and influence being a duke and duchess confer. And I *want* you to enjoy being a society beauty; the world needs to know about my extraordinary luck in meeting and marrying you, then us having the finest imp in the kingdom for our daughter. One day I shall put Jenny's suitors through hoops and hurdles and everything else I can find until one proves he might be worthy of her, if he tries his damnedest until the end of his days. We need to know how the *ton* wags if we are to do that for her and the rest of our brood one day, Ros, and for ourselves as well.'

'Why begin now? She is not eight and this one is not even born yet. I could go to town next spring for a week or two if that is what you really want, I suppose.'

'I don't want it to be a duty.'

'And I have no idea what you mean,' she said, but he was right, she did shudder at the thought. What if she met the selfish hedonist who had fooled her when she was so young she believed a libertine was only one because he had not met the right girl yet?

'Then why did you duck out of society when I left, Ros?' he challenged her.

He must have been watching more closely than she thought when they were in London this spring. She was horrified at the idea of being blackmailed or mocked by that vile excuse for a man if she re-entered high society as Ash's surprise Duchess.

'You could have brazened out our elopement and my shameful desertion,' he went on relentlessly as if he had to get the truth out in the open. 'Your stepfather would have supported you before and after Jenny was born if you had really wanted him to. He is not a cruel man and society would have sympathised with your plight and pitied our child for having a foolish boy as a father. Even in India I would have learned of my sins after a furious letter from my grandfather and would have had to come home to see the error of my ways. So why didn't you fight me, Ros? Why choose a hidden life for you and Jenny if you were *not* afraid that piece of carrion would make a public mockery of you after I had deserted you, too?'

He was relentless, as if his self-appointed mission was some sort of crusade. 'I wanted to be the person I truly am, not a pretty face wild young Bond Street Beaux like you toasted in your cups and only ever saw as an *objet d'art* you wanted to own. I wanted Jenny to grow up loved for who she is, not found fault with because her father thought her mother a liar and a strumpet and left the country to avoid her.'

'I am sorry.'

'No, you are not. You feel insulted by a smug dolt who thought he had a right to break a virgin and chose me. You have proved it by going after my seducer as if I am a possession he rendered imperfect.'

'Don't put thoughts in my head that don't exist, Rosalind.'

'And don't you call me Rosalind in that insufferably patient tone. You are looking for someone to blame for the missing years in our marriage.'

'I don't blame you.'

'No? Well, I do. I should have made you listen. I ought to have stood in front of you and refused to get out of the way until you heard me out the day I let you walk away.' Rosalind paced the room in her rage about those years apart. 'Instead I was so weak I want to go back and kick myself. I cried like a fool until my eyes hurt, until there were no more tears left. I watched you go as if that was all I deserved. You made me so ashamed of what I confessed like a naive idiot, Ash, and I let you.'

She paused, glared up at him, then looked away again. If she was not careful she could weaken and rush into his arms, tell him she was beside herself with joy because he had come back. But that was too easy. This was not a simple, quickly brushed-under-the-carpet argument. It was a battle for all they were, all they could be if he would put the past behind them and live in the now with what they could have, instead of what might have had once upon a time—if she was stronger and he was better at listening.

'If I had screamed or collapsed or had hysterics that day you would have had to stay and at least make sure I was sane and safe before you went. Instead you left me feeling so stiff and dead inside I sometimes felt as emptied out as if I had been turned to stone. I never loved any other man but you and I never meant to lie. I couldn't find the words to tell you until you told me nothing I said would ever part us and it turned out *you* lied that time and not me.'

'*Loved* me?' he asked as if the tense mattered more than the words spilling out of her, as if damming them up had only made them stronger.

'*Love*, then, although goodness knows why. You make me furious and scared and downright confused and so glorious and complete and desperate for your every touch and whisper when you make love with me. Of course I still love you, you great fool. I have never really done anything else *but* love you from the first moment I laid eyes on you.'

'Me neither.'

'Don't lie. You hated me when you left, or you would not have been able to do it.'

'I loved you as well. That was the real reason I went, so I did not break down and agree to take second-best like my parents did when they made a pact to tolerate one another in a marriage they made because he was the son of a duke and she wanted a title,' he said clumsily and from his impatient curse he must have known he had made bad worse.

It felt worse knowing that he had still loved her when he left, instead of never giving her wretchedness a second thought. It made his cruelty deliberate. 'Don't you dare say that to me, don't you *ever* tell me such a lie again,' she said in a hard voice even she didn't recognise. 'If you loved me, you would never have hurt me like that,' she told him and wasn't it a relief to feel fury push her tears back now they had got to the crux of the matter?

'You underestimate my stupidity.'

'Impossible,' she said scornfully.

'I love you now; I loved you then.'

'But you didn't love me in between.'

'I can never make up for what I did, Ros. It simply isn't possible.'

'No,' she said stonily. 'It isn't.'

'Will you let me plead and at least try to believe me?'

'I have said my piece. The Duke of Cherwell knows

my opinion of his stupid quest, there is nothing else to say.'

'Revenge…' he said and Rosalind's temper boiled over again.

'If you had wanted revenge you should have taken it eight years ago, when I might have been impressed. You let him break our marriage and never mind what you said about me lying by default, *he* is why you left.'

'No, that's not it—' he protested, but she overrode him.

'I was so desperate for you to trust me; to believe in me, Ash. Instead you remade me in your mother's image and hated me for it. I am *not* a natural liar, but my whole life was a lie after you left and how do you think that made me feel?'

'I was unforgivably cruel and abysmally stupid.'

'Was?'

'All right, then, I still am.' Ash stopped, breathed deeply, then shook his head as if fighting to find the right words.

An itchy sort of silence stretched out between them and she so badly wanted to carry on being furious. 'You are a fool, Ash,' she finally said.

'A very sorry one.'

'Not sorry enough not to forget the past,' she accused with a protective hand on the swell of her unborn child. Her fury was fading to sadness and she felt so tired she wanted to sleep, then open her eyes and pretend none of this had ever happened, except it had.

'Yes, that sorry,' he argued.

'For how long?'

'For good. I saw sense at last once I managed to track down your stepfather to Cornwall of all the unlikely places for him to be.'

'His cousin and heir lives there, I believe,' she said, startled that her stepfather had not slammed the door in Ash's face for reminding him he had ever had a stepchild as troublesome as she was to him.

'He seems to have mellowed and he made it his business to keep track of that rat after he left England.'

'Why?'

Ash shrugged as if the Earl of Lackbourne was still a mystery to him. 'Maybe he regretted being so harsh with you when you were his rebellious stepchild and, knowing your daughter as I do, I suspect you were very unruly indeed, my Ros. I think perhaps he realised after you left that he cared a lot more than he wanted to admit as well. For whatever reason he kept a close eye on that excuse for a man and I suspect he would have made his life nigh impossible if the little rat had dared try to return to this country.'

'Would have?'

'The rat is dead, Ros. Killed by the father of an even younger girl he must have been insane to go anywhere near.'

'When?'

'Two years after he left the country for that supposedly convenient posting of his.'

'Then he was already dead when I told you?' she said hollowly.

'Yes, love,' he admitted and she flinched.

'Why did he still matter so much to you though, Ash? You have risked all we had for nothing.'

'The night Jenny nearly fell off that roof I realised you two mean everything to me.'

'Really? And this is the way you chose to show it. Forgive me if I doubt it,' Rosalind said, feeling bewildered by his very odd definition of love, if that *was* what he was declaring. 'How could love make you think revenge for old sins against me would do us any good?'

'So you would know he could never blight your life again. I can never take back my own ridiculous conduct when I accused you of breaking up our marriage by lying. I was not man enough to make you feel better about what had happened to you back then, so I used my little sister in the most unforgivable way to load all the blame on you and walk away with my hands in my pockets, as if I had done nothing wrong, just like the rat.'

'So, if I understand you, which seems impossible right now, by the way—he was supposed to make up for your sins and his own, like a scapegoat?'

'I suppose so. When you put it like that it seems absurd. Perhaps every few years a fit of insanity takes over my life, Ros. Maybe you should have me confined to an asylum or hide me in the South Lodge guard tower when I get one of these stupid ideas in my head.'

'Oh, you idiot,' she said with a great sigh and shook her head at him. 'You are just a man and it strikes me you all have pockets of madness in you from the day you are born.'

'Thank you, I will be sure to tell our son you believe so one day. But how else was I ever going to prove I truly love you, Ros? After what I did to you when we were little more than children?'

'My knight in tarnished armour?'

'Exactly—more of a Don Quixote than a Galahad,' he confirmed. 'But I love you with all I am and ever will be, Ros.'

'Only if you love me with what you were as well.'

'Must I? I don't much like the heedless young idiot.'

'All of you.'

'You are an implacable woman, Rosalind Hartfield.'

'We Duchesses are well renowned for it.'

'Oh, very well,' he said and to her astonishment her tall and proud Duke sank on to his knees and looked as if he was about to mean every word he said, but could not quite bring them on to his tongue for nerves.

'I must look enormous from down there,' she said with a self-conscious squirm and hoped Joan managed to keep Jenny and her entourage out for a bit longer.

'You look wonderful,' he argued, shifting position as if his knees might be hurting him a little on the wooden floorboards of this rather spartan hired house that was all there was available at short notice even for a duchess.

'Get on with it, Ash. You must have had a long day dashing about the countryside and you might seize up and get stuck down there.'

'True, and I had best hurry before Jenny interrupts us. So, will you marry me, Ros?'

'Why?' she asked, looking down into his laughing, loving, pleading smoky-grey eyes like a besotted and very surprised schoolgirl.

'Because I adore every lovely inch of you; because you are the most beautiful woman I ever laid eyes on; because you are the mother of my children. Most of all because I love you with everything I am, was and will be. Oh, and the lawyers say we should probably marry again to make sure the baby can never be challenged for the duchy if it happens to be a boy.'

'And you were doing so well...'

'Until that bit?'

'Exactly.'

'Would you rather I lied?'

'No, I had already worked it out for myself. It's just hard to admit your dragon Great-Aunt Brilliana is right.'

'I know. Now will you say yay or nay so I can get up? I'm not as young as I used to be.'

'I know exactly how old you are, don't forget and, yes, Ash. I will marry you once a week if that is what it takes to keep us and our family secure and content for the next fifty years or so.'

'We had best persuade Plumstead to retire then, I don't think his nerves or his knees would stand the strain.'

'Neither do I. Now get up before yours get stuck like that, or someone comes along and catches us behaving like loons.'

'Personally I think I look like a dignified duke with serious family responsibilities, but if you want to be a loon you can be. Anything you do is wonderful if you agree to be my Duchess for the rest of our lives.'

He got up lithely and grinned like the boy she first recalled, all wolfish charm and wicked humour. 'You are quite right, though, you have got even fatter since I saw you last,' he added and there it was, all the pieces of them slotting back sweetly into the places they belonged. Her unease these last few weeks as she sensed gaps and wrong bits in the wrong places died and she actually believed this was real. They really were going to be as happy together as two erring humans could be.

Struggling not to laugh with this feeling of almost too much happiness fizzing inside her, she smacked a nearly playful hand against the ruffled tawny pelt at the nape of his neck she usually found fascinatingly responsive as a lover and wife. 'You wait until you see me in a couple of months' time if you think I'm big now,' she said ruefully and kissed him before he could add worse to his unflattering description.

On tiptoe and with six or seven months' worth of baby dancing about in her womb, she had to put her hands on his shoulders to prop herself up far enough to reach his warm and waiting mouth, but it was worth it. Oh, yes, it was worth everything they had put one another through since their eyes first met across that crowded ballroom now. Their kiss was long and loving and more like a vow than a kiss, but they had been apart for almost a fortnight and they were human, so it was fortunate Jenny had a fine collection of seashells and the monkey on a stick Joan had bought her on their way back from the beach to keep her amused for long enough for her parents to prove their love very thoroughly before she finally got home.

'Why was your door locked when we got back, Mama?' Jenny asked when her parents finally came downstairs to the hired parlour hand in hand. 'And your eyes look all shiny,' she added almost accusingly, as if she sensed her parents had found a place where she was definitely not invited.

'We lost a penny and found sixpence, my Jenny,' Ash said with a grin and she forgot to be offended he had been away longer than he promised and threw herself at him in a joyful rush.

Rosalind watched Ash swing their little girl around, then hug her and give her a great smacking kiss on the cheek before he put her down again. Her child would never need to hesitate on the edge of a room and wonder if she was welcome. She realised how different Jenny's childhood was from her own emotionally insecure one and here was that huge bubble of happiness again, almost too huge to keep inside. A duchess dancing to music only she could hear with her husband's baby now very obvious in her belly was a spectacle the world, and their daughter, should not have to witness.

'How would you like to be a bridesmaid, my love?' she asked, with a shake of her head at Ash as if to say *No, we are not keeping this secret*. If they had to do it again the whole world was going to know Asher Hartfield loved Rosalind Feldon this time and their time of secrets was well and truly over.

'Who for?' Jenny said, although she was jigging on the spot at the delightful thought of being dressed like a small princess and wondered at and on show for a whole day. Didn't that prove she was a far more secure child already than Rosalind had ever been?

'Us,' Rosalind said and when Jenny looked puzzled she added, 'Your Papa and I have realised we love each other so much we want to do it all again.'

'Isn't it time someone else had a turn?' her daughter said, looking very bewildered about the whole idea.

Ash could not hold back his roar of laughter and even Rosalind had to smack a hand over her mouth to stop herself joining in as Jenny looked puzzled and a little bit offended, but finally agreed to forgive them if they let her pick her own bridesmaid's dress.

Epilogue

'Happy?' the Duke of Cherwell asked his not-very-blushing bride as he boosted her up into their best carriage as best he could now she was very pregnant indeed.

'So happy I don't even care that I look like one of Monsieur Montgolfier's hot air balloons,' she told him blissfully as she shook rice and rose petals out of her unbound hair. Fertility symbols seemed redundant when she felt nearly ready to pop with his baby dancing about in her womb like a prize fighter. And it was her wedding and she was a duchess and Ash liked her unbound hair so he would just have to put up with it not being so in private for once.

'You are a wicked girl,' he told her as he climbed in after her and sat down to watch Brilliana staring down at the bridal bouquet she had caught automatically and lost for words for once in her life.

'Maybe she and Plumstead will get married now he doesn't have to get her to write a sermon for him every week. They might miss one another.'

'Poor man, doesn't he deserve a peaceful retirement after so many years of being ordered about for his own good?'

'Nonsense, he won't know what to do with himself. He will not be allowed to retire into his former parish, don't forget. He would have to take her away.'

'What a delightful thought.'

'I can dream,' Rosalind agreed as she settled back into the corner seat to wave at their assembled tenants and friends, and there was Jenny, with Judith Belstone holding very firmly on to my Lady Imogen's bright cerise bridesmaid's dress. A promise was a promise and at least they would be able to find her even in a crowd.

'Oh, so can I, love, so can I,' he said and pulled her into his arms, or as much of her as he could get hold of in one go, as he told her when they had managed to fit as neatly against each other as was possible right now.

'I know all about your dreams. Look where they got me,' she said with a wave at the white wild silk rippling over her belly where their child was visibly impatient to be born. And again, it was her wedding, so if she wanted to wear white this time, she was the Duchess in charge here so who was going to argue? Not her besotted Duke or their daughter and she had decided not to listen too hard to Brilliana for the sake of her own peace of mind.

'It got me married to the love of my life,' he said softly between nibbling her right ear because they were away from the crowds now and on their way back to Edenhope for their much-delayed wedding breakfast, 'and father to a future pugilist and his big sister.'

'I know, isn't it wonderful?'

'No, it's perfect. My ideal wedding to the finest Duchess in the land.'

'Certainly the biggest,' she said as she lay back against him and watched Edenhope grow closer and even the scaffolding was decked with flowers and bunting for her special day.

'If you hurry up, we can use the bride cake for the baby's christening.'

'Pinch me, Ash?' she asked, suddenly serious as she wondered how it was possible to be so happy after all those years without him.

'And have half of Edenhope lined up to accuse me of injuring their Duchess? I'm not that brave and I would far rather love you for the rest of my days,' he said.

'Me, too,' she said dreamily.

'It would be nice if you promised to love me back.'

'I just did that in front of a lot of witnesses.'

'So you did, but it wouldn't hurt if you did it again.'

'I do love you, Ash. I always have, I always will.'

'Me, too,' he said with all the seriousness he had in him in those dear grey eyes of his and she believed him.

* * * * *

If you enjoyed this story,
don't miss these other great reads
by Elizabeth Beacon

A Wedding for the Scandalous Heiress
A Rake to the Rescue

And why not check out her
A Year of Scandal miniseries?
Starting with

The Viscount's Frozen Heart
The Marquis's Awakening